Hard Lies

Steve Rush

Published by Steve Rush, 2023.

HARD LIES

First edition. March 28, 2023.

ISBN: 979-8215619407

Written by Steve Rush.

To my wife, Sharon.

Chapter 1

Denise Tyler tugged off the engagement ring and threw it at the mirror. Her likeness rejected it with equal tenacity. The platinum dinged off the glass and bounced a couple times on the dresser's mahogany surface. A sparkle flashed off the three-carat diamond as if the princess-cut stone knew what she was going through and winked approval.

A satin robe dangled around her. Wet hair clung to her cheeks. The paper rattled as she pulled out the note for another look. She gripped it with both hands to steady it. She squeezed her forearms against her sides. The shakes continued. Why did Jeremy write this? How could the man she intended to spend the rest of her life with want to do this to her? Each word sliced away any semblance of merit she had for him. The statement in the third paragraph weakened her beyond anything the disease she suffered from had done to her: "Leave the family memories of her, nothing else."

Denise rubbed her throat and slid the hand to her chest. The rhythm of her heartbeat increased. Paralysis seized the muscles in her legs. Flushed, she plopped on the foot of the bed, teetering on the brink of hyperventilation. She thumbed through the other pages in the file. Halfway through the dozen pages, Denise let the file fall from her hand. Jeremy Guerdon was living a double life. His secret boosted her will to leave even though leaving assured her fate.

Her opportunity diminished if Jeremy returned home before she could get out. His enclosure of control had stifled her too long. Denise refused to vow "love, honor, and obey" to him after reading about his intent. The discovery of Jeremy's life as a hired assassin snapped any chance of that.

Denise grabbed her cell phone off the nightstand and pressed number five. Two rings. Three. Four. Her dad's hello interrupted the fifth ring and kept her from teetering off the brink of sanity.

"I've got to get out of here. Where are you?" Denise parted the wine and gold drapes on the floor-to-ceiling window next to the bed and checked the street.

"D.C."

"I'm leaving, Dad. I'm coming home."

"What happened?"

"Can you meet me in Baltimore?"

"I suppose. Where? Your apartment?"

"Yes ... no! Make it the airport. I don't want to leave my car at the apartment complex."

"How soon will you be there?"

"Maybe around midnight. Meet me at baggage claim. I've got to hurry."

"Are you okay?"

"I will be."

Denise ended the call and rushed into the walk-in closet. Release felt as good as the faded jeans she decided on and slipped into. The baggy ones he despised made her feel more at ease. She pulled on a Dodger's jersey, leaving it unbuttoned until she finished snatching clothes off hangers and out of drawers and gathered necessities for her exodus.

Everything Denise needed to carry with her fit in two leather bags. She jammed her feet into a pair of white sneakers, hooked her arm under the straps on the bags, and rushed out of the room.

She made it halfway down the stairs when light flitted across the front of the house and flashed through the first-floor windows from right to left. A small car sat in the driveway alongside her

Acura. Denise retreated up the stairs. She squeezed the handrail with every measured step. If only she could see more of the car than the front. Denise lingered two-thirds of the way up the stairs afraid to move, thankful she had turned off any light that might give away her location.

The car's headlights stayed on. Denise checked her breathing and listened. The sound of a door closing and clack-clack rhythm on the cobblestone walkway sent her clambering to the second floor.

Denise crouched where the rail attached to the wall. She had a clear view of the front door. She peered through the spindles. She hugged the bags to control the tremors. Anxiety forced her to whirl away from the corner. She slumped against the wall. Her legs felt boneless as she slid to the floor.

Oh, God. Was the front door locked? She couldn't remember.

Another look provided an answer. It wasn't what Denise hoped for. The door opened. The barrel of a pistol jutted through the space between the door and jamb.

Adrenalin rushed from her core to her extremities. Denise rolled to the right and pushed herself up with resolve and strength not available to her moments earlier. She hurried through the bedroom and out the open French doors onto the deck. She skittered down the stairs and raced around the house to her car.

Denise jerked open the driver's door, heaved the bags inside, and dove into the seat. She fumbled the keys. "God help me." The visitor was nowhere in sight. Good. She'd feel better once she got away from the house, out of the city, and beyond anything and anyone having to do with Jeremy Guerdon.

The familiarity of her old car comforted her as she gunned past the dark sports car and into the street. The Acura's tires squealed upon transitioning from cobblestone to asphalt. The engine whined. It strained to meet her demand. No traffic clogged her egress.

Motion at the front door caught her eye. A female leaped off the stoop toward the car parked in the driveway. The woman yelled something. Denise couldn't make out what. At that moment, she didn't care. The face. She recognized the face. He sent *her*? Was she a new girlfriend? Denise had noticed the way Jeremy eyed the brunette at the last two or three socials they attended.

So, this is how you're playing it.

ANGELA DONAVAN PAUSED long enough at the driver's door to glimpse the Acura as it dropped over the hill out of sight. She hopped in, wedged the pistol under her thigh, and started the car. The Infinity G37 seemed to crank and back into the street in one instant. The car swayed side-to-side. Short barks came off its tires when they grabbed and held onto the roadway surface.

Angela jammed the brakes on the far side of the hill. The G37 slid to a stop. Angela jerked her head left and right, trying to figure out which route Denise may have taken. She turned left and caught a flicker of a taillight at the far end of the street to the right. The G37 whipped through the turn and surged forward.

The street ended at the next intersection, giving Angela more options: left, right, or turning around and heading back. Streetlamps illuminated empty streets in all directions. The Acura was nowhere in sight.

Instinct prodded Angela to whip through the neighborhood in search of Denise. Cover as much ground as possible in the shortest amount of time. The possibility of some irate resident noticing the car and calling the police to report a wild driver prompted her to call off the chase.

Besides, she had the contacts needed to locate the Acura no matter where Denise fled to in it. Angela opened the console and pulled out a satellite phone, punched in a series of numbers, gave the computer voice on the other end a code, and listened through three rings.

An answer on the other end put her in touch with the person she wanted to talk to—a contact she knew only as Simon One. "Denise ran. No sign of anyone else at the residence ... I agree ... Yes, I tucked the widget under the rear bumper. I'll find her no matter where she goes."

Chapter 2

"**D**enise? Sweetheart? Are you here?"

Jeremy Guerdon draped his gray Armani suit coat over the handrail at the foot of the spiral stairway and placed his right foot on the first tread. He checked his breathing and cocked his head, listening for any sign of Denise in the house. No answer. Maybe she failed to hear his call.

No footfalls on the hardwood floor in either the living room or dining room. No sound of her calling out to him or coming to greet him from the second floor. The stereo was silent. No hum to CMT. He never knew her to go to bed before eleven.

"Denise! I'm home," he called louder. "Where are you?"

Jeremy loosened his tie, twisted his neck, and unbuttoned the top two buttons of his white shirt. Perspiration trailed his face. He checked the thermostat on the wall opposite the staircase. The digital face read eighty-two degrees.

"What is this nonsense?"

After flipping the switch to "Cool," Jeremy searched the main floor. He rushed from room to room. Everything piece of furniture stood in its rightful place—exactly the way he liked it. The one thing he didn't care for was the eerie sensation of something amiss bubbling inside his chest. He hated the feeling aloneness gave him. Uneasiness raked his spine. The emptiness reminded him too much of his childhood and the mother who abandoned him to raise another man's children.

The awkwardness of silence elevated the eeriness to anger. Jeremy dashed to the stairway and clambered up two at a time. He paused at the top to listen. The copper wind chime on the deck outside the master bedroom clinked in the breeze.

Jeremy pulled the pistol from the small of his back. The bedroom door was five strides from the end of the banister. The carpeted floor made no sound under foot. Inside the master suite, he paused and flipped on the light with his left hand. He kept the weapon trained on the room at arm's length in front of his chest.

The French doors stood open, allowing entry to the tinkle of copper and the muggy July air. Jeremy lowered the gun, hurried around the poster bed covered with navy blue comforter, bypassed his favorite Queen Anne chair, and peered out onto the redwood deck. Headlights streamed up and down the street on the other side of a patch of trees two hundred yards away. He checked the ground below. Still no sign of Denise.

He stuck the pistol in his waistband and pursed his lips. He jerked the chime from its hook and slung it over the rail. A sparkle on the dresser caught his eye when he turned back to the master bedroom. The next breaths came in waves. He caught a breath and exhaled in a huff.

"How dare she," he said through clenched teeth. The three-carat diamond glittered under the accent light situated atop the beveled mirror. Denise had purposely left on the light. He sensed it. She wanted him to find the ring. Her act sent a clear message. Jeremy picked up and clutched the ring in his palm until his fingers turned white. He felt the heat of anger flush his cheeks. Arterial pressure boxed his eardrums.

He leaned against the footboard and pondered his next move. Then he noticed the door leading into the walk-in closet. It stood ajar.

Jeremy slapped the ring down on the dresser and rushed to the closet.

The first thing he saw when he flipped on the light was the corner of the blue folder sticking out over the edge of a shelf to his left. She must have left it there. Big mistake. Things started making sense. He wondered how she had discovered the file. Jerking the folder from the shelf, he flipped it open and checked to see if anything was missing. Everything was there, though out of place. The note he had written—the one he figured Denise probably thought implied her end—lay on top.

Although it pleased him to imagine how she felt upon reading it, he wished she had not found it. One more week was all he needed. One week and his job would be finished. He could dump Denise and pursue the babe Richie had introduced him to back in May.

Denise knew his secret. That changed things. Breaking off the relationship was no longer an option. He would have to take time to hunt her. Maybe he should make this happen over a few weeks or even months. If it came together the way some of his other jobs had, he would add suffering and torment to her life according to his forte before finally killing her in grand-finale style.

Content with this new idea, Jeremy scanned the double rows of designer clothes. Every piece seemed to be there. Each spaced two fingers apart the way he insisted she hang them. Not a total loss. He fingered the fabrics, going from one end to the other, thinking how nice Angela would look in them.

Two wooden hangers dangled on the rod at the far end on the left. The two things he hated to see Denise wear were gone. Jeremy threw the file against the wall. He stomped to the master bath where he splashed cool water on his face. He toweled dry, wadded the towel, and chucked it into the tub.

He had to find Denise. He flipped open his cell phone and scrolled through the call log. He reached the number he wanted and hit the call button.

"I told you to make sure she was here ... No, she's not here. You think I'd be calling if she was, you idiot? Meet me behind Sal's old place ... Yeah ... Be there in forty-five minutes. Tell Richie. I want him on this."

Jeremy Guerdon had a personal message for Denise. *Be careful who you talk to, Denise Tyler. I'll be seeing you. Soon.*

DENISE LOOSENED HER grip on the steering wheel on the outskirts of Highland Park. She sighed. The next side street she came to led to the turnpike. She checked the rearview mirror. The dark car was nowhere in sight. Denise looked left, right, left. Another glance at the rearview mirror reassured her. No car lights loomed behind. She jerked the steering wheel. The car shot up the entrance ramp.

Once Denise passed through the tollbooth, she switched on the radio. The first song after an infomercial was "Take Me There" by Rascal Flatts. The tune seeped into her heart. The lyrics planted a yearning beyond any boundary. Denise wanted magnetism and irresistibility. She needed a man she could trust.

Tears blurred the pavement illuminated by the Acura's headlamps. The future resembled the darkness beyond the light. Love and its splendor remained a mystery to her. She needed both to take her as far away from Jeremy as possible.

"Take me there," Denise mouthed at the song's end.

Overtaking traffic concerned her. Relief came only after each vehicle cruised on by. No one paid any attention to her. Glances at the mirrors kept her on edge for the first half hour. Denise eased her grip on the steering wheel and adjusted the seat for hours of driving. No one followed her as far as she could tell.

How terrible might her life have turned out to be? What's so wrong? He'd wanted to know last night. Denise hated Jeremy's gruff voice. She loathed the way his lips jutted when he talked. The concern had nothing to do with any of his provisions. She had no problems living a life of luxury. But not when it meant being attached to him.

Jeremy often compared her to a Ferrari, but his antics made her feel like a stockcar. Nothing original. He acted as though he wanted endorsements of others stuck on her life. A necessity, he'd always say right before that'd attend another one of his socials. It's all about acceptance. In her opinion, approval and acceptance of his lifestyle assured a life of constant sorrow. Denise knew she'd be forever sorry if she gave in to a pious fraud.

If he wanted titillation, let him follow his pug nose and troll the streets after dark. Maybe he'd contract some STD or worse. The "or worse" carved a few ugly thoughts in her mind. It made her grin.

Every mile behind the Acura meant one mile closer to home. The only home she'd known for the last two years—a tiny efficiency apartment in Baltimore—sounded first-rate at the moment compared to the life she left behind. Denise actually looked forward to arriving there. She longed to cuddle in her own bed. She imagined her head nestled on a feather pillow similar to the ones she lay on at the Plaza Hotel.

Denise entertained the thought of moving back to Knoxville and finding a secluded cabin somewhere close to her parents—emphasis on seclusion. Forget luxury, except for the pillow, and maybe a few small items of interest. A lady must have some fringe in life.

The speedometer needle jumped past seventy-five twenty minutes earlier. It hovered near eighty. The Jersey Turnpike was nothing but open road by the time she reached the Twin Rivers exit.

Ominous clouds crept in under the quarter moon and blocked its light. Denise imagined the billows being Jeremy's arms—muscles filled with hate, closing in on her.

A New Jersey State Police car headed in the opposite direction alarmed her. The sudden chill made her foot leave the accelerator for a moment. She glanced at the side mirror. The trooper passed, never touched the brakes.

Denise resumed her speed. She let down the windows and reclined her seat back one notch. She propped her arm on the beltline and she used her open hand to funnel the coolness straight to her face. The air whisked her dark locks behind her shoulders as if waving goodbye to her former life. And Jeremy.

The ends of the hair tickled her skin. It reminded her of how much she wanted to fall in love with a true gentleman. How nice it would be to have his hands and fingers caress her neck and shoulders. Kiss her with soft lips. Commit only to her and their future.

The scent of rain filled the Acura after she crossed into Delaware. Denise filled her lungs with its freshness. She let off the accelerator and slowed the car to sixty at the first drops. A deluge a mile farther forced her exit. The exit ramp led up to a couple of convenient stores and fast-food restaurants. Denise pulled into the parking lot of the convenient store. She parked on the near side with the Acura nosed toward the road.

The clock on the dash changed from ten fifty-nine to eleven o'clock. She was only a few minutes away from Maryland had she stayed on the highway. It was a little more than ninety minutes from there on to Baltimore.

Rain pounded the metal and glass in a soothing rhythm. After a few minutes, the torrent lessened to a light shower. Denise watched the formation of water on the hood between swipes of the wipers. Beads of water dotted the surface.

The next thing she saw enthralled her. The beads leaped and danced on the hood when subsequent drops met them. Water danced over the entire surface of the hood, leaping and dancing, leaping and dancing until time to leave the stage. They leapt in oneness across the metal and off to their destiny. It bested anything she had ever seen on Broadway.

The rain stopped after six or seven minutes, but the effect lived on. "That's what I want," Denise said aloud. "I want a true-to-life water dance. I need a water dance partner."

Denise got back on the turnpike. She reached for the volume control on the stereo and by mistake pressed the seek button. The tuner leaped to the next station. A woman's voice said, "Is there any such thing as a perfect man for you?"

"Good grief," Denise muttered. "Exactly what I need. Some radio hotshot spouting off about the goodness in men."

The voice continued before Denise could change the dial. "What do you want in a companion? Think about it while we take a break. Then we'll be back to take your calls." Denise withdrew her arm. She pressed the back of her head against the headrest and adjusted her grip on the steering wheel.

What did she want in a companion? For starters, he had to be a man with a heart that would beat in rhythm with hers. She had to look into the gateway to his soul and see honesty. Unlike Jeremy, this one would express and nurture a commitment to a lifetime of faithfulness instead of self. And share a love-paved path to infinity.

"Let's get back to the perfect man issue for a moment and then we'll hear what our callers have to say. A man like we've discussed simply doesn't exist in our world, ladies..."

Denise cut her eyes to the radio. "I can imagine, can't I?"

"But I'll offer this advice. Trust your heart. Let destiny paint your future with love. Hang the portrait in your heart. It's easily seen on the outside when you do. There is someone for you out there somewhere. You'll know it when you meet him. He's your soul mate."

The word soulmate tumbled through her mind and down to her heart. If ever she met the reflection of her heart in someone else, she would know at that moment. It wouldn't be the same as it was when she met Jeremy Guerdon. That was at a business dinner. Jeremy had acted kindly. He treated her with respect that evening and until he proposed marriage a year later. She wished now she hadn't attended the event. If only she had listened to her instinct. And her dad.

Soul mate. If she owned a red carpet, she would roll it out for that man to enter her life. Would she ever find such a man? Would she ever meet her soul mate?

"Take me there."

Chapter 3

The 747 carrying Daniel Baker touched down in Baltimore shortly before midnight on Thursday evening. The flight from La Guardia to Baltimore-Washington International took an hour and fifteen minutes. Not enough time for Daniel to settle down and get comfortable.

The Dodgers arrived in Baltimore one week following the all-star break to begin a three-game weekend series with the Orioles. Daniel figured he might surprise his old teammates with a visit—after his dreaded meeting with the orthopedic surgeon.

The navy blazer, khaki slacks, white shirt, and yellow print tie complemented Daniel's physique. He deplaned and shuffled up the ramp to the terminal.

Mixed emotions about being in Baltimore put Daniel on edge. He prayed it would get better. The appointment tomorrow with Dr. Caracas would be his last. Caracas was to give Daniel the final assessment and prognosis. Daniel accepted what the doctor's answer was going to be and no longer dreaded it. Besides, it had been seven years since tragedy ended his baseball career.

A group of ten to fifteen people loitered around Starbucks. Some carried banners or sported Dodger paraphernalia. Daniel stopped at the Starbucks counter. He sat his leather bag at his feet and ordered a vanilla cappuccino. No foam.

One teenager decked out in Dodger blue from head to feet waved his arms at Daniel. "Hey, Mr. Baker."

"Hi." Daniel returned the teen's smile.

The boy elbowed another teen. "You know who that is?" Without waiting on a reply, he continued, "That's Daniel Baker, one of the best rookies the Dodgers ever had until he got hurt."

Daniel paid for the cappuccino and tested it for taste. Perfect. He picked up the bag, waved at the boys, and strolled toward the terminal exit. The boy's words "until he got hurt" stung him. He went from being near the top of two categories—batting average and home runs, and leading in RBIs—to zilch on the last day he donned the uniform.

The knee still bothered him. He shortened his stride and took deliberate steps. About every third or fourth step on his left foot, he purposely shifted his knee. A twinge hinted for him to stop.

The crowd dwindled to a few stragglers by the time he neared baggage claim. A middle-aged man sat alone off to the right. The distinguished-looking man with silver temples wore black slacks and a dark blue shirt. He held open a copy of *Fortune*.

Daniel continued toward the exit at a leisurely pace wishing someone was there to meet him. A yearning for female companionship tugged at him. Work at the Centers for Disease Control kept him from anything more than an occasional lunch or dinner with co-workers of the opposite gender. Even in their company, the emptiness in his heart made him feel like an outsider. Most females he worked with were older, career-minded, or had families of their own.

The man lowered his magazine and rose to his feet. "Dr. Baker?"

Daniel jerked around his head and met the man's warm gaze. Wrinkles etched the man's forehead. The man smiled and extended his right hand.

Daniel said, "I'm sorry. Should I know you?"

"Not exactly. At least not yet, anyway. Clifton Tyler. I believe my secretary talked to you a couple of weeks ago."

Daniel remembered the call. "Cyclodactin."

"I'd like to sit down with you and discuss the possibility of a venture."

"It's abrupt, don't you think? Cyclodactin is still in the test stage. We're not even sure it will work."

Clifton stuck his right index finger and thumb in the breast pocket of his shirt and came out with a business card. He presented it to Daniel. "Believe me, Doctor. I've seen dozens of drugs hit the market and fade away over the years. This formula is the most promising to come along since the discovery of penicillin."

The first thing to catch Daniel's eye on the card was the city—Knoxville, the same place he planned to visit upon leaving Baltimore. Daniel refused to believe in coincidence. As far as he was concerned, things happened based on design, divine or otherwise. Caution suggested he hesitate before jumping to any conclusion about Clifton Tyler and the man's enthusiasm for Cyclodactin.

"How do you know about the formula?"

"I have contacts all over North America. When word leaked out about Cyclodactin, one of them called me to see if I'd be interested in trying to get with you and work on a marketing proposal."

"What do you mean, 'leaked out'?"

"Poor choice of wording, Doctor. Forgive me for the insinuation. I was in Denver with a colleague when he received the first lab reports. He asked me to look at them and offer my opinion on its viability."

"And?"

"Incredible. You definitely have something worth pursuing there. I'll clear my calendar whatever day you agree to. Call the number on that card and ask for my secretary, Pattie."

Daniel glanced at the card. The question on his mind was whether he should trust this stranger. Tyler's opinion matched what others had voiced about Cyclodactin. The reference to penicillin stretched it a bit in his opinion, but otherwise the drug did pique more interest among those capable of making it a success.

Clifton Tyler's advance reshaped Daniel's attitude into a shield. There was no way he would let this Tyler fellow or anyone else steal this product. He expended time, effort, and more money than he dared think about on the project and would use as much or more time, effort, and funds to protect it.

Tyler's pitch raised his curiosity beyond what he wanted to admit. "I'll listen to your plan under one condition," Daniel finally said. "You pay all expenses portal to portal."

A grin on Clifton Tyler's face expressed approval. "Name your price." He pulled out a second card and handed it to Daniel. "You have his consent."

Daniel stared at the card in disbelief. The name on the card was Simon One. He thought this chance meeting was more than a coincidence. "Let me think about it, and I'll call you."

Daniel shook hands with Mr. Tyler and walked off. He wondered if the man's enthusiasm in any way matched Cyclodactin's worth. Somehow, he got the feeling it did.

A Baltimore police officer paced beyond the row of flight arrival-departure monitors. The officer's face was weathered from years exposed to the elements. He wore a bored expression as he rocked on his feet. Airport duty lacked the luster of working the streets and dealing with what cops refer to as real crime.

"Good evening, Officer."

The officer acknowledged Daniel's greeting with a nod then jerked his head to the right. His expression softened. Something caught his attention.

Daniel saw her as he turned to go through the exit. She graced the edifice with her presence. He froze in his Rockport's at the sight of her. She wore a Dodger's shirt and jeans. He wondered what number embossed the back.

The officer sucked in his belly.

Deadlocked and feeling unable to move, Daniel's eyes would not leave hers. *Incredible. I wonder if she is as special as she looks.*

She was twenty feet away when her eyes met and fixed on his. Half a dozen steps later, she stopped within arm's length. "Excuse me. I'm here to meet someone and I'm running a little late. Do you have the time?"

The curve lines of her face accented high cheekbones and eyes the color of blue ink. Light revealed pale streaks in the iris that the artist's brush left behind. They shimmered when she smiled. A tiny scar etched the outer edge of her left brow. The blemish took nothing from her beauty.

The attraction magnetized his heart. He felt his heart shutter as if it opened and invited her into its emptiness. He swallowed and finally uttered, "Yes." Daniel lifted his left wrist to display the gray face of his watch. The warmth in her voice equaled her stunning presence.

The woman flipped her hair behind her left shoulder. She glanced at the time and without delay returned her eyes to his.

He felt heat rush to his cheeks and ears. Every joint in his body loosened as if their cells somehow separated and gravity's power failed to keep them together. He swallowed again, tilted his head to the left. "There's a gentleman sitting right around the corner. That may be—"

"What makes you think I'm meeting some guy? You think I'm some chick out here to meet her sugar daddy?"

Daniel opened his mouth to reply, but his brain refused to supply any words.

"What's the matter? Afraid to answer?"

He jammed his hands in his pockets and wished for relief from the lurid feeling. "Actually, yes." His eyes still fixed on her. "What are you like on a bad day?"

She pouched her lips, which quickly formed a half grin. The sparkle in her eyes brightened when she blushed. "My worst day's not so bad anymore. Got to go. Nice, thank you."

The woman struck off in the direction he'd motioned. He saw number 33 on the back of the replica jersey. Hair covered the name, although he didn't need to see it. He recognized his old teammate's number. *Why couldn't it be number twenty-seven? And say Baker instead of Wright?* If she had recognized him, she didn't let it show.

"Wait! I didn't get your name."

Too late. Questions blazed through Daniel's mind. One thing was for sure: meeting her was nice. Very nice.

The image of beauty like he'd never seen before burned in his mind. His heart demanded it dwell there, focus on those vibrant eyes. He wondered if he would ever see her again. The thought of even a remote chance sent hope soaring.

"If only," he muttered, stepping through the automatic doors onto the sidewalk.

"Did you say something, son?" A tuxedo-dressed man waited next to a white limo parked at the curb. The back door stood open as a way of welcome.

"Thinking out loud."

"It must've been some thought by the look on your face."

"She was, um, I mean, ah, it was."

"Sure." The limo man raised his hand and pointed a finger at Daniel. "That's a preoccupation. You're hooked, my friend."

Hooked. If that's what hooked is, it sure feels good. It feels wonderful.

"Here." The limo man offered him a business card. "You never know."

"How right you are." Daniel read the card. "Tennessee. Never been there." He slid the card in his shirt pocket and wondered if Tennessee was where she called home. He had detected a slight twang in some of her words, something he equated to the city side of Southern.

The limo man—Luke Lanier according to the business card—spoke with a Southern drawl.

"Maybe you should come visit us sometime. Take in a tad of our renowned hospitality. That's all it'll take, you know. Once you set your feet on our soil, you may never want to leave."

Daniel missed home in Cripple Creek, Colorado. The Rockies beckoned his return to their sky-piercing peaks.

"Maybe sooner than you expect, Mr. Lanier."

"Be sure to look me up when you do. I promise to provide you with a first-class tour."

"You got it."

He adjusted his bag's strap on his shoulder and trekked along the sidewalk until he located the shuttle that would take him to Hertz.

"HI, DAD."

Clifton Tyler looked up as his daughter hurried toward him. He chunked the magazine on the chair next to him and rose to greet her. "Hello, sweetheart." He kissed her right cheek. "How's my girl?"

Denise embraced him and buried her face on his chest. His shirt soaked the tear from the corner of her eye. "I'm doing ... How's Mom?"

"She's fine. She wanted to come, you know, but didn't want to leave because of all that's going on right now with the business and your grandmother."

"How is Nan?"

"She's hanging in there. She went back to visit her doctor two days ago for a few minor complaints, but the report was good. It sounds like she may be with us a while."

"That's good.

"You have everything?"

"Yes. I'm ready to get out of here."

"Luke got us a limo. Dalton flew up with us to drive your car back in the morning. They have no flights available tomorrow, so we'll have to drive home."

Denise opened her purse and pulled out her keys. She removed the Acura keys from the key chain and handed them to him. "Let's go. I think you'll like my place. It's cozy."

Denise and Clifton made their way out to the limo. Clifton placed his overnight bag in the limo driver's hand, handed the Acura's keys to Dalton, and settled in the rear passenger's side seat. She waved at Dalton and slid in on the opposite side. She tucked her right foot under her left leg.

They pulled away from the curb when Dalton emerged from the parking lot behind the wheel of Denise's Acura. Once they reached I-695, her dad said, "You seem preoccupied."

"I'm fine," she lied, wetting her lips.

"No, you're not. It's him, isn't it?" He shifted in his seat, quartering toward her. "That's why you wanted me here."

Denise felt his look drilling into her head. It was the same one he had the day he caught her in a lie when she was nine. That was twenty years ago. The icy look that frightened her then was probably more from hurt than anything else.

"It's over, Dad."

He slapped his thigh. "Praise the Lord."

"My sentiment exactly. Except."

"What?"

"He won't let it go."

"Sure, he will. He has no choice. Ignore him. Refuse to take any of his calls. Act like he doesn't exist. He'll finally get fed up and move on to something else."

"You're wrong, Dad. He's not the man you met. He's the epitome of bad from his heart outward. He hides it well. He's good at playing the part of a true gentleman in public."

"What is your plan?"

The limo stopped at the top of the exit. Denise stared at the red signal. The rhythm of the turn signal matched the pulsating throb in her head. "I don't have one."

"Come stay with us."

"I can't."

"Of course you can. You'll be safe tucked away in the hills."

"He'll find me, Dad. Don't you understand? When he does, he'll have a heyday."

"What have you gotten yourself into, baby girl?" Concern altered his tone. He leaned toward her, reached over, and took hold of her forearm. "Who is this guy?"

Denise pulled away. She leaned her head against the window. Coolness leached from the glass to her skin. She flicked a tear with her eyelid to keep it from dropping to her cheek.

The lights in one building on Baltimore's west side resembled a giant crossword puzzle. It soon faded from view. She felt the same way the building's appearance came across to her: void of answers.

Chapter 4

The alley behind Sal's Diner on Staten Island opened to an area large enough for three vehicles and a dumpster. The way the open area was situated hid Jeremy's Jaguar when he parked, nose out, against the brick wall connecting the diner with adjoining buildings. There was no view of the space from the street.

Jeremy shut off the headlights and waited with the engine running and the air conditioner on max. He kept the windows up to keep from smelling the stench of rotting food coming from the dumpster where half dozen rats fed on scraps that didn't make it in the container.

A half-full Heineken rested on the seat. Jeremy laced his fingers around its neck and swigged it about every thirty seconds. He guzzled the remaining half, rolled down the window, and chucked the bottle at the dumpster. The rats fled when the bottle shattered. They returned seconds later, nibbling on scraps.

A set of headlights filled the alley, followed by the appearance of a black Impala. The sedan swung around and stopped between Jeremy and the dumpster. The driver rolled down the window and blew out a plume of smoke.

"You're late," Jeremy said, getting out of the Jaguar, clutching another open bottle. "You know how I feel about being prompt. Being late causes setbacks. I don't like setbacks."

"It's my bad," Richie said from the front passenger seat. "I was in the middle of something when I got your call."

"And that should keep me waiting? Who this time?"

Richie rotated leftward on the seat, hung his left arm over the seat back, and leaned far enough forward to make eye contact with Jeremy. "A twenty-two-year-old I met out on Long Island last week brought her mama over for dinner and desert. Mama's a really attractive woman. Big hooters. Fake, but nice. She's better in the sack than the daughter."

"Until I interrupted," the driver said, his words tailed by a chuckle.

"Yeah. I could've been there still if the stupid phone hadn't rung."

"This is more important." Jeremy's tone sounded cold and hard. He leaned against the top of the car and kept his head low enough to see under the roof rail.

"Harry told me what happened on the way over here. Any idea where Denise might be headed?"

Before answering, Jeremy straightened, chugged the beer, and hurled the third-full bottle. Green glass sprayed the brick wall and pavement. "Probably Baltimore. I'm headed down there after we finish here. I want you to go to Knoxville."

"What's in Knoxville?"

"Her parents. Her father's some hotshot business executive that runs his own company. I have all the details written out for you."

"Her mama?" Richie asked.

"Never seen her."

Richie cocked a brow and smirked. "If she looks anything like Denise, I might have to have a little fun first."

Jeremy pulled a manila envelope containing fifteen thousand dollars from his rear pocket and tossed it on the seat between the two men.

"Keep hard-n-happy in check, Richie. Get down there." He pointed at the envelope. "Use this money to buy a used pickup. Make it something full-sized like an F-150 or a Dodge Ram. Call me to let me know when you have the truck before you do anything further. I mean it. The address for Tyler's business is in there. We're doing this my way."

Chapter 5

Denise cowered on one end of a tweed sofa in her apartment. She tucked her legs under her. The fabric poked her exposed skin. The foam in the cushion was flat and split from many hours sitting in that same spot while she wrote her feature articles for Trend magazine. It felt nothing like the smoothness and softness of the leather sofas she had gotten used to while staying in Jeremy's house.

She situated a small pillow between her head and top of the sofa, pulled a Volunteers blanket around her and tucked it under her chin. Sleepiness tugged at her body. She dreaded going to bed for fear a nightmare might invade her sleep.

Her dad sat on a matching chair sipping cranberry juice from a plastic cup.

"Kidneys bothering you again?"

"It's nothing. A little aggravation, that's all."

"I don't know how you can drink that stuff."

"It's not so bad. Helps prevent stones."

"I think I'd rather have the stone."

Clifton peered over his reading glasses. "No, you wouldn't either. Imagine a cat clawing your insides. Worst pain you could ever have, believe me."

Though used to pain caused by Sarcoidosis, Denise feared the harm Jeremy might be planning for her. She imagined a maze of terror with excruciating surprises and a result outside the realm of belief. Knowing Jeremy, the terror he would unleash on her would surpass anything she might ever imagine. A tincture of doubt blurred her thinking. It made her wonder if leaving him this way was the right decision. Perhaps she misconstrued his intent.

The image of two words lingered in her mind's eye: "Kill Denise." Nothing implied in that statement. She pictured it with clarity. The scene shuttled her to the reality of the jeopardy she found herself in.

Denise flipped off the afghan and ran her fingers through her hair. She needed something to calm her. In stressful situations, nibbling on comfort food usually helped take her mind off things. Those were the ones never listed on any top ten health food lists. These were foods full of glucose or saturated fats, the taste-good, figure-blowing items fitness gurus dared put in their mouths. The apartment contained none. The only provisions in the kitchen were the package of coffee her dad bought at the convenience store and the outdated box of cocoa mix in the cabinet she noticed after they arrived at the apartment.

Denise loathed coffee. "I think I'll make some hot chocolate. Would you like some?"

Clifton raised the cup and tapped the side with his index finger. "Thanks, but it won't taste good after this."

"I guess not."

"You feeling any better, baby girl?"

"Being here helps some," she said on her way to the kitchen, dragging fear-filled thoughts with her every step. She filled a pan with water, set it on the eye, and adjusted the temperature.

"I talked to your mom. She ordered me not to come home without you. She said to tell you that your soul mate will come along at the right time."

Soul mate. There it is again, she thought, dumping hot cocoa mix in a cup she pulled out of the cabinet.

"When you first met Mom, what was your first impression?" She longed to hear again the story of how they met. It always warmed her and kept her from getting lost in and overwhelmed by circumstances.

"I thought she was the most luxuriant beauty I had ever laid eyes on. When she smiled, she beamed like a reflection of rays from the morning sun off a crystal lake. I don't know how else to explain it. You got your smile from her, you know."

Denise leaned over the pan and saw her reflection in the water. "As pretty as hers?"

"Every bit as pretty, if not more. But don't you dare tell her I said that. She was the delight of my days at UT. Prettiest girl in Knoxville. Still is in my book."

Waiting for the water to simmer, Denise closed her eyes and tried to picture what he was saying. The images kept blurring, Daniel's face floating over them like a double exposure.

"I was studying at the university. I'll never forget what happened that day. I hesitated to go that evening. We had finals all that week, and I was behind on my study time, as usual."

Denise peeked around the corner at him. He bobbed his head. "Too much time wanting to do other things, you know."

She stirred the mix as she poured water into the cup. "Guess I get that from you."

"Bad habits in your genes? Not good, baby girl."

Steam floated above the cup. Denise let it cool a couple minutes, then savored the drink to the last drop, listening to her dad yak about the past. Her lungs ached. She again wondered what kind of night lay ahead for her. Maybe the cocoa would help her sleep. She carried the cup to the kitchen, rinsed it with tap water, and set it in the sink.

"Well, anyway," he continued, "I guess fate changed all that. The telephone call from President Reagan that afternoon and being with your mother that evening sure altered my course."

"The president called you? I never knew that."

"Congratulated me for an award."

"Wow. That's great."

"It was a remarkable change toward my future. Connie influenced me that evening. Still does, thanks be to God."

"That's great, Dad. I'm glad to see you and mom so happy. I hope I can have that someday." She crossed to the couch where she again huddled on the end.

"You will. Give it time. The right one may be right around the corner."

Denise leaned her head back on a pillow. There was no way she was going to get involved in another relationship. Still, the face of the man she met at the airport hovered in front of her no matter which way she looked. And she didn't want to dismiss it. A tingle worked its way through her chest. It seemed to settle on top of her heart.

"You never know, Denise. You may meet Mr. Right any day." He paused and took another sip of cranberry juice. "Did I say something funny? What's with the grin?"

An involuntary smile played on her lips without her even realizing it. "What grin? I'm not grinning."

"Oh, yes. You were. See, there it is again. You can't stop."

"I can't help it. He's got me all out of whack."

"Who?"

"Some guy I saw at the airport."

"Sounds like more than some guy to me. Want to fill me in on what I'm missing here?"

"He had incredible green eyes. They made me completely forget what I was doing for a moment. He had a gentle look about him, a pleasant-sounding voice. And there was a deep dimple in his left cheek that, when he smiled, melted me right there. I can't believe he saw me looking like this. Look at me. I must look like a slouch."

"Oh, no. Don't you worry none. You look fine. Tell me about him. What did he look like?"

"Handsome. I think he was wearing a navy blazer and khakis. I remember his smile and a dimple in his left cheek."

"You know what? I saw him not long before you got there. He came through the terminal while I was waiting for you. He spoke to me as he passed. Seemed like a nice young man."

Nice. Very nice indeed, Denise thought.

"Did you get a name?"

"Not enough time. I wish I had. I really wish I had."

"Don't worry." He gave her a sly look. "If it is meant to be ... you'll have another chance to meet him. I'm sure of it."

She saw the look but dared not ask. He was holding something from her. She was certain of it.

Another chance. If only she could have another chance. She would get his name and find out everything she could about him. The idea followed her to the bedroom where she stripped down to brassiere and panties and slipped into bed.

The tingle zigzagged down through her abdomen and settled between her legs. She closed her eyes and pictured the face, the dimple. The images relaxed her, escorted her to dreamland.

Twilight. Water dashed against rocks in the shallow part of a wide river coursing through Cades Cove.

Denise stood at the edge and stuck a toe into the water and jerked away. She gradually submerged one foot, waited a few seconds and eased in the other foot.

The thigh-deep flow splashed off boulders jutting above the surface. Those below the surface were worn smooth from centuries of water flowing over them, leaving them slippery under foot.

She waded to midstream, reached for his waiting hand, and climbed and perched on a massive rock, facing him.

Cool air gave her shivers.

He pulled the blanket he sat on from under him and draped it around her shoulders.

Denise opened her eyes. Rolled up in the sheet, she cuddled the pillow and basked in the dream's agreeable nature. She listened for sounds coming off the river. The only things audible were tires singing on the nearby highway and her dad's snores coming from the living room.

The red glow of the clock displayed 3:33.

FIVE HOURS AFTER GAINING and locking the signal from the Acura, Angela Donavan steered her sports coupe into the parking lot of the Courtyard Baltimore. She circled the lot and located the Acura parked five spaces from the front entrance. The car faced the building.

She circled a second time and found an open space in the opposite row. She backed in and stuffed the pistol and holster in an overnight bag.

A sleepy-looking clerk no older than twenty-five in hotel attire with close-cut sandy hair greeted her as she approached the check-in counter. "May I assist you?"

"I would like a room."

The clerk yawned. "Sorry. It's been a long day. Double shift's about done me in. Let's see here. Single or double?"

"Single. Please make sure it overlooks the parking lot."

He typed something on the keyboard and waited, staring at the screen. In a moment he said,

"Ah, yes. Here we go. May I have your name?"

"Erika Webb," she lied.

"Okay, Ms. Webb. Address?"

Angela gave him an out-of-town address and the phone number of a pay phone at LaGuardia Airport.

"And how will you be paying for the room?"

"Cash."

"All right. Your total is $117.56."

She paid, took the elevator to the third floor, and located her room on the front side of the hotel. Once inside, she dropped her bag on the bed and marched straight to the window. She whipped open the drapes.

Denise's Acura was parked in line with the window. Angela's position provided a clear view of the car and vehicles on each side.

She opened her bag. The satchel contained more surveillance-type equipment than clothing—binoculars, ten-megapixel camera, satellite telephone, listening and tracking devices. Angela removed the binoculars and set them on the chair next to the window. She changed into a nightshirt, set the alarm for five thirty, and crawled into bed.

Light poured into the room through the open drapes. She preferred to sleep with them closed but kept them open in case she needed to jump up for a look. Angela dozed until the alarm buzzed and startled her. She slung her legs off the side of the bed and dashed to the window. The Acura was in the same spot as it had been when she went to bed.

Angela slipped into a pair of jeans and a pink tee with MIT on the front. She pulled on socks and worked her feet into silver running shoes. The gnarl in her stomach quickly reminded her she had eaten nothing since the previous afternoon. The situation necessitated she stayed within sight of the Acura since she had no way of knowing what room Denise occupied or when she might leave the hotel.

Angela pulled the drapes, but left a gap wide enough to see through. She slid the chair next to the window where she could sit and see the vehicle.

The wait was short. Two males ambled, one behind the other, on the sidewalk a couple of minutes before six o'clock. The one in the lead looked to be in his late teens. The other was older. When they reached the Acura, the teen unlocked the doors.

She gazed through binoculars to get a close-up look once they were in the car and facing the hotel. Neither one looked familiar. The driver backed the car out of the space and turned south when he entered the street. Angela lowered the binoculars and leaned back in the chair. The device Angela had placed on the car to track Denise was now on its way somewhere without her.

Where are you, Denise?

Chapter 6

D aniel slapped the clock on the nightstand, wondering why the alarm failed to wake him. He spun out of bed. His stomach growled seconds after his feet hit the floor. Late again. He rubbed his trim waist. "Sorry. You'll have to wait."

He hopped on one foot, forcing the other through the twisted leg of a pair of knock-around pants. He pulled on a shirt, brushed his teeth, grabbed a towel, and scampered down three flights of stairs to the athletic room.

The door leading out of the stairway opened in on him before he reached it. A man burst through and brushed against him when Daniel sidled to miss the swinging door. The man scowled. His deep-set eyes, square jaw, and pug nose portrayed a sense of pride. His choice of clothes and shoes shouted lavishness. The jolt Daniel felt from the man's shoulder sent a message of muscle.

"Pardon me." Daniel studied the man. Something about him upset the balance between suspicious and ordinary. In Daniel's mind, the scale plunged in favor of distrust.

"Watch where you're going next time, pal."

He glared at Daniel and skittered up the stairs. A bulge mid-back of his suit coat censored any retort from Daniel. The way the silk waved over it left no doubt about what it was. The last thing he needed was to mix with an armed whomever. Besides, one appointment with a doctor this morning was enough. Although in a one-on-one Daniel might have a chance, the gun vaulted advantage the other way.

Daniel lingered in the doorway until he heard a door open and close two or three floors above him. He crossed the hallway to the workout room. The encounter with the stranger made him feel like he had gotten a look at evil in the flesh.

The key card cleared entry into the fitness room. Stale air mixed with body odor filled his lungs. After a warm-up on a treadmill for fifteen minutes, he progressed through two sets of exercises with free weights and machines. The pump invigorated him. He felt ready for anything. He dried the sweat from his face and arms and flexed his left leg. The knee joint moved freely, without a hint of anything wrong.

He twirled through the maze of machines, hopping over benches in a laughable dance.

"*Dancing with the Stars*, here I come." He pictured a judge's score of triple threes and imagined Len Goodman's opinion. "Your quickstep is fantastic for someone who looks like they're high-stepping through a quagmire."

DENISE STRETCHED AND kicked off the striped comforter that covered her from the waist down. The ceiling fan wobbled with every rotation. The motion imitated the way she felt after the half-in, half-out-of-it attempt at sleep. And indecision about what to do based on unknowns. The motion fanned her body.

The constant hum mirrored the way she felt about her state of affairs. No matter which way she ran or how fast, she ended up stuck in the same doldrums.

Denise showered. Angst clung to her. She lifted her head and studied her image in the mirror. The same figure she had before putting on designer clothes faced her. The young woman from Tennessee realized what a misfit she became in the present situation, suppressed by a hedonist. My life's important too, she thought, shoving strands of damp hair off her bare shoulder.

Some things had been nice. The three-story house had an Olympic-size pool. A bank account provided unending resources. Jeremy had bought a new Mercedes convertible for her to drive and two closets filled with in-fashion clothes and more shoes than she ever thought she would have to choose from.

No. Jeremy's goal was clear enough. What's the difference? Fear nagged her even when he wasn't there. Fear was one thing. To live another minute in the home of a killer was terror she could do without, especially since she knew he had named her as a target.

A rap on the door snapped the trance. "Just a minute."

"Checking to see if you're up," her dad said through the door. "How about breakfast? I thought we'd grab something before we pack your things and head south."

"Hold on." Denise shoved out of bed and ransacked the middle drawer of the chest for something to put on. She came across a Knicks T-shirt, the same one Jeremy bought for her on their first trip to Madison Square Garden. She whirled and slung the shirt under the bed, never wanting to see it again. "Let the next tenant find it," she mumbled.

She slammed the drawer and opened the one above it. The navy fleece suited her about as much as it complemented her curves. The choice was between the fleece and the Knicks tee, and there was no way she'd ever don that shirt again. She pulled on the fleece, hiked up the sleeves, and slipped into the pair of jeans she had worn the night before.

"Dad?"

"In here, baby girl."

Denise traipsed to the kitchen in bare feet and propped against the counter. Her dad turned his head in her direction. "Little warm for that, isn't it?"

"I'll be fine in the AC." The last thing she wanted to think about was clothes, especially where she left most of hers. That's when she spotted the two bags stacked next to the front door.

"I think I will change into something else."

"What? Did you forget about those?"

"How silly of me. I was so out last night, I forgot I even brought them in."

"Well, it's another day, so let's put all the other stuff behind us. There's no need to concern yourself about anything except what's waiting for you from this moment on."

That's what scares me, she wanted to say, but decided not to. If he had any idea what Jeremy was capable of, he'd suffocate her with protection, paparazzi-style.

"Ready?" he asked when she came back through wearing a navy chiffon blouse in place of the fleece. "It's a long ride."

"Sometimes long can be good."

Every mile traveled meant another mile farther away from him. She wanted to forget Jeremy ever existed in her life. One thing made it impossible for her to forget: his intent to kill her.

Chapter 7

Jeremy arrived at Liege Ville Apartments and found a space to park at one end of a building angled to the one in which Denise had leased a studio apartment. He checked his wristwatch on his way to the back of the Cadillac—9:05 a.m. He popped open the trunk and removed a canvas bag containing a pair of gray coveralls, Danner work boots, and a Ravens hat.

He loped to the laundry room at the rear of the building, finding the room void of living beings. The room reeked of bleach mixed with the smell of laundry detergents.

The hinges squeaked when he shut the door. Jeremy slipped out of his Mezlan loafers and pulled on the coveralls over his charcoal slacks and navy shirt. He removed the boots from the tote, put them on, and stuffed the loafers in the bag. He tucked the bag out of sight, plopped a cap on his head, and strolled across the property to find Denise.

The coveralls had the name "Danny" stitched on the left breast and King Heating & Air on the right. Anyone seeing him might not give him a second look.

A key copied from the one Denise kept separate from those on her key chain opened the front door with ease. The apartment smelled of coffee. Jeremy sneaked to the kitchen and peered inside. Condensation clung to the inside of an empty four-cup coffeepot on the counter next to the stainless-steel sink. The heating element felt warm when he touched it.

He stroked his left jaw and ran his fingers behind his ear into his black hair. The facts suggested a departure time of less than thirty minutes earlier. He figured fifteen or twenty.

A copy of *The Baltimore Sun* on the oval table lay open to the sports section. Jeremy rotated the paper on the laminate wood surface and scanned the articles. Someone had circled a Baltimore Orioles ad. Orioles and Dodgers. One o'clock.

Jeremy pondered going to the game. Why not? Denise was probably headed to Tennessee, and there was no reason for him to rush after her. Let her seek comfort with her parents. They would call the authorities at the first sign of trouble. Everyone involved might expect him to go after Clifton and Connie Tyler to get at Denise. What they might expect was not what they would get.

Time to put his thoughts together and form a plan was his. Let them smother in worry. He could take all the time necessary and do things his way.

DANIEL PULLED OPEN the door to Dr. Caracas's office, signed in at the window, and wrote his arrival time of 10:23. He grabbed a seat on the only available chair next to a woman with a swollen foot. The woman fluffed the side of her graying hair and adjusted the rimless glasses on her nose.

Daniel filched a copy of *Sports Illustrated* from among the assortment of magazines on the table to his left. An article about the baseball commissioner piqued his interest.

The woman next to him cleared her throat and shifted in her chair. When Daniel kept reading, she tapped his right arm. "Mind handing me one of those, sonny?" Her hand shook as she indicated the stack of magazines to his left.

"Not at all. Which would you prefer?"

"I don't care. I need one to scratch my leg. I can't bend enough to reach it otherwise."

The door leading to the exam rooms opened and a nurse dressed in purple scrubs poked her head out and scanned the room. "Mr. Baker, the doctor will see you now."

Daniel handed a magazine to the woman and pushed out of the chair, rolling the *Sports Illustrated* in his left hand to take with him. The woman thanked him and said, "You must be important. I never get called back without having to wait thirty minutes or more."

"That's because you always arrive way before your appointment time," said the woman sitting on the chair opposite her.

"Be glad I'm half crippled over here, Justine, or I'd bop you one good time."

"Don't pay any attention to them," the nurse said to Daniel. "They're old friends. Second door on the right." She indicated with a flip of her hand. "He'll be with you in a few minutes."

Daniel dropped his pants and sat on the exam table in his boxers, a routine he'd learned after eight or nine appointments at the same office. The linear scar on the left leg exhibited the only visible evidence Daniel's career-ending injury. He massaged the area around the scar. What might have been was long gone.

His phone rang. He glanced at the caller ID. It was his mother. "Hi, Mom."

"How did your appointment go today?"

"I'm here now waiting on Dr. Caracas to see me."

"Have you talked to Anne? She said she was going to call you and let you know she prayed everything would go well for you this morning."

"It's still early out there."

"Not for Anne."

The door opened, and the doctor stepped in the room.

"I've got to go, Mom. The doctor's here."

"Headed out to the game today?" Dr. Caracas asked. He greeted Daniel with a handshake, scooted forward on a stool, and palpated Daniel's knee.

"I am if you let me out of here on time."

"You'll have plenty of time. How's the knee feel? Any problems since I saw you last?"

"A twinge now and then lets me know it's still there if I twist the wrong way on it."

Caracas had Daniel perform a series of stretching exercises while he examined the leg. Afterward, he scanned Daniel's medical records and looked at the latest set of X-rays.

"Everything's healed well and looks good. We've done all that needs to be done for you here. I'm releasing you today. Deb will give you your discharge papers."

Finally. No more appointments.

"Thanks, Dr. Caracas."

The doctor stuck out his hand. "Enjoy the game."

BY THE TOP OF THE THIRD inning, Jeremy Guerdon had downed his second Bloody Mary and finished a rough draft of his to-do list. The box at Camden Yards provided ample quiet to contrive each part of the reprisal. He watched the Orioles bat in the bottom half of the innings and refined each entry between innings and while the Dodgers were at bat.

The quest to locate Denise topped the list. He figured that to be the easy part. Where could she go except home to Tennessee? The ranch owned by her parents a few miles south of Knoxville seemed the most likely place.

Next came the pleasure part. Taunt Denise. Terrorize her. Several ideas came to mind, but he put only choice ones on the list—things like providing plenty of reading material since Denise liked to read.

Gifts too. Especially chocolate. Her favorite treats included chocolate in some form or other. She made it easy for him to come up with ideas. He was going to enjoy this. That's more than he could say for her.

He played fair and gave Denise some leeway. He could warn her in some manner before going through with each thing on the list then precede each one with a clue, make some obvious, a few subtle, and wait to see if she heeded any of them. Whether Denise might find and regard some or all was not his concern. Doom awaited her either way. He figured on drawing this out for weeks, maybe even months to bring it to fruition. Holy terror only began to describe what he had in store for her.

"Another Bloody Mary for you, sir?" A knockout with frizzed blonde hair, adorned in a black blouse and orange skirt, bent forward with a Bloody Mary perched on a silver tray.

"Sure. Can you make it a double? That should top me off for now."

"I took the liberty." The girl twisted her upper body and bent lower to place the drink on the table next to his notepad.

Jeremy lifted the drink from the tray and thanked her while his gaze stayed on her silicone-amplified cleavage eighteen inches away from the tip of his nose.

"You must be an important man. Are you always working, or do you take time to play?"

Without moving his eyes from her chest, Jeremy covered the pad with his forearm, unsure if she saw anything on it. He wasn't about to take any chances. Loose ends provide pieces that may need to be tied together. He finally heaved his eyes to meet her browns. "Name the time. I'll be there."

"Oooooh. How about a seventh-inning stretch? I have access to a killer motor home."

"Then I will take you on a trip sure to make headlines."

Chapter 8

Jeremy left his seat in the sixth inning and ambled to the RV. Loud cheers erupted behind him. He scanned the parking lot before he climbed into the Berkshire motor home.

"You like?"

Jeremy turned his head left, right, and scanned the RV's interior. The unit smelled new. "Nicely decorated, but I prefer—"

"Not this thing, silly. Me."

Although Jeremy cared nothing about knowing her name, he played along. "What should I call you?" He leaned over the counter and parted the custom shutters. "You haven't told me your name."

The girl snickered. "How about Bloody Mary?"

"Perfect." If she only knew how well the name fit her.

Bloody Mary laced her fingers into Jeremy's left hand. She unbuttoned her shirt while she led him through a hallway barely wide enough for him to pass through without canting one shoulder.

The hallway opened to an eleven-by-fourteen bedroom. A mauve and lavender print comforter covered a queen bed situated with the head abutting the rear wall. Bloody Mary spun, let go of Jeremy's hand, and plopped on the bed. She tucked her left leg under her right thigh and patted the bed.

"Don't be shy. It's comfy. No one will bother us in here. Come on, try it."

"One thing for me first." Jeremy admired her lips and lowered his focus to her cleavage.

Bloody Mary acted as though she understood what he wanted. She propped on one hand and leaned backward. The shirt gaped open. "Better?"

"You're making this effortless for me."

"This is supposed to be fun, not work."

"Close your eyes."

Bloody Mary obliged and tossed her head rearward. "I'm ready, handsome. Take me."

Jeremy eyed her slender neck. Carotid arteries pulsated under taut, freckled skin. He edged a knee between her thighs. He caressed them and slid his hands under her short skirt.

Bloody Mary spread her legs. Her body quivered at his touch. She moaned and wiggled in pleasure when he moved aside her thong.

This was too easy. Jeremy removed his right hand from under the skirt. He drew his arm back and smashed his right fist into Bloody Mary's throat. The impact crushed her trachea. Her eyelids sprang open. Disbelief gushed from her eyes. She collapsed onto the bed and grabbed her neck with both hands. Jeremy backed into the hallway and watched her struggle to suck in a breath. She gagged. She coughed. Flailed her arms and kicked her legs.

Blood trickled from the corners of her mouth. The body that once absorbed pleasure as if it was nourishment thrashed in agony. The thrashing stopped after forty-five seconds. Blue tinged the outline of her red lipstick. Pupils expanded as if to allow death's entry through them.

Jeremy watched Bloody Mary's last breath gurgle out. One day he planned to watch Denise suffer the same fate. Why shouldn't she? Like Bloody Mary, her future held no benefit to him. Why should he let her live?

Soon. He had other plans first.

A roar came from the stadium. Fireworks streaked and boomed overhead.

Jeremy washed his hands in the lavatory. He snatched a handful of paper towels from the roll on the kitchen counter. He dried his hands and swabbed the handles to remove any fingerprints.

Every window he peered through offered the same result. No one loomed in sight of the RV. He turned the doorknob and cracked the door, checking to make sure the door would lock when he shut it. He wiped the knob clean and pocketed the paper towels before descending the steps. He would get rid of the waste somewhere else. He bumped closed the door with his elbow and ambled to his rental car.

PLAYERS STREAMED INTO the locker room at the end of a one-run loss to the Orioles. Shirts flew to the floor. Cleats banged against locker walls. None of the players had much to say following the Orioles' two-run, walk-off home run.

"Well, look who's here." One of the bullpen coaches spotted Daniel, hobbled over, and hugged him. "How's the leg?"

"Baker hates to be reminded. You should know that by now, Charlie," said one of the outfielders who played on the team when Daniel sustained the injury.

"So, Baker, how is the leg?" The outfielder propped a forearm on Daniel's shoulder.

"Good to see you, Dwyer. Still looking light on your feet out there. The knee's fine. I had my last appointment with Dr. Caracas this morning."

"Somebody should get a uniform for this guy. Hey, rookie," Dwyer called to a sandy-haired infielder recently called up from the Las Vegas 51s, the Dodgers AAA team, "let Baker have that jersey. He's starting tomorrow in your place."

"Aw, man. I just got here." Sandy-hair started unbuttoning the shirt, blank-faced and staring at Daniel.

The locker room erupted with laughter.

"It's a joke. You're safe for now," Daniel said.

Sandy-hair grinned and looked around the room. Players and a coach focused on him. "Worse than finding a red ribbon hanging in my locker. Cut. Cut. Cut."

That garnered more laughs.

"I haven't seen Cars around. What's up?" Daniel asked Dwyer.

"I don't know. He got a phone call before batting practice and started acting all weird. He was scratched from the lineup at the last minute."

"Did he say what the call was about?"

"Not to me. He wasn't in the dugout at the end of the game, and he wasn't in here. Between you and me, he's been acting strange lately. That's from observation. He's been ... standoffish. I haven't said anything to him about it. Give me ten and I'll be ready."

Ten minutes later, Daniel and his former teammate strode out of the locker room toward the team bus. Outside, they noticed a crowd gathered in one section of the lot. Police officers barked orders to disperse the throng closest to an RV parked under a canopy near the Dodger's team bus.

Blue lights flashed at every exit. Vehicles jammed the lots, their occupants waiting to be on their way.

A man and a woman wearing vests with "Police" on the backs stretched yellow crime tape around the RV and tied each end to the bumpers of uniformed cars positioned precisely at the curb. A mixed group of stadium employees in Oriole attire huddled close to one of three Baltimore Police cars parked nearby. Two females sobbed. One collapsed into the arms of a security guard.

"What's going on over there?" Daniel heard one woman ask. The woman stood on the curb. She had one arm propped on the shoulder of a gray-headed man wearing a Ravens t-shirt.

A man standing in front of them turned and said, "They found one of the female concession workers dead in that RV. Somebody said she was murdered."

"Is no place safe anymore?" the woman said.

"What a cluster." A man in a brown tweed sport coat and striped tie whisked through the crowd until he reached the company of a uniformed sergeant. Daniel figured the man was a detective. The man wheeled around with arms out, a pad in one hand and a pen in the other. "Has anybody gotten a handle on this mess yet?" he said to no one in particular. "How 'bout somebody giving us some room to work here?"

"We're working on it." The sergeant left the man in the brown tweed and approached Daniel's group.

"Sorry, people. You might as well find some place to relax. You're going to be here until we have time to get your names and such. I apologize for any inconvenience. The only ones permitted to leave are the players and coaches. Their whereabouts at the time this happened are not in question. The rest of you will have to wait here."

JEREMY WATCHED CARSON Wright hesitate in the entryway outside the dim-lit tavern before finally jerking open the door. Carson paused inside the door and pulled a plain ball cap down over his eyes before weaving through tables filled with happy-hour drinkers to the bar where he slid onto a stool.

"Over here." Jeremy motioned to a booth from the far end of the bar.

Carson spun on the stool, pushed off, and followed Jeremy to a secluded booth in the opposite corner. Jeremy slid in first with his back to the wall where he could see most of the tavern and the front entrance. He shifted to the inside to keep from sitting on a split in the vinyl cushion. Carson settled in across from Jeremy.

"Let's dispense with any chitchat and get on with this. I don't like it here. What am I going to do if somebody recognizes me?"

"Exactly why I chose this dump, so don't worry. The people who come in here care about one thing and only one thing—a cheap high. Even if they do see you, they won't remember it tomorrow."

"I hope you're right."

"I am."

"How do you come up with places like this? This is not your style."

"Different approaches keep the water stirred up."

Carson peeked under the brim of the cap and glanced around the tavern. "Something needs to stir this place. It's stagnant in here. Smells like piss."

"Forget the smell. Are you still hot on Judith Lanier?"

Carson bobbed his head. "So-so I guess."

Jeremy leaned forward. "You guess? That's not good enough."

"We still talk some. Why?"

A server with thin arms, long bony fingers, and stringy hair sauntered up to the booth. Jeremy ordered a Bloody Mary. Carson asked for a screwdriver. They continued their conversation only after Jeremy watched the server strut beyond earshot and go behind the bar.

"I'm going to Tennessee on some business," Jeremy said. "I thought I might drop by to see her."

"Why do you want to see Judith?"

"She knows Denise."

"Uh-uh. No way. Leave Judith out of whatever it is you're planning."

"I'm not going to hurt the girl, Cars," Jeremy said, though he knew he would do whatever deemed necessary to find Denise despite the frown on Carson's face.

Carson shifted on the seat. "You promise?" His voice sounded weak.

"I don't believe in making promises. You know that. Now give me her address. I need her home address and place of employment."

"I don't have a pen."

"I swear, Cars. I've got to fix you." Jeremy removed an ink pen from his breast pocket, slapped it down on a napkin, and shoved the pen and napkin toward Carson. "You're never prepared. Write them down on this."

Carson fiddled with the pen and tapped the point on the napkin a few times. He finally scribbled something on the paper, scratched through what he had written, and wrote some more.

"Write it where I can read it."

"I'm trying to remember. I can't think of the house number."

"The street's good enough for now. Put down her old man's name for comparison."

Carson slid the napkin to Jeremy, still clutching the pen in his fingers. Jeremy eyed what Carson had written and shoved the napkin across the table. "Her phone number, too."

The server returned with their drinks while Carson added Judith's cell phone number below the address. Jeremy again eyed her.

"You like that?" Carson asked after she walked off.

"Wouldn't want to be seen out anywhere with her, but in the dark, she looks decent enough."

"You are nuts."

Jeremy picked up the pen and stuffed it in his pocket. He checked the information Carson had written, folded the napkin, and slipped it into the front pocket of his slacks. "I hear Southerners like nuts."

"Trust me. They won't like you."

Jeremy looked at the Bloody Mary on the table in front of him. It reminded him of the girl at the stadium and the seventh-inning stretch in the motor home. "Everybody likes me, Cars. I'm a likeable guy."

Chapter 9

The day after her 450-mile trip from Baltimore, Denise picked up her car at her dad's office where Luke and Dalton Lanier had left it. She drove to visit Judith Lanier, her best friend from high school who worked at the Barnes & Noble in Suburban Plaza on Kingston Pike.

She arrived at nine fifty. The brunette at the check-out counter checked the time and said, "Ms. Lanier is scheduled to be here at ten."

Denise perused the bargain shelves and tables while she waited for Judith. Whenever a certain title piqued her interest, she flipped it over and read the back cover, thumbed to the opening paragraphs. She repeated this a dozen times or more. Nothing fit what she thought her dad might like to read.

Denise strolled to the customer service counter and stopped in front of a PC at the far end of the counter.

She typed in "John Sandford" and waited for the screen to fill with results of her inquiry. In her peripheral vision, she noticed a young man mosey over to a computer system catty-corner to her. He typed on the keyboard, scratching the side of his face while he waited for a response. His steady side glance stayed with Denise as if she was what he was aiming to find.

Denise backed away and returned to the section she was first looking through. The man did not turn away or hide his interest in her when she glanced toward the customer service counter.

When he saw her eyes fleet past him, he shifted to the end of the aisle. "My, oh my, oh my. What agency do you work for? Ain't you one of them models? You must be."

Denise knew what he wanted—the same thing they all want: an easy lay. Uncomfortable with his leer, she abandoned her post at the computer and browsed the selection of paperbacks for the one she figured her dad might like. The seeker followed her but kept at a distance. One glance had told her all she needed to know about him: hair clean but unkempt, yellow polo shirt unbuttoned, rust-colored denims, and boat shoes with the toes worn. She figured he was a college frat boy looking to make his quota for the month. Maybe assure bragging rights.

"I'm talking to you, missy."

Denise ignored him and continued to scan titles of one of her dad's favorite authors. Several piqued her interest, but she decided on *Rules of Prey*. She hoped he didn't have a copy.

She flipped it around for the frat to get a clear view of the cover.

"You should first learn the rules," she said and tossed her hair behind her shoulder. "You'll not find what it is you're looking for with me."

A Barnes & Noble employee sorted books on the other end of the shelf. His cart blocked the aisle. That left her with no choice. The only way to the register led her by the frat boy. She turned toward him and started by hoping he wasn't the aggressive type and would let her pass.

She was wrong.

The frat boy sidled to block her passage, propping his hand on the top row of books. "C'mon now. Be nice to me."

The move caught Denise in mid-stride. Her right foot landed at an awkward angle. She bent forward and threw out her right arm to brace against the opposite bookshelf. Her hand fell on the latest

Stephen King release. This should do. She clutched the hardback, jerked it off the shelf, and shove it between the stalker's legs.

"There, creep."

Denise slammed her left forearm against the stalker's temple and stepped over the crumpled man. She heard him mutter what she figured was the b-word between moans. She didn't care. He deserved it.

"Is everything okay over here, miss?" Judith Lanier asked with a look of concern, responding to the commotion and seeing the crumpled man writhing on the floor. Her face brightened.

"Denise? Hey. When did you get in town?" They hugged. Judith patted Denise on the back.

"Yesterday."

The frat boy pushed to his hands and knees. He scrunched his brows and glared at Denise and Judith. Hate boiled the vitreous fluid in his eyeballs. "I'm going to sue you. And this stupid store."

"The manager has warned you twice already about your conduct in here." Judith jabbed her finger at the frat boy. "Now you'd best leave or I'm calling the police. Come on, Denise. Let's get a latte and chat about that hunk boyfriend of yours."

A CLAP OF THUNDER RUPTURED the clouds over Knoxville, Tennessee. The downpour sent Jeremy scampering for cover. Raindrops pounded the parking lot and Jeremy, before he made it a third of the way up the walkway to the double-glass doors leading into the reception area of Clifton Tyler's company.

Jeremy pulled open the left door and swiped water from his sport coat. Fake trees flanked the entrance and a set of wooden benches to the right accenting the stone-tiled floor and a circular receptionist desk adjoining the wall to the left. No one occupied the desk at the moment.

A gentleman who looked to be in his sixties with a scruffy beard wearing a blue plaid shirt and tan Duck Head pants sat on the nearest bench. A tan sheath attached to his belt held a bone-handled hunting knife. The man gave Jeremy a tobacco-stained grin. "Raining out there, is it?"

Jeremy twisted around and glanced through the floor-to-ceiling windows at steam rising from the asphalt. "More like a steam bath, old timer. I can't imagine anyone wanting to live in a place like this."

The man's grin changed to a scowl. "You dad-blame urbanites come down here and act like we're all noddies. Let me tell you something, Mr. Yankee man. I may be old, but I know a few things. I ain't ready for the grave yet."

Jeremy swaggered up to the man. "Oh, yeah?" He pulled out a photo from an inside pocket of his jacket and flashed it in front of the man's face. "Then tell me where I might find her."

The man grunted and rubbed his whiskers when he saw Denise Tyler's picture. The Statue of Liberty towered in the background. "Mister, if I knew where to find something like that you think I'd share the information with the likes of you? Why, I'd get shed of my ole lady for one like that, good cook or not."

"Have you seen her?" Jeremy poked the photo with his index finger.

The man leaned back and crossed his arms. "I might've."

"Where?"

"Oh, around town, I guess. Been a while, though."

"How long?"

"How long, what?"

"Since you've seen her?"

"Can't say." He pointed to the photo. "Let me see that again."

The man whipped out a pair of glasses from his breast pocket, wiped the lens on the front of his shirt, and propped the spectacles on his nose. He held the snapshot in both hands and bent forward, resting elbows on his knees.

"Yeah. I remember her. Her name's Denise, I think. My son, Chad, dated her a time or two. Three or four years ago I believe."

"And where might I find Chad?"

The man tightened his lips. He paused for five seconds and said, "Clark's Grove."

"Address?"

"Williams Mill Road."

"You think he's there now?"

"Yep. I'm sure of it."

"Great, Thanks."

Jeremy hurried to his car. He pulled out a street atlas for Knoxville and surrounding area and checked the index for Williams Mill Road. He was pleased to learn Williams Mill Road wasn't far from where he sat.

Five minutes later, Jeremy lingered at the entrance of Clarks Grove Cemetery. He growled and slapped the roof of the Charger. He rubbed the nape of his neck with his left hand. His face burned. Time wasted chasing Chad—a stoic nonentity.

The cell phone buzzed on the seat. He snatched it off the seat and pressed the call button. "You better have some good news for me."

He listened to Richie drone about the truck bought with the money Jeremy gave him for twenty seconds and cut him off.

"That's enough about the sale, Richie. Where are you now? ... Richie ... Richie ... Shut up and listen. I want you to go to Woodson Drive. Be there at noon and look for a black limousine. Lincoln. It'll most likely be parked in front of 264 Woodson. Do the preliminary. No more, you got it? ... Good. Do it and get back to me ASAP."

"WHAT'S BEEN HAPPENING with you lately." Judith perched at a table, arms out in front of her with a cup of espresso in her left hand. "We hardly ever get to see each other anymore."

"When did you make assistant manager?"

"Last month. I'm quitting next week. I got my real estate license."

"Good for you, Jude."

"What's up with you and that Jeremy guy? You sure threw a weird look my way when I mentioned him. I thought he had you up there in Jersey somewhere."

"He did. I'm taking a break."

"Yeah right. You never took a break from anything in your life, Denise Tyler. What's going on? Tell me or one way or the other I'll pull it out of you. That's why you're here, isn't it?"

Denise stared across the store.

"Listen, Denise. Unload it. That's the easiest way."

There was no easy way to tell Judith the truth. How do you explain something like this? How do you say, He's a heartless killer without saying he's a heartless killer? "I wanted to stop by here to see you for a minute."

"That's nice. Now tell me the truth."

"That is the truth, Jude."

Judith shifted the chair to her right and leaned forward. "Okay. Give me more truth, then."

"I can't."

"You never had a problem before."

"This is different." Denise pushed back the chair with her legs, picked up the bag holding her purchase. "I've got to go. I'm sorry. I can't do this to you." She left Judith sitting at the table and sprinted out the door.

A mile down the road, Denise pulled over and stopped. She sat in the Acura and stared at the Smoky Mountains in the distance. Anxiety settled in her chest. The swell raked across nerve endings too sensitive to endure anything else after scraping across coarse sandpaper. Denise's heart felt like a skewer impaled it and held it over a fire.

Would Jeremy get her or would stress incite the Sarcoidosis in her body and increase the chance of her mortality? What was she to do? The only way for her to beat back Sarcoidosis was another prescription. She loathed how steroids made her feel and added fluid to her body. There had to be something else out there to take instead of them. Why couldn't somebody come up with a drug without excessive side effects?

Denise merged into the traffic on Kingston Pike. It was eleven o'clock, too early for lunch, but she needed nourishment. She craved companionship. She imagined the next thirty minutes in her mind: stroll in alone; sit and stare at the empty seat on the other side of the table; eat something she had no taste for; and if possible, leave with optimism. The one sensible answer she could think of at the moment was Sal. Sal knows. He should be able to direct her out of her dilemma.

A waitress seated Denise in the corner booth. An antique jukebox played a song by Jim Reeves. She recognized the sound of Sal's favorite singer from past visits. The smooth voice hardly affected her mood. Denise hunched over the house salad. Her fork rested on the lip of the bowl.

"Why you look so sad, my friend?" The tone of Sal's Italian accent provided the first part of what she needed. Perk the ears for gifted dialogue.

"Sad countenance makes for raisin face, like mine," Sal continued in his patent way. Not at all like Jeremy. "Trust Sal. A flower like you will want to keep her petals smooth. Your man will thank you for it one day."

"I had to leave," she finally forced herself to say.

Sal slid into the booth and put both hands, palms up, on the table in front of him after wiping them on the front of his apron. He waited for her to take them. When she touched his fingertips and curled her fingers over them, he said, "You did well to leave that bastard nephew. His wise-guy attitude and sludge he hangs with is no good for you."

"The only friends he ever let me meet are business associates."

"Not business you want to know. Your world is much better without all the blight he causes."

"I'm glad you feel that way. Few uncles would turn against their family in something like this."

Sal huffed. "I am protecting family, dear. You. Ruination and sorrow are what he brings, though I can't place all blame on my sister's son. She's the one let him roam the neighborhood like some stray. Rosy lips and big ordnance." Sal cupped his hands. "But sadly, no brains."

The gesture lightened her mood. She didn't know why. Leave it to Sal to know exactly what to do even when it involves expressions of offensive-type mannerisms. What she did marked her. She knew leaving New Jersey made her the target of a maniac. If only there was some way to erase Jeremy Guerdon from her memory, her past.

"Thanks, Sal. You're a good man. A good friend."

"No, Denise. Family."

His assurance made her feel better. There was nothing superfluous about Sal. That's another reason she trusted him. "Family it is then."

"Finish your lunch now." He scooted to the edge of the booth and got to his feet. "And don't fret your decision. Believe me. It's for best."

Chapter 10

The next morning, a black limousine wheeled to the curb in front of the terminal at Knoxville's McGhee Tyson Airport. From the sidewalk, Daniel recognized Luke Lanier in the driver's seat.

Luke hopped out and greeted Daniel with a wide grin as if they had known each other all their lives. "Well, I'll be. You made it here. Welcome to God's part of the world." Luke clutched Daniel's bag and extended a hand, still grinning.

Daniel shook Luke's hand. He felt calluses and strength in the man's grasp. "Is everybody down here as friendly as you?"

"Pretty much." Luke opened the rear door and waited for Daniel to climb in. "We go by what the Good Book says about friends, you know? Be one to get one."

"And love your neighbor as yourself," Daniel said, ducking inside.

"You got it. Hang around here a spell and you'll soon learn how neighborly the neighbors can be. We all look out for each other. Take care of things that need to be taken care of."

"I'll have to remember that."

Daniel loosened his tie and unbuttoned the top button of his shirt. Luke's enthusiasm was contagious. It made Daniel feel good. He was ready to have the meeting with Clifton Tyler and spend the rest of the day exploring the countryside. He yearned to see the mountains he had often heard so much about and visit renowned Gatlinburg and Pigeon Forge.

The police had taken their time getting around to interviewing him about the girl found murdered in the RV in the stadium parking lot. They let him leave after deciding he lacked information useful to their investigation. The setback prevented him from catching the last flight to Knoxville.

The plan was set. Go in. Listen to Clifton Tyler's spiel. Exchange ideas and that's it. No quid pro quo. No favors. He figured to be in there thirty minutes, maybe forty-five. Then he'd be free to do whatever and get back to the hotel for a quiet evening alone and a good night's sleep. If only the alone part was an option. Luke's voice interrupted his daydream.

"I'm sorry. Did you call me?"

"I don't mean to inconvenience or put you on the spot, but I need to ask you something. I wanted to clear it with you before I gave Miss Tyler an answer."

"Sure. Go ahead."

"Mr. Tyler asked if I would give his daughter a ride to his house at around two o'clock. I know you have a meeting with him at one. If that's okay, I'll drop her off there and then drive you wherever you want to go."

"Absolutely. I have no definite plans this afternoon. How old is the daughter?"

"Late twenties. And single, in case you're interested."

Luke swung the limo into the driveway and stopped in front of Mr. Tyler's building. Daniel opened the door and got out before Luke got around to that side of the car. He shook Luke's hand, leaving a hundred-dollar bill in the man's hand.

Luke nodded thanks. "Your bag?"

"If you don't mind, I'd like to leave it in the back for now. Save me from lugging it around."

"No problem on my end. I'll be out here when you're through."

Daniel admired the architecture a moment, sucked in a deep breath, let it out, and pushed open the door.

NOW THERE'S ONE, DENISE thought. She watched his gait from the moment he caught her eye. The way the visitor postured at the front desk and spoke to the receptionist exhibited a certain amount of ardor. The ease with which he moved gave her an idea about his desire in life. Deliberate steps carried him toward destiny. An aura of confidence, not arrogance, fortified his stride.

The visitor smiled and waved to the man dressed in a blue plaid shirt and khakis as the man hobbled by.

Denise slinked behind a planter and pulled away some of the fern's branches to make sure she had an unobstructed view of the visitor. The face played with her mind until it finally jogged her memory. It's him. Her mind flashed to Baltimore. It was the same person she chided at the airport. She hoped he had taken it the way it was intended. A jest and nothing more.

Why is he here?

That question vanished about as quickly as it took to flash across her mind. She didn't care why he was there. That he was there, standing a few feet away, suited her. She wanted to rush up to him and introduce herself. Hi. I'm Denise Tyler. We met at the airport, remember? I'd like to get to know you. A move in his direction might decide whether to go on with the notion. She could act like she was looking for something and pass on by. The plan sounded okay, but she wasn't sure if she could go through with it.

She frequented her father's office two to three times a week when she was in town. Another chance might escape her if she walked away. If she waited to see what developed, who knows what might happen. The thought grabbed and twisted her stomach. Too many ifs gnawed at her. What if this? What if that? What if there's a girlfriend? Any man with his looks must have a bond with the opposite sex. Denise was about to make her move when someone behind her spoke her name.

She whirled around. "Hi, Mr. Lanier."

"Are you okay? You look startled."

"I'm fine." She glanced toward the reception desk. Disappointment tumbled through her. The visitor was nowhere in sight.

"Your dad asked me to give you a lift home. He said about two o'clock?"

"Uh, huh." She tried to act normal. "What time is it now?"

"Twelve fifty-five. There'll be another person along for the ride."

Denise cut her eyes to Luke. "Who?"

"You better hope it ain't the guy that was in here this morning." The man in the plaid shirt steadied himself against the wall. "Darn might rude character."

"Hi, Pops."

The man waved to her and hobbled around the corner. Denise turned her attention back to Luke.

"His name's Daniel," Luke said.

"I don't know a Daniel."

"I think you do, Denise. You were just staring at him."

THE SIMPLICITY OF CLIFTON Tyler's approach impressed Daniel. Clifton schmoozed as if he and Daniel had known each other for years. After initial formalities were over, Clifton rose from the chair opposite where Daniel sat and paced on an oriental rug centered between a large mahogany desk and the door of the third-floor office. Five steps one way, pause, about-face, five on the return. Another pause and repeat.

The back-and-forth didn't faze Daniel. He listened while relaxing in one of two high-back leather chairs next to a floor-to-ceiling bookshelf. The chair's contour cradled every body part in contact with its surface.

Then Clifton said, "You have a future in this business, Dr. Baker, and I'm not just whistling air up your britches. Some people in this industry would kill to have this drug under their control. This meeting alone is worth more to me than you can imagine. I'm not putting down your ability to imagine things, of course. The people I've had contact with will do whatever they can to get their hands on Cyclodactin. We can't let that happen." He paused, nodded at Daniel, turned, and stepped behind his desk.

"This contract is more than Cyclodactin being placed on the market. It stipulates where and how it will be used and on whom."

"A specific market?" Daniel asked, although he knew how the drug was to be used.

"Cyclodactin will not be available at local pharmacies, Dr. Baker. Prudence will dictate its availability; its receivership. What I'm offering is a deal I trust you won't refuse."

Daniel remembered the second business card Mr. Tyler gave him at the airport in Baltimore. The card which bore the name Simon One. "Trust?"

"Explicitly," Clifton said. A light blinked on his desk phone. "Excuse me while I take this call."

Memories of Daniel's tenure with the Los Angeles Dodgers drew him away from Clifton's statement about trust. Women loitered outside stadiums and in hotels and restaurants for a chance to be with a player. Some offered companionship for the evening. Others tendered whatever lonesome, road-weary athletes might desire of them.

Respect for women and desire to make right choices guided his refusal to get involved with any of them more than the possibility of contracting an STD. A mother's discourse on morality steered him away from accepting what amounted to a bribe, sexual or otherwise.

Although something in Clifton Tyler's tone connected with him, Daniel suspected he was no ordinary entrepreneur. The man's body language betrayed him.

This same feeling came over him the day after graduation from medical school. The offer presented to him that morning on the phone from the person identified only as Simon One opened the path to a career opportunity that would make him part of a clandestine agency. Two years of training set Daniel's future. Service at the Center for Disease Control in Atlanta led him to a breakthrough he never thought possible.

Daniel wanted to ask Clifton about Simon. He waited for a more appropriate time and pushed up from the chair the moment Clifton ended the call. They shook hands. "I'll let you know."

"Then you understand my position in this matter."

"Yes."

Clifton accompanied Daniel to the reception area. "You do plan on staying in town awhile." Clifton's tone sounded like an insistence.

"I've heard much about this part of the country. I might try to see some of it."

"Good. Luke will take you anywhere you want to go."

Chapter 11

Denise settled in the limo and opened a strawberry-flavored water and took a sip. She capped the bottle and pulled a Brandilyn Collins novel from her bag. She stared at a slip of paper stuffed next to her bookmark. Someone had written, "What's wrong with your car?" in red ink.

"Miss Tyler's inside," she heard Luke say. The statement whisked away the fog and brandished reality. She quickly crumpled the paper and let it fall between her left leg and the door and fixed her eyes on the book. The door on the passenger's side opened.

Denise gasped when she saw the face. She relished the sight of his handsome features and athletic physique. Flushed, she lowered the book. Her left thumb held her place. The thrill of having him next to her tied a bow around her heart. She felt every pulse of the carotid artery in her neck. Her throat felt dry.

"You must be Miss Tyler."

That did it. His voice soothed her aching heart, although its rhythm increased in intensity. She uttered a yes.

"I'm Daniel." She watched his eyes shift to her lap and back up. They locked on hers. "Good book?"

"Huh?"

"The paperback you have there. Interesting?"

She nodded but said, "Not anymore."

The limo pulled away from the curb. A left turn tossed Denise rightward. She threw out her hand to brace on the seat. Her fingers brushed against Daniel's arm. Her mind advised her to latch the seat belt, yet her hand stayed planted on the leather seat cushion. A strange feeling swirled up her arm and filled her chest. Daniel searched the seat for the buckle to secure his restraint. Denise followed his lead and latched hers. Luke slowed the limo as they approached Maryville Pike.

The sound of crushing metal and breaking glass blasted their eardrums at the intersection of Maryville Pike and Woodson Drive. The front of the striking pickup careened off the left front of the limo. The truck's engine revved. Tires squealed. The stench of burned rubber filled the limo. The engine noise faded in the distance. The entire incident was over in less than two seconds. For Denise, it seemed like time changed from a flash to a prolonged horror.

Dazed from being jostled around inside the car, the first thing she realized was fingers in her hair. Palms cradled her face. The sensation seemed surreal. This was another thing her ex never took time to do for her. Jeremy never caressed her face or ran his fingers through her hair. Schmooze, snatch, and grapple fit Jeremy's style. Her eyes finally focused enough to catch Daniel's concerned look inches away. He knelt on the seat next to her, leg touching her thigh, eyes following his fingers through strands of her hair.

"Can you hear me?" His gaze met her seeking eyes.

She affirmed with a nod, still unsure if the face so close to hers was real. His touch was nice, but what surprised her most was having her hand cupped on his cheek.

"Miss Tyler. How do you feel? Are you hurting anywhere?"

"What happened?" she asked, pulling away her hand and righting herself on the seat.

"Someone hit us. Are you hurting anywhere?"

"No." She checked her arms and down her body to her feet. She wiggled her fingers and toes, inhaled and exhaled. No pains. Everything worked. "I'm fine."

A moan from the front seat prompted Daniel to rush to check on Luke Lanier. He reached over the seat back and felt Luke's neck for a pulse.

"How bad is he hurt?" Denise's face poised next to the driver's headrest. The possibility of something seriously wrong with her friend's father troubled her in the worst way.

"Hold his head." Daniel clasped her hands in his and positioned them on either side of Luke's chin. "Hold it right there and don't let it move."

Daniel crawled over the seat and checked Luke's vital signs. He snatched open Luke's shirt, reached for the ballpoint pen in the shirt pocket. He hurriedly unscrewed the top portion of the pen and stabbed Luke's chest. The air in Luke's chest released with a hissing sound. Denise shrieked when Luke jerked and gasped. The release of pressure allowed inflation of Luke's left lung. His struggle for breath startled Denise more than the hiss.

"He's going to be fine," Daniel said. "I had to relieve the pressure in his chest so he could breathe. Luke, if you can hear me, take slow, easy breaths."

Luke tensed and pulled against Denise's hold. "A debt of gratitude."

"Easy, Luke. Don't talk. An ambulance is on its way."

Denise rested her head on top of the seat back. The poise and swiftness of Daniel's actions left no doubt in her mind that he knew what needed to be done for Luke.

"Heck of a job, young man."

Denise peered out and saw a white-haired firefighter perched next to the car looking over Daniel's shoulder.

"My guess is you've had some training." The firefighter paused and let out a chortle when Daniel's face turned toward him. "Wait, a minute. I know you. Hey guys, look who we have here. I don't believe it. It's Daniel Baker. Hurry. Get that gurney over here."

Daniel Baker. Should I know that name?

The firefighter hurried around to the passenger's side and opened the rear door. He reached a hand inside, got Denise by the hand, and helped her out of the limo. He asked her how she was feeling and if she hurt anywhere.

The mention of Daniel's name caused a stir among the hoard of onlookers. Many of them closed in for an eyeful and a story to tell whomever might listen. Their actions irked Denise. Bystanders pushed and shoved each other as if trying to glimpse royalty. She overheard one man ask for Daniel's autograph. The man huffed and stormed off when Daniel ignored him.

Denise admired the way Daniel focused on Luke. Rescue workers used the Jaws of Life on the driver's door to open it. Neither noise nor their actions distracted him. He assisted the EMTs with Luke's extrication and stayed alongside the gurney until they loaded Luke into the ambulance.

Denise started toward the ambulance. As she passed one of the uniformed officers interviewing a witness, she heard the lady tell the officer, "There was no way this was an accident. That truck intentionally hit them, Officer. I saw it."

Anxiety clawed at Denise. What if this was done purposely? Who would do such a thing? The notion made her woozy. She wobbled around the limo, using the side of the car for support. After a couple of deep breaths, Denise shuffled to the rear of the ambulance where the medics performed a secondary assessment on Luke.

The next thing she knew, Daniel held her in his arms. The concern she had seen immediately after the collision focused a second time on her.

"You need to go with them." He motioned toward the medics.

Denise grabbed Daniel around the neck and held on as if the Grim Reaper clutched and yanked a handful of her hair. Her body trembled. She couldn't make it stop. "Please hold me. I'm afraid."

STAGE ONE OF JEREMY'S plan failed to accomplish his goal. He watched through a spotting scope from where he set up a block from Clifton Tyler's office. The impact of the Ford F-250 into the limousine looked like a direct hit on the side he had seen Denise get into. Glass shattered and sprayed both vehicles and the street. The limousine veered right and nosed to the curb. The truck sped away and disappeared from view.

Jeremy focused the scope on the car. The tinted rear window and windows on the passenger side prevented seeing anything inside. The doors stayed closed. He wished he could see the driver's side of the limousine. His vantage point prevented it.

Passersby stopped and got out of their vehicles. Some put cell phones to their ears. A crowd of onlookers gathered on the sidewalk and in the street. They stared at the limo. A couple of them crept closer to the car as if hesitant to get near a dying monster.

Two minutes. No discernable movement in the limousine.

A fire engine pulled through the intersection and parked, followed by a rescue truck and a police cruiser. The passenger in the rescue unit threw open his door and darted to the limousine. Moments later, the same firefighter hurried around the rear of the car and opened the rear door. Denise emerged from the limo unscathed, as far as Jeremy could see from the window. He leaped to his feet, displeased at Richie's failure.

"Unreliable idiot."

He huffed, grabbed the scope, and chunked it through the open door into the adjoining room. The optics exploded when it crashed against the plaster wall. He grabbed the edge of the desk and flipped it upside down, and kicked the chair across the room.

Fury burned inside his chest when once he again looked out the window and saw Denise throw her arms around a guy's neck and rest her head on his chest. His breathing changed to deep, slow, and controlled.

"Play on, Denise Tyler. My fun's only beginning."

Chapter 12

The rapidity and stiffness of Denise's heartbeat was clear as she pressed against his chest. The closeness of this stranger and whiff of her perfume stirred Daniel's emotions. What was he to do under these circumstances? Should he hold on to her and give her a hug to let her feel secure in his arms?

"I'm here for you."

Denise turned her head from his shoulder and nuzzled his cheek. A stream of tears trickled across his jaw and down his neck.

One of the medics waved Daniel toward the ambulance. "Come on. You two need to get checked out."

Daniel agreed, more so for Denise's well-being. "Go with them, Miss Tyler."

"Will you come with me? Please?"

"Sure. I need to get my bag out of the car."

"We have to go now," the medic warned.

"Go," he said to Denise. "I'll get a ride, I promise."

The medic extended an arm and assisted Denise into the back of the ambulance. Daniel supported her from behind and closed the rear doors.

Daniel retrieved his carry-on from the limo's trunk. As he passed the open rear door, he noticed the novel Denise had been holding prior to the crash lying of the floor. A piece of paper lay on the floor next to it. He picked up the book and paper he figured Denise was using to mark her place. He thumbed open the paperback and stuffed the paper inside. The word *wrong* caught his eye.

What's wrong with your car?

Daniel stuffed the book in a side pocket of his bag and asked the lieutenant for a ride to the hospital.

They arrived at University Hospital before the paramedics unloaded their patient. Three staff members from the emergency department converged on Luke. The medic relayed her findings to the accepting physician who directed them to an exam room. The buzz centered on Luke's chest wound and how part of an ink pen came to be lodged in the man's upper chest.

A nurse helped Denise out of the ambulance and led her to a room around the corner. Daniel caught up with them at the door. The nurse directed him to wait in the hall.

Daniel paced the hall between the two exam rooms. He wanted to be in there with Denise. Concern for Luke kept his ears perked for any news coming out of the exam room where he was taken. Without privileges in Tennessee hospitals, any offer to assist either was useless. Abilities to exercise and not being allowed to use them here frustrated him. Forget liability if anything should go wrong. He ached to be in there.

He yearned to know what caused the fear he detected in Denise.

Clifton Tyler rounded the corner three minutes after the nurse closed the door to the exam room. "Dr. Baker, where is Denise? Is she hurt?"

"In there."

Clifton Tyler rushed to the door and pushed his way inside. A short time later, the door opened and he stepped out. Daniel straightened to meet him.

"Denise told me what you did for Luke. Luke's a good man, Dr. Baker. Thank you."

"You may see her now." A woman in orange scrub pants and print top made eye contact with Daniel. She held open the door to the exam room.

"Go ahead," Clifton told Daniel. "I'm going to check on Luke."

Denise sat on the edge of the exam table, head down, as she threaded the top button on her shirt. The beauty displayed in her smile when she lifted her head let him know everything turned out okay. "How's Luke? Have you heard anything?"

"All I know is what I've picked up from the staff going in and out of the room. They are about to take him for a CT scan. He'll be there awhile. How do you feel?"

"I'm fine. My left shoulder's tender. And my head. I guess I hit the window or something." She rubbed the area over her collarbone.

"That's from the seat belt." He pointed to her left clavicle.

Denise pulled the fabric away and exposed a band-like wheal the width of the belt webbing. "You were checking my head when you had your fingers in my hair, weren't you?"

"Your head slammed the window pretty hard."

"My head broke the window?"

"The window next to you stayed intact. The one in front of it shattered and sprayed us with shards of glass."

They sat in silence for the next three minutes. Daniel leaned against the counter and watched Denise with his peripheral vision, not wanting to look directly at her. He did not want to give her the impression that he was staring at her.

Denise fidgeted on the table. She twisted and stretched her back and rubbed her left shoulder.

The nurse in charge of her care waddled in breaking the silence with her singing, "Are you ready to go?" to the tune of "Are You Lonesome Tonight?" The woman went straight to the counter, where she scribbled something on Denise's chart. When she adjusted the pages against the countertop, a slip of green paper jutted out of the side.

"What in the world is this?" The nurse slid out and lifted the piece of paper, read what was on it, and jerked open the door. "Call security!"

Denise hopped off the exam table and picked up the note. She read it and looked at Daniel and again at the note. She eased back up on the exam table and stared at the floor, the note, the door, the note. Her expression concerned him. He stepped over and offered his hand to her. She glanced up at him, slid her right hand into his, and looked back at the paper.

A uniformed Knoxville police officer entered the room, nodded to Denise and Daniel, and asked about the note. The nurse and a technician followed him in. Daniel motioned to the chart on the counter. The officer slipped on a pair of glasses and bent closer to the counter. He pulled off the glasses and turned to face them. "How many people have touched this?" The officer paused at each face until he met the gaze of every person in the room.

"The nurse and I both handled it," Denise said.

"Then I need for you to come to the precinct. We'll need your fingerprints for elimination."

"Oh, you don't have to bother with that, Officer. I already know who sent it."

"You know, or have an idea?" The officer's tone implied doubt.

Daniel wanted to hear more. Everyone in the room closed in. They listened while Denise told the officer what she had learned about Jeremy Guerdon.

Fifteen minutes later, dispatch notified officers of an abandoned F-250 at the Knoxville Museum of Art. The pickup had damage to the front and left side consistent with what witnesses had described on the hit-and-run vehicle.

"Sounds like they got our vehicle," the officer said, jotting on his pad. "That's good for you folks. We now know what area to look at to find the driver. I need to get something to secure this."

"Will an envelope do?" the nurse asked.

"That'd be good."

The nurse left the room and returned with a manila envelope in hand. The officer looked at the note once more before sliding it into the envelope and folding shut the clasp. He turned to face Denise. "The way this reads makes it sound like there's more to come. We'll get this off to the lab and hopefully have this hoodlum off the street before he can do you more harm. I'd take a few extra precautions if I were you, ma'am."

"He's right," Daniel said, still holding her hand. "If this guy's even close to what you've told the officer, he has to be stopped and you need protection."

Chapter 13

Daniel agreed to stay through the afternoon and evening with Denise. Necessity prodded him more than anything else. Everything pointed to the likelihood of another attack by Jeremy Guerdon or whoever was doing this to her. Help Denise cope, keep her safe, and get her through demands placed on her shifted from priority to desire to priority. At the moment, desire and priority merged into one.

Her charisma stunned him. Whatever was happening captivated him. This was something he never expected. It surpassed anything he had ever known.

Daniel hoisted his overnight bag and situated the strap on his left shoulder. They strolled through the automatic doors onto the ramp outside the emergency room.

"Dad said he parked my car somewhere over ... There it is."

The man Denise had described to the officer was nowhere in sight. Satisfied they were safe to head across the parking lot, Daniel adjusted the strap and took Denise by the arm. He looked up and down each row before moving to the next, alert for the unexpected.

"Where are you taking me?" Daniel asked when they reached the car.

"To my parents' house. I hope you don't mind."

"Not a bit. You should let me drive."

She looked across the top of her Acura at him. "You really don't mind?"

Daniel shoved his bag over the top of the seat and let it fall in the back. One end of Denise's paperback protruded out of the pocket. An edge of the paper inside it jutted from among the pages.

What's wrong with your car?

"Not at all."

Daniel circled the car and held out his hand. The way she placed the keys in his palm expressed an interest in more than a drive to the Tyler's' residence. The tips of her fingers sent warmth through him. A feeling unlike any he ever sensed encased his heart. Denise waited while he opened the passenger door for her. She took the hand he offered to help her get in. The same feeling of warmth transferred from her fingers through his body a second time.

He noticed her watching him when he slid in the other side. Oh, how he wished he could read her mind. Did her thoughts match the feel of her sensitivity? He sensed they did.

THE ACURA ROLLED TO a stop in the left turn lane two miles from where they had pulled into the street. Denise wanted to close her eyes, but Daniel needed directions to her parents' house. She wished she could shut out everything bad in her life, pretend none of these things were happening to her, and that Jeremy was a vapor in one of her dreams. Somehow, she had to start over. She needed to make plans for a different future instead of the one forced on her.

Daniel made a left turn and whipped right into a parking lot at a strip shopping center.

"What did you do?" He put the gearshift in park. The tone in his voice gave the impression of a stalemate. He looked straight ahead, chiseled jaw locked, waiting for an answer.

Denise hesitated long enough to think about how she should reply. The wrong answer might drive him away. "What do you mean?"

"The crash. The way you clung to me out there. The note. Somebody's after you. Your body language screams it."

"I don't want to talk about it." Denise dropped her head and began to cry. "I don't know who to trust."

"Trust no one."

"What about you? Should I trust you?"

"I'll have to earn it. Earned trust secures a bond between two people better than any blind trust. Let me earn it."

Denise sneaked a glance at him. If he was like Jeremy, his face refused to show it. The tenderness she saw in his eyes squeezed her heart. It made her want to be near him that much more. Kindheartedness burned from his eyes in a way she'd never seen in another person.

"I'll think about it. If I ever start to trust you, I hope I'll not be disappointed."

"Me too. Whenever you're ready—"

"I need time."

"Fair enough."

A man of understanding was another thing she needed in her turned-upside-down life. She wondered if Daniel might be the one.

"TAKE A RIGHT HERE." Denise indicated a paved driveway. Daniel steered the Acura into the turn.

The Tyler's property comprised of sixty acres of knolls covered with mountain laurel and mixed hardwoods and fifteen acres of open pasture. A split-rail fence surrounded the property and lined the asphalt drive on both sides up to the remodeled farmhouse built by Connie Tyler's father. Summersweet lined the way to the house, each one covered with bright flowers that emitted a sweet fragrance. More colors filled an oblong garden stretched in front of a huge front porch and extending to a detached garage.

"Somebody has a gift," Daniel said.

"My grandfather owned a nursery. He left it to my mother. She and Grands run it now. Adds natural beauty to the old place. What do you think?"

Nothing like your beauty, he wanted to say. "Certainly does. Smells nice. Not too overpowering."

Denise opened a gate in the fence and closed it after they stepped through. She led the way across the edge of the pasture to the tree line. They followed the fence as it zigzagged toward the backside of the acreage. A boy's bicycle leaned against the fence a few feet from the rearmost corner.

"The neighbors," Denise said, explaining the bicycle. "They have a trail their two boys ride on."

Three fence rails leaned against a new section of fence. Bullet holes riddled the splintered wood.

"The boys declare war on your fence?"

Denise laughed at her dad's handiwork. "It's something Dad and I do."

"Is that the way you vent your anger?"

Denise picked up a piece of the wood and examined it. Three to this one, she observed. He cut it in half with three shots. "Who said anything about being angry? This is just one of the ways he and I bond."

"Shooting a perfectly good fence."

She chucked the board aside. "Better than someone who asks too many questions."

"I'll take that as a hint to shut up."

"I enjoy casual conversation."

"Just not about fences."

"No, you may talk about fences, if that's your thing."

"As long as I don't cross the line."

"Right."

"Else I may be the one full of holes."

"Right."

Farther down, Daniel spotted and picked up a shed antler. "Check this out." He held up one half of the buck's bleached-out rack. "Five points."

Denise squinted. "Looks weird."

"That's because some critter's gnawed on it. See the teeth marks? This came from a nice buck."

"How did he lose it? Did it break off?"

"They shed them every year. Grow another set during spring and summer, usually larger and with more points. They're covered with velvet until late August, early September.

"That big? That fast? And velvet? Come on now. What really happens?"

"Okay, it's not real velvet. That's what it's called because it looks like velvet."

"Amazing. I guess you hunt?"

"Two or three times a season whenever I have the chance. I love the challenge more than anything else."

"What animal presents the greatest challenge."

"Whitetail deer if hunting pressure is high."

"Any other challenge in wherever it is you're from?"

Her inflection on the word challenge piqued his curiosity. He recognized a vibe that led him to believe Denise wanted to get to know him and she hoped there was no one he might be attached to somewhere else.

"Not interested in any there."

"What about here?"

Daniel scanned the landscape and switched from there to her Nikes. His focus crawled up her curves and locked on her blue eyes. The eyes mesmerized him every time he looked into them. "The scenery makes a lasting impression."

At that moment a red-tail hawk flew over calling, Cheer, cheer, cheer, and perched in the boughs of an oak.

"The hawk approves," Denise said with a laugh, looking skyward.

Daniel looked at Denise. *So do I.*

When they returned to the house, Denise filled the blender with ice, strawberries, peaches, and vanilla yogurt and made smoothies. Daniel sat catty-corner on the one end of the sofa, twenty-ounce cup of smoothie in his left hand, staring at Denise lounging on the other end, legs folded under her. Her hands cradled a smaller cup of the drink on her lap. Daniel noticed a faraway look on her face. "Are you okay?"

"I will be." Denise sipped the smoothie and put the half-full cup on the coffee table centered in front of the sofa. "I'm glad you're here."

"Me too."

"You mean that?"

"Yes. And I can't explain why."

"Why doesn't matter. It just feels good to have someone I can talk to that won't snap at me every time I have something I want to say."

"Is that the way it was with him?"

Denise sighed and slumped farther into the corner of the couch. She sat in silence while Daniel waited patiently for her answer. Tears filled her eyes and spilled onto her cheeks. "I've never told anyone anything about mine and Jeremy's relationship—ever."

"You don't have to go into any of that with me, Denise. We can sit here and talk about whatever you want to talk about, or we could just lean back on this cozy sofa."

Daniel adjusted the pillow behind his back and crossed his legs at the ankles.

"You're not at all like Jeremy."

"You make it sound as though we know each other."

"I see it in your eyes. I've noticed it the whole time we've been together today."

"If that guy treated you as badly as I imagine him, based on your reactions—"

"It wasn't that way at first. He played the part of a perfect gentleman. I was led to believe that he was the CEO of a company that he and two of his college buddies started in 2008. They planned a celebration dinner after some acquisition of another company, and one of my friends invited me to go with her. She introduced him to me during dinner, and we chatted until almost everyone else had gone for the evening, including my friend. I never saw her again after that night."

"What do you think happened to her?"

"I'm not sure. I tried calling her. All I got was her voice mail. I went by her condo. She was never there. I drove to where she worked. Her boss said they received her termination notice in the mail. The lady said it came unsigned."

"It sounds like something happened to her."

"I believe he killed her."

"You think Jeremy killed your friend?"

"I know he did. I figure it anyway now that I know what he really does for a living."

Denise opened up and told Daniel all about Jeremy and their involvement, or lack of, with each other. Every emotion except happiness expressed itself. Her face reddened. She wrung her hands, balled them into fists. She cried, embraced herself, and quivered. She let her head fall back and stared at the ceiling. All the while she expressed anger and distress more than any other emotion.

She ended about an hour later with details of the evening she discovered the terrifying letter, drawn up in a ball against the back of the sofa.

"God gave us free will and the ability to reason and apply logic to things we do," Daniel said. "Choices we make follow us, and hopefully a black hole of regret won't swallow us. Whatever—"

"If you think I'll regret leaving him, you're out of your mind."

"I'm not finished."

"He intends to kill me."

"You crossed the death line."

"The death what?"

"Death line. It's self-set boundary of sorts. Cross it and you'll face a day of reckoning. Whatever you did must have put you over the line. If it did—"

"He won't stop until he's killed me."

"Or make you wish you had died. That's the harsh reality."

"I still can't figure out why. Based on the note I found that night he already had plans to kill me. I thought about leaving way before then. I should have. His note cinched it for me. I had to get out. I left and was on my way here the night I saw you at the airport."

"I'll never forget that night."

"I know I won't."

"Wearing a Dodgers jersey. I was a tad disappointed. It was not one with my old number on it."

"Twenty-seven. Am I correct?"

"You recognized me?"

"Not right away. It took me a while but I finally remembered where I had seen you. The jersey was a gift."

"Special?"

"Yeah. Jeremy wouldn't let me wear it out anywhere. He got resentful when Carson gave it to me."

"You know Cars?"

"He used to date my best friend, Judith. You'd like her. She's a blast to be around. They split a while ago. He wanted her on the road with him, but she turned him down. She's a homebody."

"Did this Jeremy fellow spring a jealous leak about Cars?"

"A deluge. That's what really started me thinking. The whelp overacted."

"Overreacted, huh."

"Justified ... Hey. Whose side are you on here?"

"You're the teacher. I'm the student."

"Here to learn what?"

Daniel smiled. "Everything I can about you."

"Well, tell me. What have you learned so far?"

Daniel eased up on one knee. "That you desire something special in your future." He leaned forward and kissed her.

Chapter 14

Jeremy had to make sure Richie had done what he was supposed to with the truck before he moved on to item two on the list. He wanted to find out all he could about the man keeping company with Denise. Three phone calls later, Jeremy located the F-250 at the police impound. Now he had to finagle his way in to confirm the VIN plates were missing from the truck.

"Agent Zumwalt?" The fifty-something security officer at the gate handed back the ID presented to him. "You don't look like any agent I ever seen. Black ops maybe with that getup you have on."

"The key, please." Jeremy held out his hand.

The man's appearance disgusted him. Flab inside a knit shirt dangled over undersized pants. Flakes of weathered skin jutted from his forehead and receding hairline. His lubed hair was parted about an inch above the left ear.

"Yeah, yeah. Hold on here a minute. You know, I got about as much use for you guys as chewed gum." The officer scrambled the keys in the drawer until he found the one he was looking for. "Impatient, and no manners like all the rest of them feds that show up here without so much as a phone call to let me know what's going on."

"Follow me and I'll show you."

"What?"

"Exactly what I'm about to do."

"Really? Let me lock up and I'm right behind you."

The guard blabbered the entire one hundred fifty yards to the truck and continued while Jeremy pulled on a pair of work gloves and checked every location on the truck for the vehicle identification number. "Am I talking too much? Let me know if I am. I don't want to be a nuisance."

Jeremy huffed.

"The old lady says I do. Talk too much, that is. Told me I should've been born a girl. I'm not really sure what she meant by that, though. Makes me wonder if maybe she'd like me better as a woman, if you know what I mean. If I was a woman ... ah, never mind."

"Has anyone else inspected this vehicle?"

"A gumshoe from auto theft at Knoxville PD called about it. Wanted to make sure nobody fooled around with it until he could get out here the next day or two. Said he figured it was stolen since the plates came off a Chrysler something or other. I think he said the truck was involved in a hit-and-run case. I doubt he'll find anything when he gets here. Nothing really to find from what I can see." The guard leaned against the open tailgate, whipped out a pocketknife with a three-inch blade, and guided the tip under his fingernails.

"Nothing except a dead body."

"What? Where?"

"Here." Jeremy clamped his hand over the officer's hand holding the knife and shoved the blade into the guard's left nostril. The guard bowed back into the truck bed. His head rested on a spare tire, his hands grasping his face. Blood gushed from his nose and mouth, streaked down both cheeks and dripped and pooled on the bed liner. The guard postured and convulsed several seconds and then relaxed with a whoosh.

Jeremy slammed the tailgate, scrunching the guard's legs between his buttocks and the tailgate. He ripped off the gloves and tossed them inside a crashed sedan in the next row.

"Your wife should've told you to quit jabbering and pay attention to what's happening around you."

The notion prompted Jeremy to take out his phone and send a text message to Denise.

THE WARMTH OF DANIEL'S lips launched another tingle through her body. The kiss opened lines of communication to every body part and filled the lacuna in her heart. She wondered if Daniel felt it. The steady contact suggested he felt something. A display of affection, not the least bit of pretense, shrouded her from everything outside the moment. Its intensity shoved aside her anxiety and fear of Jeremy Guerdon.

A rattle of keys and the sound of a key inserted in the side door lock stalled her on the edge of weakness. The kiss did something to her. Daniel's kiss made her feel like she was more than some object set on display and she wanted another and another.

Connie Tyler opened the door.

"Hi, Mom."

Connie let the keys slide from her fingers onto the table and set her Rebecca Minkoff handbag next to them. The pale-yellow button-up dress trimmed in white and dark hair pulled back on one side gave her a look of someone much younger than fifty-two.

"Are you alright? Your father phoned me about the accident. Let me look at you." Connie ran her hands up and down her daughter's arms while she gave Denise a once-over with her eyes.

"I rushed to the hospital, and they told me you'd been released. Are you sure you're okay?"

"I'm fine, Mom. I got checked out at the hospital. Everything's fine."

"Who's this?"

Daniel had risen to his feet and stood at the end of the couch. Denise unfolded her legs and sprang off the sofa. She guided her hand into his.

"Mom, meet Daniel Baker."

"Does your mother know you're here, young man?"

"Umm." Daniel pumped Denise's hand.

Denise nudged him. "Loosen up. She's only kidding."

"I'm an orphan," Daniel said and sucked in his cheeks.

Redness mottled Connie Tyler's face. "I apologize, Mr.—"

"Doctor."

"I'm truly sorry, Dr. Baker. I truly am. I would've never..."

"No apology necessary, Mrs. Tyler. And yes, I talked to my mother this morning. She knows I'm here."

"Daniel." Denise nudged him again. "That wasn't very nice."

"Well, not here exactly," he continued. "I told her I had some business in Tennessee."

Connie Tyler strode up to Daniel and patted his left cheek. "Finally, someone with a sense of humor." She looked at Denise. "I like him, Denise." She cut her eyes at Daniel. "He's quite handsome."

Denise thought so too, but for her Daniel was more than a nice-looking man. His personality appealed to her. She especially liked the confidence he exuded at the crash scene and at the hospital. His remarks about trust made her want to trust him that much more.

The tone on her cell phone indicating an incoming text message interrupted the mood. Denise reached for the phone and hit "View." Two words on the screen shocked her heart.

"New boyfriend?"

Tremors shook her. The text reminded her of the note at the hospital. Its words, *A tap for attention*, flashed through her mind. She figured Jeremy was watching her. What would he do next? He probably saw Daniel with her and surmised that Daniel was a new love interest. What was she thinking when she got Daniel involved, putting him in harm's way?

Denise darted out the front door.

Daniel pursued two strides behind. He kept pace with Denise until they reached the corner of the fence perpendicular to the driveway. There he overtook and circled in front of her. Denise sidled right to continue. She covered her mouth to hold back sobs rumbling inside her, threw out her other arm, and braced on the top rail.

"The text was from him, wasn't it?"

"Please," she said, pulling her hand away to speak. "I've put you in danger. You've got to get away from me." She clamped both hands over her mouth, closed her eyes, bowed at the waist, and slumped against Daniel.

"You're the one in danger. I'm not leaving you like this."

Daniel draped his arm around her and led her across the yard. She knew where he was guiding her when she caught a whiff of a fresh coat of sealant on the gazebo. When he paused, she lifted her leg and stepped up eight inches between yellow angel trumpets and over to a five-foot swing.

"Sit here," Daniel said. "Take a deep breath and savor nature's bounty."

The first deep breath of lacquer-saturated air irritated her lungs. She opened her eyes and exhaled a sputter of coughs.

"Sorry. I guess that wasn't such a bright idea."

"It's all right. The smell is not too awful. I like it here. This is one of my favorite spots," she said, dabbing tears with the sleeve of her shirt.

"I hoped it might be when I spotted it."

Denise shifted to one side to give Daniel room to sit next to her. "Are you always this way?"

"What way do you mean?"

"Sensible."

He eased in next to her. "Sometimes. Thanks to my mom."

"I like it. Thank her for me. Now it's your turn." Denise pushed her feet against the floor, putting the swing in motion. The links of chain in the eyebolts overhead squawked in rhythm with their fore-and-aft movements. "Occupy my mind with things about Daniel Baker."

Chapter 15

Jeremy sensed a need to move. Somewhere near Knoxville. He wanted a place to settle into while there; some place he could work on his things to do without distraction and monitor Denise. Since no acquaintances or family lived in the area—talking to his uncle Sal about staying with him was out of the question—and hotels failed to suit his need, Jeremy would look for a suitable shelter.

He cruised the outskirts of the city. At two thirty, Jeremy pulled up to an iron gate in front of a stucco ranch on the northwest side of Knoxville. The house stood some eighty yards off the street. An eight-foot fence surrounded the property. The fence was flanked on the inside by rows of cypress trees. He wrote the information from the real estate agent's sign on a scratch piece of paper, called the number provided, and arranged to meet the agent at her office on the south side of the city.

He wheeled the Lincoln into the driveway and parked twenty-five minutes after making the call. Red hair and curves stood next to the open driver's door of a green Honda, keys in hand. She wore too much makeup for his taste.

"Mr. Rubano, I presume?"

Jeremy coursed between the cars and met her in front of the Honda. He offered his hand and flashed a mouth full of bonded enamel. "Anthony, please."

"I'm Judith Lanier. Would you like to go see the house first?"

Jeremy thought about the napkin in his pocket bearing Judith Lanier's name and phone number. "I'm settled on it."

Judith described the house with enthusiasm as they strode up the steps and through the front door of the real estate office. "It has several features I know you'll enjoy. It has hardwood floors throughout—except the baths and kitchen, which are tile—large bedrooms, plenty of open space in the family room with vaulted ceilings, kitchen with new stainless-steel appliances, full basement, state-of-the-art security and intercom systems."

The way her hips swayed excited him. He slowed, allowing her to cross the room well ahead of him. "Perfect," he said, referring to her gait, not the features she described in the house.

"Pretty near is. Coffee?"

Jeremy declined her offer and dropped to the chair next to the desk that displayed her nameplate. "Let me say, Ms. Lanier, I prefer to lease the property, but will purchase it if necessary."

Judith raked through file folders in the top drawer of a wooden file cabinet, snatched out a folder, and nodded. "I think we might arrange something for you, Anthony."

He loathed the way "An-tha-nee" rolled off her tongue. He wondered if Southerners ever said anything without a drawl or twang.

Judith pulled out the chair from behind the desk, slid in, and rolled up to the edge. A picture of the house topped the file. She brushed aside the photo, rummaged page after page until finally locating and pulling one near the bottom of the stack. "What length were you thinking about for a lease?"

Six months would give him ample time to complete his to-do list. He only needed five. The last thing on the list—kill Denise—wouldn't happen until a week before Christmas. Until then, his plan contained plenty of things to make her life miserable. And her family's as well.

"Six months."

Jeremy missed New York City. Hillbillies and rednecks cruising around in pickup trucks with oversized tires and flying rebel flags made him jittery. He didn't trust them. Most people he'd met since he arrived seemed nice. Their niceness made him suspicious of them. The thing that concerned him: they carried guns. Some even displayed their long guns on racks mounted to the cab for the world to see. Those displays left no doubt as to the owners. He had heard stories. They act as protectors. He figured whatever. If they enjoyed life, who was he to argue? He could handle it for five months.

Judith locked fingers, frowned, and said, "Most of our clients require at least twelve months on a lease unless it's a lease-purchase situation."

"How soon will I be able to move in?"

"Give me three days. I should know something by then."

DENISE NESTLED DANIEL'S side and rested her head on his shoulder. For two hours he talked, starting with his high school days in Cripple Creek, Colorado, on to being drafted by the L.A. Dodgers after his sophomore year at the University of Colorado and the career-ending injury he suffered at Camden Yards.

"What then?"

"I went to medical school. Growing up I wanted to become a baseball player or a doctor."

"Where do you work?"

"The Center for Disease Control in Atlanta."

"My Dad's business has something to do with them if I'm not mistaken. Is that the reason you were at his office?"

"That's why I was in Baltimore the night you asked me the time. The next day, I had my final appointment with the physician that performed surgery on my leg."

"What did the doctor say?"

"He said it had healed well and looked good, though he strongly suggested that I not try to play again."

She cringed when he mentioned the injury but was relieved to hear it should cause no problems for him in the future. The inflections and tone of voice caressed her soul. The solace she needed came from an unforeseen source.

The pink and lavender pattern hovering near the horizon accented the effect his presence had on her. The wind whisked away the scent of lacquer and replaced it with the essence from the Tyler's flower garden.

"Are sunsets in Cripple Creek anything like this?"

"They would be if you were there to share them."

The words formed a balm penetrating the exterior of her heart and easing the ache she had lived with since before leaving New Jersey. Could this possibly be a glimpse of future bliss?

The wind settled to a breeze after the sun dropped below the horizon. The hideous odor of lacquer returned and strengthened around the gazebo with the increase of humidity. It didn't seem to matter. They sat there a couple minutes in silence except for the squawk-squawk of the chain overhead.

A melody Denise recognized by the fourth note purred in Daniel's throat. The hum reminded her of the night she heard the Rascal Flatts' song on the radio during her drive to Baltimore. She joined in when he got to the chorus and cocked her head to catch his reaction. He smiled and forced up the volume. At the end, he coursed right into another one of their hits.

"Rascal Flatts fan?" she asked.

"Have been ever since they released their first CD."

"Do you sing?"

"I enjoy singing. Put it that way."

"I'd rather listen. That way, I'm not embarrassed if I mess up by forgetting the lyrics or if I sing off pitch."

"I don't imagine anyone would notice. They'd be captivated by your beauty to notice how you sang the song."

Denise felt heat flash her cheeks. One song on the CD talked about a girl wearing the guy's old shirt. She wondered if she would ever slip into and claim one of Daniel's.

"What are you thinking about? You're blushing."

She turned her face into the breeze. "Nothing."

Daniel pushed to his feet. "I have to go. If you have a phone book, I'd like to look up the number for a taxi."

A longing gripped her. It made her want to latch onto Daniel. She wanted additional time with him, any amount of time she could get. She offered to take him to the hotel. A feeling of contentment filled her heart when he accepted the offer.

She leaned her head on his shoulder. "You saved my life, Daniel Baker. I owe you big time."

"Maybe you'll return the favor someday."

It'd be my pleasure.

Chapter 16

Pleasure of a different kind held Jeremy's attention when he met Judith Lanier in her office four days later. A folder lay open on her desk, turned where Jeremy could read it.

"Sign where I've highlighted and the house is yours, Mr. Rubano."

The pen scratched the document in the appropriate places and dinged on the desk when he set it there. He looked up and noticed Judith's rapt gaze. She had her eyes fixed on his well-developed arms, chest, and shoulders, perhaps caught up in the way they filled the tan polo.

"Celebrate with me." Jeremy slipped his fingers under her hand and took it in his. "Allow me to prepare dinner for you tonight." His thumb brushed the back of her hand.

Judith acted surprised by the advance and invitation. She pulled her hand away, tucked the documents in the folder bearing Jeremy's name, and pulled open a file drawer. Her hand shook as she thumbed through the files until she came to where she wanted to put the contract.

"I'll be here until seven."

"That's no problem. I'll plan everything for eight."

Judith shoved a finger and thumb between the files and wedged Jeremy's file in place. She bumped the drawer closed with her leg.

Jeremy lowered his eyes to the leg, bare up to five inches above her knee. He pictured her kicking off her heels and sashaying around the desk, leaning to kiss him before she hiked up her skirt and straddled his lap. Unable to resist his charm, she would give herself to him right there in her office. No comparison to the lack of ladylikeness portrayed by Bloody Mary. Move over, Cars. I'm staking a claim to your old territory.

"Mr. Rubano." Judith swung her legs behind the desk. She straightened in her chair. "Anthony?" The accent snapped him out of the muse. Why did she have to say it like that? "Maybe we should make it another time. I have tons of work to do here."

Jeremy rose from the chair and acknowledged with a short nod. "Another time then." He pulled open the door.

"Are you disappointed?"

He half-turned toward her and said, "You have your reasons." He closed the door. He made it to the bottom step when Judith opened the door.

"Mr. Rubano, excuses won't keep me from dinner. I'll be there at eight."

JEREMY PUSHED BACK the drapes covering the front window to the left of the door in time to see Judith point her car at the corner of the house and park it. He checked his watch—8:03. He opened the door and watched her plant high-heeled feet on the concrete, pull herself out of the car, and stroll up the stone walkway. The green print blouse lay open a couple inches, enough to show the upper curves of her breasts. A silver necklace adorned her freckled neckline.

Jeremy stopped halfway down the front steps. "Stunning," he said, pleased she was on time.

"Fashionably late, to be truthful," she replied.

"Just the way I like it. Close enough to being on time without making me wait and wonder if you're going to show or not."

They stepped through the door. Jeremy engaged the deadbolt. Judith set her wallet and car key on the entrance table. "Something smells good. What is it?"

"Pheasant. Ever had it before?"

"Once. My brother brought back several from a hunt he went on last year."

"Mine's a special recipe. I'd tell you, but then you know what I'd have to do to you."

Judith laughed. "Ah ha, a killer chef. I guess you'd better keep your recipe a secret then. Are you good at keeping secrets, Mr. Rubano?"

Jeremy felt a tingle roll down his back when Judith's fingers played across his left shoulder and the nape of his neck. He liked her. Part of her persona mirrored his. She paraded her wares with class.

He picked up a meat mallet. "Secrets and lies are like this mallet. Hard ones crush the heart. I'll never admit either."

They shared a laugh. Jeremy kept multiple secrets hidden, and no one would ever know any of them unless he allowed it. Issues pertaining to secret societies and henchmen known only to the ones involved topped the list.

"Excuse me for a moment," he said and motioned to the kitchen. "Dinner requires my attention."

"When do you suppose I'll get your attention?"

"You got my attention the very first time I laid eyes on you. Let me check on things in there and then I want to show you something."

Judith slipped her hand into his. Hot hands, he thought as he led her to the kitchen. The feel of her skin reminded him of Denise, though not an adequate substitute.

He paused at the bay window in the dining room. Clouds dotting the evening sky faded from bright colors to dull shades, though their splendor failed to register in his mind. Jeremy's focus centered on Denise. The lack of her presence in his life doubled, maybe even tripled, his desire to load her into a chariot that would take her to her final destination. Heaven or hell mattered none to him. The time was his to choose, and whichever transport arrived first and suited his purpose at the appropriate moment, Denise would be on it. Then he would pursue Angela, make her his priority. Desire for Angela smoldered in his heart, waiting for the embers to erupt with their first sexual contact. He wondered why.

Judith broke the trance when she pressed against his back. She rested her chin on his shoulder and whispered, "Beautiful, isn't it? Look at the mix of light and color. In time, it will all fade into night. Where do you think they go?"

"They skirt unseen amidst the eroticism of night."

"Unseen, yes, but not unfelt."

The softness of her breasts through his shirt and her warm breath on the side of his face let loose a freshet of lust for the redhead. He turned and faced her. Attractive. Witty. He knew of no real reason she should die. Not tonight. He might train her to be a female counterpart if she would lose the accent.

"Definitely not unfelt." He pulled her close and pressed against her. Lust prodded his body. The desire to have her burned within him. He wanted them skin-to-skin, in bed, on the sofa, wherever.

"You'd better check on the bird."

"I suppose you're right."

Jeremy released his hold and paused before going into the kitchen when she asked, "What kind of business are you in?"

"Public relations." He continued on into the kitchen, removed a dish from the oven, and set it on the granite counter.

"You don't seem the type. Being a people-person, I mean."

"I don't believe in following the usual patterns. I prefer creativity. That's what keeps people alert." He lifted the foil off the dish. "This is done."

"Aware and unaware at the same time?"

"That's a great way to summarize it. The way I do it, I'll have clients expecting one thing and then I astound them with something altogether different."

"Surprise Incorporated."

"You're good. Surprise Inc. I like that."

Jeremy retrieved two hand-tossed salads from the refrigerator and handed them to Judith. He removed a green bean casserole from the oven, dipped steamed carrots into a bowl, and placed both dishes on a round table set in front of a bay window.

"It all looks and smells great, especially this." Judith dipped a spoonful of casserole onto a plate.

"My mother's recipe," he lied.

"Delicious. I'll bet your mother's a sweet lady."

"She made me what I am."

"What? Full of surprises?"

For the first three or four minutes, Judith nibbled the food on her plate in silence. Jeremy noticed her picking at the food and said, "Something wrong with my cooking?"

"Everything's delicious. I'm just not ... It's nothing."

"Maybe I should have fried a chicken and smashed some potatoes," he quipped, hoping the suggestion would put a smile on her face. "I need somebody to teach me how, though. Otherwise, I doubt it would be edible."

Judith propped her fork on the rim of the plate. One side of her lip curled upward.

"My mom knows how better than anyone. Chicken has a nice golden crust on the outside made with a buttermilk baste. Bite into it and it's juicy and tender on the inside."

"What about your dad? What kind of work is he in?"

Judith frowned. "He was working for a pharmaceutical company."

"Was?" Jeremy feigned concern. "Cutbacks?"

"An on-the-job injury. He's in the hospital."

"I hope it is nothing serious."

"He almost died."

"That's terrible."

"Needless," she added.

"Why do you say that?"

She nudged the plate an inch farther from the edge of the table, leaned forward. "Because it was. Some thug in a pickup truck rammed into the company car he was driving. If it hadn't been for a doctor riding in the car with him, he would've been a goner. I'd give anything to know who hit him."

The story sounded familiar to Jeremy. The driver of the limo Richie crashed into had to be carried from the scene in an ambulance. Was the limo driver Judith's father?

"Do the police have any leads?"

Judith shook her head. "The driver of the truck fled the scene. The police found the truck abandoned in a parking lot."

"What kind of vehicle was your dad driving when he had the accident?"

"A limo. And it wasn't an accident. The way my friend described it, the truck hit them on purpose."

Jeremy leaned back in the chair. Collateral damage.

"I'm sorry about your dad." Jeremy intended the statement as empathy, not an apology. He was not about to apologize for setting up the deed that put her dad in the hospital. He planned to complete every task on his list no matter the cost to Denise or anyone associated with her.

"They're looking for the man, but I know they won't find him."

"That's no way to think. Think positive."

"I try. I hope they catch him and kill him."

"Wow. That's extreme just for someone leaving the scene of an accident."

"Extreme or not, I want him to pay for what he did."

"I think maybe they should slit his scalp across the crown of the head, insert a stick like an Indian feather, and make him fly an I'm-a-Nimbus flag for five years."

"It'd have to be at least ten. After then, drive the stick through his brain."

Richie doesn't need his brain. He never uses it. Why not?

"I'll have my people design one," Jeremy said.

After dinner, Jeremy noticed Judith kept glancing at her watch. He said, "I'm sorry to have to do this, but I have an appointment in an hour."

"I guess PR keeps you pretty busy, huh."

"I'll finish my current project by the end of the year. Then things will change."

"Oh? What then?"

"Satisfaction."

Chapter 17

The serenity Denise sensed in Daniel's presence secured a calmness she had never known before meeting him. They talked on the telephone every day. They spent one afternoon together the first week and shared Friday and Saturday the next week. In between visits and telephone contacts, Denise spent time at the gym honing her skill in the martial arts.

The Saturday of the second week, Denise finally slept through the night without a nightmare waking her. She attributed the night of undisturbed rest to Daniel's tranquilizing goodnight kiss. Her body had mystically absorbed the kiss, which ensconced her in a splendiferous cocoon.

Denise awakened Sunday morning unsure if life still inhabited her body. Sunlight squeezed through slats in the shutters. She had to shield her eyes and look around the room to see if it was, in fact, her bedroom and not heaven. Once her pupils adjusted to the light, the antique dresser inherited from her great-grandmother assured her of her whereabouts.

She rolled out of bed and pulled on a white satin robe. She shuffled to the kitchen. The coolness of the tile felt nice under bare feet. Denise opened the refrigerator door and tried to decide what she wanted from among its contents.

"Hey, you."

Denise lifted her head. The sight of Daniel put an irresistible smile on her face. She bumped closed the refrigerator door and twisted off the top of a V8 V-Fusion Peach Mango.

"You're early." Her focus jumped to the phone in Daniel's left hand. The smile faded.

"What's the matter?"

She noticed his hesitation. She felt certain that he was about to leave. The phone in his hand assured it. The moment was finally upon her. Mission accomplished as far as she was concerned. Or at least the task was well on its way. Love amused itself during their time together. It propelled them along the same path: head on toward destiny. It developed into a union somewhat extra than what she had hoped for in the beginning.

"Tell me." She took a sip of juice, capped the bottle, and set it on the counter. The concern in her tone intensified.

"I have to go."

"No. When?"

"Now."

"Why now? Can't it wait?"

Daniel shook his head. "The department secretary notified me of a problem. Something to do with the new project I'm working on. If I don't get it taken care of in the next couple days, I might lose everything I've done on it."

"Does this thing have anything to do with my dad?"

"Not exactly." He flipped open the phone and closed it. "I kind of expected him to say something about our meeting. It's been two weeks, and he hasn't mentioned it."

"That's his way. He'll wait on an answer in your time, not his."

"That's unusual for a person in his position. The ones I've met with won't leave me alone, and I hate it. The project is not finished, and yet they prod and pry at me every other day, wanting in on the venture. They all want to know if I've decided."

"Not Dad."

"That's nice to know. What about you?"

"I believe in persistence. I'll pry, prod, anything and everything possible to find out. It may not be the answer I want, but at least I'll know. I'll then deal with it and move on." She laughed. "You can tell me your decision. I won't say anything."

"Bug me all you want. My way is the less said, the better."

"The trust issue, huh."

Daniel smiled.

"I bet I can get the answer out of you." She saddened her face and pouched her lower lip.

"Use your smile, Denise. Pouters turn me off."

"Who's pouting?" Connie Tyler turned the corner and crossed the room to the coffeemaker. "Morning, Daniel. You're here early. Going to church with us?"

"I just stopped by to see Denise."

Denise lifted the bottle off the counter, twisted off the cap, and swigged juice.

Connie filled a mug with steaming coffee, opened the refrigerator, and pulled out a quart of milk. "What's going on, Denise?" She topped the coffee with a splash of milk and returned the carton to the refrigerator.

"Nothing, Mom. We were discussing something about Daniel's job. Will you excuse us, please?"

Connie lifted the cup, blew over the top of the coffee, and took a sip. "Duty calling you away, Daniel?"

"Mom."

"Okay. Okay. I'll not stand in the way of progress." She left them alone in the kitchen.

"Is this better?" Denise put on a smile.

"Fake."

"One thing you have to learn about me, Daniel Baker. There's nothing fake about me. I'm all me from head to toe. What do you say?"

"If this fails, your dad and I both lose."

Her eyes brightened. "You are going into business together."

"This is more of a venture."

"That makes you a risk taker."

He ran his fingers through her hair. "I take risks only when necessary." He pointed to the juice. "Is that stuff good?"

"Try it."

Denise pulled out a juice glass from the cabinet, removed a new bottle of V8 V-Fusion from the refrigerator, and filled the glass. She handed it to Daniel while she sipped from her bottle. Daniel put the glass to his lips. As soon as he tasted the juice, he turned up the glass and emptied it.

"More?"

"About half." He held the glass for her to fill. She poured beyond what he'd asked and capped the bottle.

"Where are you going to from Atlanta?"

He drank the juice, reached over her, and set the empty glass on the counter. As he passed her ear, he whispered, "Somewhere in the depths of your heart, if you'll allow it."

"That's not possible."

"Why not?" Disappointment leaked out in his voice.

Denise slid her hand into Daniel's right hand and turned his palm against her chest. She wrapped her right leg behind his knee. "Because you're already there."

JOY SWELLED INSIDE Daniel when her lips met his. A girlfriend of her class and beauty surpassed his hopes. The times they had kissed before never affected him like this one. This kiss bonded them as if a cord sewed together their hearts.

In a first line of defense, be aware of the enemy and rely on acuity.

The satisfaction of knowing Denise was safe at her parents' house had yet to reach fulfillment stage for Daniel. He hated leaving. The thought of not knowing whether something might happen to her while he was away disturbed him. Daniel scoured the acreage as soon as they stepped out onto the front porch. He was going to miss being in Tennessee. More than anything else, he was going to miss spending time with Denise.

Humidity hung heavy in the August air. The rising sun intensified it, making the temperature feel warmer than the reported eighty-one degrees.

Denise slipped her arm under his. Her silence expressed what was going on inside her heart. He understood the feeling and put his arm around her shoulders as they lumbered to Daniel's rented Malibu.

Denise tugged him toward the Acura. "I need to get something out of my car."

Daniel stepped ahead when they got to the Acura and reached for the door handle to open the passenger's side door. He tensed his muscles and stopped short of the handle. Goose bumps rose on his arms. He glanced at his bare forearms. Hair stood as if drawn by static electricity. The sensation crawled to his neck and up the back of his head. He pulled away and backed a step toward the house. The legs of his slacks clung to his shins.

"Daniel?"

He shushed her with raised hand, palm toward her, and motioned her away from the car. Denise slowly retreated three steps, crossed her arms, and shifted her weight to one leg.

"What are you doing?" she asked when he stooped to look under the car.

Daniel hunched next to the car long enough to scan the undercarriage. He straightened, eased around the rear, and again checked underneath the Acura. He ran a hand along the inside of the bumper until he came in contact with a dime-sized cylinder. He peeled the thing off and got to his feet. He dropped the gadget into a pocket on his way around the far side of the car to keep Denise from seeing it and asking questions he wasn't inclined to answer at the present time.

"Find anything?

"Look at my pants."

"It's static cling. What'd you do, forget a dryer sheet?"

Her grin made it difficult for him to let her comment irritate him. "Might be if they weren't dry clean only."

"Then what caused it?"

The piece of paper he discovered in the limo came to mind. *What's wrong with your car?*

"Better call the police. There's a device under the car. Looks like an electronic apparatus. It has wires coming out of one end."

Daniel had also recognized the box and knew the reason for it being there was to strand Denise and make her an easy target. While they waited for a deputy to arrive, Daniel asked Denise about the bookmark.

"It was on the back seat of the limo when I got in it that day. I figured one of Luke's passengers must have dropped it. My car's been running fine. Still is."

"For the time being."

A Blount County Sheriff's patrol car arrived at the Tyler residence within two minutes of Denise's call. Lanky and with pearl hair in need of cutting, the uniformed man delayed getting out of the car. He paused at the driver's door once outside the car, said something into the radio mike, waited on a response, and tossed the mike onto the seat. He stayed there another ten seconds or more before he approached Denise and Daniel holding a notebook in his left hand.

"You folks the ones that called?" he asked in a gravelly voice. The man coughed and strained to clear his throat. "Sorry about that. Got a summer cold. I've never been able to figure out how anybody can catch cold in the middle of summer."

"Yes, sir," Daniel said. He ran his hand in the pocket where he put the disc. He knew this small tracking unit was not Jeremy's work. Only certain federal agencies had access to them. He was not about to let the officer get his hands on it. "I found something under the car that does not belong there. You can probably get to it best from the driver's side."

"Let me take a look-see." The man's knees popped as he hunkered and stuck his head under the rocker panel. "I see what you mean." He uncurled, rolled his head on his shoulders, checked the time on his watch, and penned something on the pad.

"Well? What is it?" Denise said.

The man closed the notepad and strutted for his car. "I'll be right back."

"You think he knows what he's doing?" They watched the man lope to the rear of the cruiser, pop the trunk, and return with a pair of pliers. "He worries me."

"Look at the way he moves," Daniel whispered. "He exudes confidence."

To the man, Denise said, "It's not going to blow up, is it?" She leaned into Daniel and clasped both hands on his left when he pulled it out of his pocket.

"Not to worry, ma'am." The man braced against the car and dropped to his knees. In less than fifteen seconds, he pulled the contraption from its hiding place and showed it to them, pliers clamped onto the wires leading from the device to a rectangular sensor.

"This is what's known as a tickler. It's triggered to activate when anything gets within a set distance and then emits a signal of electrical pulses. It's harmless, unless you have a pacemaker. Your car won't start with one of these turned on and within twenty feet of it once the engine heats it up. If you'd gone anywhere, you would've been stranded. Any idea how it got there?"

"We have an idea." Daniel looked at Denise to see if she approved. She nodded for him to continue. "Jeremy Guerdon, white male, hails from New Jersey. What about fingerprints?"

"Jersey, huh. He ever been arrested?"

"Not that I'm aware of," Denise said.

"The surface looks clean, but we'll check it anyway to be sure. If we find any useable prints, we'll run them through the system. I have to be honest. Fingerprints won't do us much good if he has no arrest record. I'll tag this as evidence, and we'll see what happens."

The man wrote something on a card, placed the evidence inside a paper bag, and stapled the card to the top of the bag.

"You folks have a nice day now."

As they watched the deputy's car turn out of the driveway toward the city, Denise turned to Daniel. "Maybe I should pack a bag and go with you to Atlanta."

"Why do you say that?" He felt her hand tighten and knew she was not about to let him leave without resistance.

"Because I don't feel safe unless I'm with you."

A blast startled them. A plume of grey smoke rose from the far side of the hill in the direction the patrol car had gone.

Chapter 18

"Stay here. Call 911," Daniel said and raced toward the explosion. He vaulted the fence and sprinted through the pasture cut across it at an angle. He topped the rise and saw the patrol car engulfed in fire. The car sat half-on and half-off the road on the left side.

Heat stifled him when he got to within fifty feet of the vehicle. Orange and yellow flames curled out of window openings around the roof. Smoke filled the interior, making it impossible to see inside. Components sizzled and popped as the fire spread. The heat's intensity prevented Daniel from getting any closer than fifteen feet. He circled the car around the rear. A door lay crumpled in the opposite ditch. The door was off the right front of the police car.

Denise approached the scene from the driveway. Daniel met her thirty feet from the inferno.

"Is he suffering?" The reflection of flames enhanced the sadness he saw in her eyes.

"I've not been able to get close enough to see inside. The blast should have rendered him unconscious. If not, the flash fire sufficed to kill him pretty much instantly."

"I hope he didn't suffer. He seemed like a nice man."

Daniel wasn't convinced. He had noticed how the man reacted to Jeremy Guerdon's name.

Sirens wailed in the distance. They grew louder as they neared from two directions. Thirty seconds later, fire and rescue units swarmed the scene. Daniel recognized one of the firefighters. The lieutenant he had met at the hit-and-run scene climbed out of the rescue truck. He surveyed the fire and motioned to two firefighters on the fire engine where to direct the hose. Two uniform patrol cars, an unmarked car, and another fire truck converged on the scene.

"He didn't have a chance," Daniel told the lieutenant.

"Most never do. That's the sad thing. Stay here. The sheriff will want to talk to you." The lieutenant patted Daniel on the shoulder and marched off to assist his crew.

Denise and Daniel huddled on the opposite side of the road until Sheriff Price arrived on the scene and called them aside. They gave their statements to one of the deputies while the sheriff listened.

"Whoever this man is, he's not one of ours," the sheriff said.

"Are you sure?" Surprise wrapped Denise's voice.

"The patrol car was stolen off our lot sometime this morning before the day shift came on duty. We have no idea who this person is. All my people are accounted for."

"He acted so legit," Denise said.

"Like he knew what he was doing," Daniel added for effect.

"How did he know to answer our call to your office?"

"Probably monitored the radio traffic when the call went out."

"He must've been close. He was here within two minutes of our call," Daniel said.

"Did either of you notice anything unusual or that seemed out of place about the man?"

"His accent," Denise said. "Definitely not from around here."

The sheriff looked at Daniel.

"Crisp," Daniel said.

"In what way?"

"The way he enunciated his words."

"Anything else?"

Denise and Daniel looked at each other and shook their heads.

"Hey, Sheriff." A deputy, face dingy from the smoke and uniform smelling like he had been inside the car when it went up in flames, nudged between them and the sheriff. "We have a problem."

"What?"

"There's no one in the car."

The sheriff locked his gaze on Daniel. His face reddened, and he reached for Daniel's arm. "I think you'd better come with me."

Denise stepped between them. "We've given you our statements. What more do you want from us?"

"The truth would be nice."

"We told the truth. I called 911, and the man I described to the deputy came to my house just like we said. He removed something out from under my car, put it in the trunk of that, and left."

"How do I know you're telling me the truth?" To the deputy, the sheriff said, "Check the trunk as soon as they knock the fire down to see if there's anything in there that don't belong. Call me and let me know what you find. These two are going in with me."

Sheriff Price led Daniel and Denise to his unmarked car. Daniel sensed this might happen and wedged the disc he had taken from underneath the Acura between two fingers.

"Hands on the car; feet apart."

The sheriff searched Daniel while a deputy patted down Denise. Satisfied they were unarmed, she opened the rear door and motioned for them to get in. The shift toward the door gave Daniel the chance to slip the disc in his pocket.

"What are we going to do?" Denise asked.

"It will all work out. You'll see."

"At least they didn't put handcuffs on us."

They arrived at the sheriff's office on E. Lamar Alexander Parkway at ten fifteen. A deputy escorted Daniel to an eight-by-eight interview room. The sheriff flipped two switches on a panel next to the door. He called a deputy to accompany Denise to his office and sat down at the table across from Daniel.

"Now, you be straight with me and I'll be straight with you. Tell me about this thing you found on your car."

"It looked something like a car stereo," Daniel said.

Although Daniel knew something about ticklers from experience, he wasn't about to tell the sheriff or anyone else. He suspected the device the moment static popped his finger. The static-cling cinched it.

"I didn't see it well enough to give you any more than that."

"Car stereo, huh? Any knobs or buttons on it?"

"The way the man cradled—"

Radio traffic interrupted Daniel's answer.

"Hold on a minute, Mr. Baker." The sheriff pressed the button on his shoulder mike. "Go ahead, twenty-one."

"The trunk's clean, Sheriff. There's nothing in there."

The sheriff looked at Daniel. "As you were saying?"

"Yes, sir. The way the man cradled it under his arm prevented me from getting a good look at it."

"How did you know this thing that supposedly was under the car was under there to begin with?"

"Let me start from the beginning."

"Please do."

The sheriff leaned back in the chair and crossed his arms. His posture let Daniel know they were not going to be believed.

"Denise and I walked up to the car. I reached for the door handle, and a spark popped my finger. It felt like static electricity. At first, I thought little about it and was about to pull the door open when my pant legs sucked against my legs. I backed away and finally looked under the car. That's when I saw this thing strapped under there."

"Okay. So where is this thing now?"

"I told you. The man we thought was one of your deputies took it and drove off with it. Thirty seconds later, we heard the explosion."

"Tell me this, Mr. Baker. Why you two?"

"Recent threats."

"What threats?"

"It started with a hit-and-run. Call the Knoxville Police. They'll confirm it."

"Where did it happen?"

"Maryville Pike and ... Woodlawn?"

"Woodson," the sheriff corrected.

"That's it."

"When?"

"Two weeks ago."

Sheriff Price jotted the information on a pad. "Sit tight. I'll be right back."

A uniformed deputy wearing sergeant chevrons on his sleeve stormed into the room. The sergeant, hair the color of red grapefruit and nose the shade of cyanosis—from too many six-packs Daniel surmised, not the lack of oxygen—kicked the chair vacated by the sheriff and leaned on the table with both arms.

"You're going to tell us what we want to know if we have to stay here the rest of the day and all night." The deputy slammed a fist onto the table. "I mean what I say, do you hear me? Nobody steals and blows up a police car on my watch and gets away with it. Nobody! Just because you played in the big leagues, don't pull the wagon around here, sonny boy. You're on my turf now. I'm talking dirt roads and back woods where Eric Rudolph thought he could hide without getting caught. We showed him."

A second deputy, who looked as though he might be the sergeant's brother, entered the room and joined the piñata fest.

Daniel leaned back in his chair and watched the sergeant's face redden. Threats missed their mark. He imagined them strapping him to the table and clamping his nostrils closed with an industrial-sized stapler. Their jargon and rants coerced no negative responses from him. He considered them nothing more than ankle weights. They presented no evidence against him or Denise. Five minutes passed since the sheriff left the room.

"I'm watching you, fella," the sergeant finally said. He motioned to the deputy and stomped out of the room.

Daniel watched the minute hand move past twelve minutes before Sheriff Price returned holding the thing in his left hand.

Denise stepped in around him.

"You're free to go, Mr. Baker. My deputy here will drive the two of you back," Sheriff Price said without apology and left the room.

"How did they find it?" Daniel asked Denise while they followed the deputy out of the building.

"One of the deputies spotted it on top of his patrol car when he came out of a restaurant at West Town Mall."

"No one saw anything?"

"I heard the deputy say he was in and out in less than two minutes. I asked the deputy in the room with me about it, but she told me they couldn't talk about an ongoing investigation."

"They let me go because they found the mechanism?" he asked, knowing it wasn't the reason.

"I don't think so. The sheriff got a phone call and stayed on the line for five to six minutes. I could see through the window from where I was sitting. He had a scowl on his face at first. That quickly changed and his face paled. The rest of the time he was on the phone he never uttered a word."

"Strange."

"The deputy said the caller's name, but I'm not sure I heard it right. I thought she called him Simon One. Do you know anyone by that name?"

Trust flashed through his mind. He couldn't tell her he knew the man. Simon One trusted him. This matter extended all the way to the White House. Earning her trust would end if he lied to her.

"Simon One is an odd name. I'm positive I'd remember someone with a tag like that." Daniel checked his watch on the way out the door. "I've got to get on the move."

"You're right. We should be in Atlanta before dark," Denise said and slid her hand into his.

"We?"

"Yes, we. I told you I'm going with you."

Chapter 19

For the past two weeks, Angela Donavan obeyed a directive from Simon One and kept a safe distance from Denise Tyler, yet close enough to perform any duties required of her when called upon. From her vantage point in the parking lot of Blount Memorial Hospital, Angela raised her camera equipped with 80-300 zoom lens and captured images of the couple when they exited the building.

She discerned a new love interest in Denise's life from the way Denise clung to and kissed the guy outside the Blount County Sheriff's Office. He was handsome. The man's smile and gait reflected naturalness of a nobleman. She watched as he lifted Denise off the ground and spun around. Graceful movement indicated physical fitness. The abrupt emergence of the man in Denise's life struck Angela as strange.

Simon One mentioned the male during their conversation, though not by name. She sensed he was withholding information from her when she called him to let him know of Denise's detainment by the Blount County Sheriff. Somehow, the tracking device from Denise's car went with her there, although the Acura was not located anywhere near the building. If Simon One knew the man's identity, Angela dared not question his lack of disclosure. He had his reason.

A deputy led Denise and her companion to a waiting SUV. The way they angled from the point of exit to the car gave Angela clear view of their faces. She snapped a half dozen additional shots of them. Everyone except two focused on the male. The deputy opened the passenger's door. Denise slid in. The man climbed in after her. The deputy got behind the wheel and pulled out into the street.

The telephone call to the sheriff prompted Denise's release somewhat sooner than expected. Influence again prevailed over status quo.

Angela tucked the camera safely in a case and directed the car onto the parkway. She stayed within sight of the sheriff's SUV and tailed the deputy and her two passengers to the Tyler's residence. Angela watched the deputy pull up to the house, let out the two passengers, and drive away. The signal on the monitor moved with them.

Thirty minutes later, Denise and the male came out of the house. They got into a light-colored sedan. Angela checked the monitor for movement. The sedan turned north out of the driveway. The blip on the screen maintained its position—stationary. Angela dropped in behind the car and followed the Malibu to the car rental return near the airport. From there, she tailed the shuttle carrying them on to McGhee Tyson Airport.

The moment the couple passed through the terminal doors, Angela whipped to the curb and threw an ID card on the dash and got out of the car. Any officer seeing the item there would not have the vehicle towed to impound. She grabbed a bag from the backseat to fit in with the crowd and ambled through the nearest set of doors. It wasn't long before she located Denise at the ticket counter. Once the couple turned the corner en route to their gate, Angela approached the ticket agent who had assisted them.

"Excuse me. I need to know what flight the lady and gentleman you just helped is booked on."

"I'm sorry. I'm not allowed to give out that information." The fluffy-haired brunette looked past Angela. "May I help the next person in line, please?"

Angela straightened her arm, palm raised, toward the man at the head of the line. "I'm not finished here," she said to the brunette. She scribbled a name and ten-digit number on a piece of paper and slid it across the counter.

"Type this into your system."

The brunette shoved the paper toward Angela. "Are you crazy?"

"Do it."

"I don't think so."

"You have ten seconds."

The ticket agent bobbed her head side-to-side and cocked a smirk. "Or what?"

"We'll finish this conversation in your boss's office."

The brunette snatched up the telephone receiver and put it to her ear. "I'm calling my supervisor."

Angela nodded. "Suit yourself."

The line behind Angela lengthened while she waited on the supervisor's arrival. The second person in line grumbled. The thirty-something male raised his arms and slapped his thighs.

Others joined his dismay, expressing their displeasure. The brunette's superior arrived moments later, took one look at the paper, and punched in the number Angela provided.

"Yes, sir," the supervisor said into the phone, gazing across the counter at Angela. "I'll see it's taken care of ASAP." To the brunette, she said, "Give the lady anything she wants."

Chapter 20

The streetlights along Clifton Road flickered on minutes after sunlight furled the city of Atlanta in a haze of twilight. The sun's departure brought little relief from the August heat. Humidity rode the molecules of air, making it feel heavier than normal. Beads of sweat popped out on Daniel's forehead before he reached the front entrance to the CDC.

Denise tried to persuade him to let her tag along to see where he spent most of his working hours. Any other time, he would have agreed. He wasn't sure what this new development entailed and decided it best to go at it alone.

He got two rooms at the Omni Hotel instead of taking Denise to his apartment where anyone searching for her might find her.

The CDC's new department head met Daniel in the front lobby. The man could have passed for one of Snow White's dwarfs with his dumpy stature and white hair that curled over the collar of a loose-fitting olive pullover. Round, wire-rimmed glasses sat mid-shaft of the man's nose.

"I got here as soon as I could, sir."

"No problem," the supervisor said, holding open the electronic security door. "Time is on our side, son. Cultures don't grow any faster than nature will allow. C'mon and I'll let you in on what we've done with the samples."

Daniel shortened his stride as they ambled down the hall. "Any ideas what might have gone wrong?"

"Let's step in here first." The department head motioned to an office around the corner to his left. He used a pass card to gain entry into the ten-by-ten office. The space was equipped with a wood desk, short-backed leather chair, a bookshelf holding supplies and a row of books on the bottom. Two armchairs faced the desk. He plopped to the chair behind the desk. Daniel closed the door and followed his lead, pulling a chair and sliding it against the wall before lowering himself on it.

"We have a crisis brewing, and I need your input," he said. "If we can't nip this soon, we'll be faced with disaster."

"I thought this was about Cyclodactin."

"It is."

"What's the crisis?" The department head was silent. Daniel repeated himself.

"Sabotage. Someone's gotten to the samples."

Daniel leaned forward. "Here?"

"Now you know why I couldn't tell you about it on the phone."

"How is that possible?"

"I would imagine someone with itchy palms."

"Money?"

"Know of a better motivator?"

"What about the surveillance videos?"

"No good. There's a nine-minute segment missing. Someone used a passkey stolen from one of our techs to gain entry. She's in the hospital in critical condition, and word is she may not survive. Whoever did this went straight for your files."

"Why Cyclodactin? There are plenty of other things to make money off of than an unproven formula. This makes no sense."

"Could be its potential, but I don't think that's it."

"What then?"

"You." The department head leaned forward, rested his arms on the desk, and laced his fingers. "I believe somebody's after you,

Daniel. I like you. I did what I did for the benefit of those involved, and you've proven yourself beyond what anyone here at CDC thought you could. You'd better keep an eye over your shoulder because people with enough influence to cause something like this are not playing around."

"Neither am I." Daniel slammed the chair back and jerked open the door.

He marched to the secured area of the lab where he kept most of the research information on Cyclodactin and samples of the drug. Two females and a male intern huddled around one of the workstations off to the left. They giggled after Daniel passed through the door and wove through the maze of tables filled with microscopes and other medical devices. He wondered if they knew what was going on and were laughing at his misfortune. It hardly warranted a category of bad luck. Losing this discovery meant disaster.

The trio's snickering continued even after Daniel entered his workstation and closed the door. He glared at them through the glass and watched as they tinkered with a new piece of equipment and poked at each other. They paid no attention to him as he grabbed the file containing the research materials from the cabinet, pulled the samples, and situated himself in front of a microscope.

The three quieted when Daniel slammed a fist on the stainless table. He lifted a hand in apology. The intern stared at Daniel, mouth open, and turned his attention back to the ladies. One lady said something to the intern Daniel could not hear. The intern lifted a file box from the table behind him and followed the ladies out the door.

For the next thirty minutes, Daniel checked and rechecked samples. Additional tests returned similar results. Malaise tore at him every time he examined a segment and realized the quandary it left him in. He dropped his head after looking at the last one in the group. Nineteen of twenty-three samples showed evidence of tampering. Two were imperfect and had to be trashed. The main batch of the trial product proved worthless to him or anyone else.

Two remained. Daniel tested each for viability. The evening turned around for him the moment he examined the final sample. What Daniel saw opened the door to everything he'd hoped would come together.

Somehow, the saboteur had missed it.

THE ROOM SERVICE ATTENDANT wheeled the cart holding their evening meal to Denise's door at 9:46, a moment after Daniel rounded the corner. The man raised a fist to knock when Daniel called to him. He was not about to take any chances of the man being someone other than what he appeared to be.

"Let me take that for you."

"Allow me, please. I don't mind." The man spoke with an English accent.

Daniel unfolded a twenty-dollar bill and presented it to him. "The lady may not be dressed."

"I understand, sir. Thank you, sir. Enjoy your meal."

Daniel rapped on the door. "Room service," he said, trying to mimic the Englishman.

Denise pulled open the door and stood there dressed in a white blouse and faded jeans. She was barefoot, with her hair pulled back and held in place by a clip. He wanted to forget everything except taking her in his arms, feel the warmth of her body, and gaze at her until his eyelids refused to allow him another waking moment. He wondered why anyone would want to harm her.

Denise grinned and moved out of the way and lifted the cover from one of the entrées as the cart rolled by—roasted chicken, baked sweet potato, lima beans. "It smells good. Let's eat. How was your meeting?"

Daniel situated the cart next to the table and uncovered two additional entrées. He stared at broiled flounder on a bed of wild rice, coleslaw, and steamed green beans on one plate; a filet and baked potato on the other. "Three? I hope you're hungry."

Denise laughed and pulled a chair out from the table. "I couldn't make up my mind. I thought we could sample each one. How did it go?"

"Enlightening," he said, not wanting to elaborate on what he had learned at the CDC. "I'll tell you about it later. Let's dig in and enjoy the rest of our evening."

DENISE WATCHED WITH interest as the fork's tines speared a slice of roast chicken. Daniel lifted the meat to his mouth. He chewed slowly and deliberately, savoring the full flavor. Excellent table manners, she thought. He chewed and swallowed before speaking, sipped water without slurping, elbows tucked at his side instead of propped on the table. Daniel's physical and sensual conduct appealed to her. As she watched him, her insides began to tingle.

She glanced at the clock on the nightstand—10:11.

Daniel set his fork in the middle of the plate and pushed the plate two inches from the edge of the table. He raised the water glass to his lips and drank the remaining water, allowing the last bit of ice to slide on his tongue.

She glanced again at the clock. The red numbers changed to 10:13.

Daniel wiped his lips on a cloth napkin and dropped the napkin next to the plate.

The urge to act on her feelings grew stronger every passing minute. Whether she should make the first move or wait on Daniel kept racing through her mind. Now that he had finished his meal, there was nothing to occupy his hands, or his mind, except her. Destiny, she thought. Two people fall in love and commit to each other. That's the normal progression for people in love, wasn't it? She looked around the room. The setting exuded perfection. They were alone in a hotel room. At the right moment, they might indulge in the act of lovemaking.

Daniel sat three feet away, legs crossed, smiling at her. She pondered ripping off her clothes to watch the effect it would have on him. She reached up and fiddled with the top button on her blouse. The longer she considered it, the more she felt squeezed into a cleft.

The chair tumbled backward and banged against the wall when she jumped to her feet.

Daniel jumped up. "What's wrong?"

Denise dashed to the bathroom. She slammed the door and locked it. She hunched on the edge of the tub and buried her face in her hands. Hot tears seeped between her fingers and trickled down the back of her hands, forearms to elbows propped on her knees. After three or four minutes, she lifted her head, stood, and stared at the mirror. She swiped tears from her cheeks with her fingers and dried them on the legs of her jeans.

Why am I here? Am I ready for this?

AFTER GOING TO THE bathroom door twice and hesitating each time, Daniel returned a third time and tapped on the door. "Talk to me, Denise."

"I shouldn't have come," she said in a broken voice. "I've burdened you with my problems and that's not fair to you."

"I don't look at it that way."

"That's the way it is. How else can you see it?"

"Remember what I told you about trust?"

"No ... yes. Trust ought to be earned."

"How am I doing so far?"

"It's not you. It's me."

"What can I do to help?"

The lock button rattled and the lock disengaged with a click. The door opened. Denise kept her head down and rushed into his arms. She clamped her right hand on her left wrist behind his back, pressed her face to his chest. "Hold me."

He slipped his arms around her. Warmth blended with softness touched his chest. The fragrance of her hair and skin filled his lungs. He swept her hair aside and kissed her neck. She shivered and tightened her hold on him after his breath breezed the back of her neck and whisked under the collar of her blouse.

"I'm scared," she said, turning her head and pressing her other cheek to his chest.

"You have a right to be afraid. Who wouldn't be in your position? The threat is real." He rubbed her back.

"A bond has formed between us."

"That's a good thing."

Denise pushed away. "Any other time I'd agree. Right now, I'm not sure I'm ready. I'm sorry—"

Daniel turned to see what sidetracked Denise. Smoke drifted under the doorway. It rose inside the room, hovered near the door.

"Bathroom!" he motioned. "Wet the towels and hold one over your nose."

Daniel put his hand, palm forward, against the door while Denise hurried into the bathroom. The door felt normal to the touch. The gaseous cloud reached his nose. One whiff let him know this was not emitted from a fire in the hotel. This was something else. They were enveloped in a life-threatening trap.

Chapter 21

The door leading out of the bathroom offered Denise an unobstructed view of the room's entrance. She opened the faucet and stuffed two towels in the sink while she dampened a third in her hands. She held the towel over her mouth and nose and watched smoke billow under the door.

Daniel engaged the inside latch on the jamb. The person out there had somehow gained access to a key card. The lock clicked. Light increased around the jamb. The door swung inward as far as the latch would allow it.

A jolt against the door from the hallway was subdued by Daniel's foot and left shoulder. A second effort proved futile. The cloud swirled around Daniel. He coughed. The intruder's third attempt overpowered Daniel and knocked him to the floor. He rolled to his feet and bolted toward the door.

Denise lowered the towel and screamed. A man entered the room. A second man, somewhat taller, stood to one side behind him. A breathing apparatus covered each man's face. The first wielded a gun in his left hand. The gunman approached Daniel while the other stayed in the doorway.

"No!" Denise yelled.

She threw the towel at the man with the gun to distract him. She leaped out of the bathroom and planted her heel on the man's jaw. The gunman's head snapped to the side. He stumbled and braced against the wall. Denise followed up with a fist to the throat. The man gasped and placed his free hand to his neck. He shoved off the gasmask, eyes wide in disbelief. Fingers released their grip on the weapon. The pistol dropped to the floor.

An accomplice rushed through the doorway. He reached for the gun. Daniel stepped on the man's wrist and kicked him under the chin. The man moaned and fell back. The fog in the hallway consumed him.

"Did he run off?" Denise asked.

"Not likely."

She jerked another towel off the rack. The smell eked through it no matter how hard she pressed it over her nose. The scent gagged her. She remembered the ones in the sink and swapped the dry one for it.

"How'd they know we were here?"

"That's a good question. I checked in under assumed names." Daniel bent over the man on the floor. "Where'd you learn to fight like that? You pummeled this guy."

The gunman postured on the floor, arched his back, and continued his struggle to take in a breath. Blood-tinged froth oozed from the corners of his mouth. His eyes bugged. He was dead.

Denise looked at Daniel. She could see and hear his struggle to breathe. It was painful to watch. The gas-saturated air burned her throat and lungs.

"A guy in one of my college classes was a master in martial arts. He taught me."

"You handled yourself like a pro."

Daniel picked up the soaked bath towel and tossed it over the steaming canister outside the threshold. His breathing was labored.

"Take this," Denise said, handing him a towel from the sink.

He braced with hand on the door handle and put the towel to his face.

The accomplice burst out of the fog and tackled Daniel. His shoulder caught Denise and banged her against the wall. She lost her footing, rolled off the corner, and fell between the bed and the wall.

Denise watched the man and Daniel jab, punch, wrestle, and kick each other for ninety seconds. Daniel finally rolled to his feet. He pulled the man to him by the front of his shirt and slammed the heel of his right hand on the man's nose. The man reeled in pain for a moment and then collapsed in silence.

Denise moved to the foot of the bed and put her hand on the small of Daniel's back. "Dead?"

"If not, he'll wish he was by tomorrow."

"Who are these guys?"

"Nobody. That's the point. They're expendables hired to do a job."

"Jeremy?"

"That'd be my guess."

"Thank God they failed this time. What are we going to do now? With them?"

"I'll call security. Let them take care of it."

Security officers and Atlanta Police uniformed officers and detectives from homicide division, emergency medical personnel, and a representative from Fulton County Medical Examiner's Office converged on the hotel room.

The comatose accomplice received treatment from medics on the scene. They transported him to Grady Memorial Hospital.

Officers and detectives rammed question after question and some accusations at Denise and Daniel. Most of them aimed their questions at Daniel. He gave direct answers. No response offered anything to the investigators more than what was asked. His answers brought looks of antipathy on their faces more so than when he said, "I don't know."

At four thirty, another police officer entered the room. "A Ms. Donavan is in the lobby and wants to speak to you," he said to the lead detective.

"Tell her I'm busy."

"I already told her that. She said she didn't care. She demanded to speak with you ASAP."

"She'll have to wait."

A voice on the portable talkie interrupted their conversation. The detective stepped into the hall. He returned three minutes later. He slapped closed his notepad and swiped his fedora off the table. He gave a stern look to Daniel, smirked, and stomped out of the room.

"Was that about us?" Denise asked the officer.

The officer smiled and said, "Y'all are free to go."

Chapter 22

Daniel sent text messages to Denise every day since their trip to Atlanta ten days ago. Each one was filled with things a woman in love desired to hear. She listened to his voicemails two or three times a day. The sincerity in his voice lured her. It prodded her to want to call him each time she heard them instead of responding with text messages.

The cell phone clunked onto the kitchen table when Denise let it fall from her hand. She picked it up and poised her thumb over the number two on the keypad. Yesterday's message from Daniel bested all others he had left her.

The puffiness in her face finally abated from what it had been during the first regimen of steroids. She hated taking the pills because of the bloating effect they had on her body. She stopped taking them after the sixth day. Swollen sarcoids in her lungs hampered her breathing to the where she had difficulty taking in air. Those in her neck triggered hoarseness in her voice. If she talked to Daniel, he would know she was battling illness and would want to be there to help her.

Denise set the phone on the table after deciding not to speed-dial his number. She loped to the refrigerator. Though the refrigerator was full, nothing satisfied what she wanted. After flitting from one item to another, a half-full bottle of mango juice caught her focus. Saddened by seeing Daniel's favorite flavor, she let the refrigerator door close.

Not being with Daniel brought gloom and misery to every conscious moment. She missed him. Being alone in the house while her parents spent Labor Day away intensified the feeling. Her heart tightened with each second that transitioned from present to past. The ache forced her lower into a realm she couldn't believe she was letting herself sink into.

Enough time wasted with her charade. No more, she decided, and marched to get her phone. Tears blurred her vision. No matter. She hit the top middle number and put the phone to her ear. As soon as she heard his voice on the line, she said, "I have to see you, Daniel. I can't—won't—go through another night or day without you in my life." Denise paused, felt relief remove the ache from her heart with his response of where to meet him. She hurried to her bedroom to change clothes. "Give me fifteen minutes and I'll be there."

Denise tossed the phone on the bed. She opened drawers and banged them closed. Hangers flapped against the shelf above the rod they hung on when she stripped off a shirt from one and pulled a pair of jeans off of another. She wiggled out of her nightshirt, jerked on her outfit, and grabbed a hairbrush from her purse. Hair clung to its bristles as she whipped the brush through her hair and slapped it down on the dresser.

She snatched up her phone and purse and whirled back to the dresser where she sprayed her neck and wrists with Happy. Denise ran out the door to her car. Something in her peripheral vision drew her attention as she stuck the key in the ignition. She looked to her right and screamed. A crow's head dangled from the rearview mirror. She shoved open the door and scrambled out. Her foot caught on the rocker sill and pitched headlong onto the lawn. She rolled onto her back, panting, digging her heels into the ground to get away.

The crow's head swayed on the strip of ribbon as if mocking her attempt to break loose from its power. She knew how it got there. Its meaning perturbed her. Jeremy had exacted no threat or harm to her for two weeks. Now this. Was the crow a warning of something worse to come, or Jeremy's attempt to keep her away from Daniel?

Love for Daniel emboldened her. No matter what Jeremy planned to do to her, she was not going to let it stop her from following her heart. "Your silly token's not going to work on me, Jeremy," she yelled and pushed to her feet. She jerked the ribbon off the mirror and slung the crow's head over the fence. "Perish in hell with the rest of your kind."

She hopped in the car. The engine barely had time to turn over when she jerked the gearshift. The Acura's front end swung leftward as she backed around a flowerbed. Tires screeched and the car lunged forward. Out on the road, Denise felt inside her purse for her phone. She found it and dialed Jeremy's number.

"HELLO, SWEETHEART. It's so nice of you to phone me." Jeremy motioned for the two guys with him to leave the table. The thugs from Newark, dressed in black from head to toe, pushed back their chairs and sauntered to the bar.

"I may be a sweetheart, but I'll never be yours." Her words blared in his ear. "I got your message. Is that the best you've got? Do you really think you can scare me with antics like that?"

"I—"

"Your use of I *is* right, Jeremy. Everything you do hinges around what brings you pleasure. Well, this time and from here on out, things are going to be different. My life belongs to me and not you or anyone else will ever tell me what I can and can't do. You hear me? No one."

Jeremy felt heat fill his face. He motioned to the server for another Bloody Mary. "Listen a da—"

"No. You listen. You treated me like some prize you won at a poker game or something. Bought fancy clothes and paraded me in front of your friends. Did you ever once stop to think how those things made me feel? No, you didn't. I know you better than you think I do. I learned a few things by being around you. Things I despise. I've had it with you, your friends, and your parties. You gallivant until the wee hours, flirt with some woman that started hanging around everywhere we went. Who is she? Was she the one you sent to the house? Was she supposed to kill me that night?"

"I don't know what you're talking about."

"Deny it. I expect nothing less from you. You tried then and you tried in Atlanta. Well, let me tell you this, Mr. Jeremy Guerdon, if that's even your real name, I'm denying you what you want. I'm denying you everything that has anything to do with me. It's my life and you can't have it. You'll never have it as long as I live and breathe."

Wind noise filled the phone followed by silence. Jeremy jammed the phone in his shirt pocket. He gritted his teeth and huffed at her audacity. He stared at his associates perched on stools at the bar. They waited for his signal, which he gave them after brooding another thirty seconds.

He gulped the fresh Bloody Mary and banged the glass on the table. "Change of plans, guys," he said once they were seated at the table. "Go on back to Jersey. I'm staying in Tennessee for another week. I'll see you then. I'm coming back here as soon as baseball season is over to see Carson."

Jeremy pulled a handkerchief from his pocket and rubbed it over the Kruggerand coin ring on his right ring finger. The younger of the two associates leaned forward and braced on the table. Strands of black hair fell across pockmarked cheeks and dangled in his close-set eyes. He forced the hair back with stubby fingers and tucked it behind his ears. "You still want us to find Angela?"

"Why wouldn't I?"

"I don't know. I thought maybe you changed your mind."

"This one never changes his mind, kid," said the older thug. "You got a lot to learn." To Jeremy the old man said, "I heard she asked about you at the Waldorf's party last Thursday night. Word is, she acted like she really missed seeing you. After fifteen minutes, she left in a dark blue or black sports car. Alone. If the dame's anywhere between here and Boston, I'll find her." The man, old enough to be Jeremy's father, extended a calloused hand. The tips of hard-worked fingers wrapped around and touched the thumb when Jeremy shook the man's hand and smiled.

"I knew I could count on you." Jeremy reached into his pants pocket and pulled out the keys to his car. "Put the tickler in the trunk. I still may have use for it."

The thugs rose to leave. The old man swigged the last of his Heineken and said, "That hillbilly sheriff's still searching for the phantom. I bet the crow's head scared a flood out of her. Any word yet?"

"That was her on the phone."

"Angela?" the young one asked.

Jeremy snarled. "Keep up or you're out." He turned to the old man. "Denise mentioned a woman coming to the house the night she ran off. I wonder if it might have been Angela."

The old man laughed and smacked Jeremy on the back. "I guess that should tell you something. Angela wants you all to herself. Sounds like she's out there trying to wipe out the competition."

The thought made Jeremy feel good inside. "My kind of woman. Maybe I should have asked her to go to Atlanta instead of sending those numbskulls. All they did was get caught peeing upstream and paid for it with their lives."

THE ACURA ROLLED TO a stop near the one-room Sam Houston School House. Denise spotted Daniel, released her grip on the phone and let it slide onto the console. She pushed open the door, hardly noticing the navy sports car parked two spaces from the end. She ran to the oak stump carved into the likeness of the old schoolmaster where Daniel held her in his embrace. His arms felt good around her. Joy flushed away the anxiety that gnawed at her during their time apart when she turned her face to his and accepted his kiss.

"Forgive me. I didn't intend to hurt you by staying away so long. I didn't want you to see me in my condition. I won't blame you if you don't want me because of it." She felt his arms tighten around her.

"I'm not letting go, Denise. No matter what."

"I have something I need to tell you. I want you to trust me and I know you won't if I keep it from you."

"You think my knowing whatever it is will drive me away?"

"I don't know. I hope not."

"Then tell me."

She sobbed and said, "I have Sarcoidosis. It flairs up a couple times a year, and it is especially bad when I have to deal with that and this August heat and humidity at the same time. The medication I have to take causes me to retain fluid. All I want to do when that happens is find some place to hide and not let anyone see me. Plus, I've been wary about starting a new relationship after what I've been through. I tried to push it out of my mind, but it didn't work. The only thing I wanted to think about was you."

His kiss to the top of her head gave her a feeling of relief. The embrace meant comfort. The kiss delivered assurance.

"When were you diagnosed?"

"The week after my twenty-second birthday. It's in my lungs. Sometimes I'll find knots under my skin and in my abdomen. The doctor said there's a low mortality rate of about four percent."

"I see it as a ninety-six percent survival rate. Those are odds I can live with."

Daniel's optimism sounded good to her, especially the live-with part.

"Let's take a ride in the mountains."

Chapter 23

Denise and Daniel made their first trip to Newfound Gap in the Great Smoky Mountains National Park six weeks later.

"I feel better than I've felt in a long time." Denise stood next to Daniel at Clingmans Dome, the highest point in Tennessee at 6,642 feet. "What do you think? Is this enough to make up your mind?"

She coaxed Daniel into buying or renting in Tennessee, although he decided a week ago to look for something in the areas around Townsend or Pigeon Forge. He enjoyed the way Denise schemed to get what she wanted. He played along with her.

"It is beautiful, but ..."

"But what?"

"I'm not sure I want to live here," he teased.

"Come on. What's not to like, except maybe the humidity? Fall colors. Snow in winter. Friendly faces everywhere you look. Nice place to raise children. Living here's good enough for me."

"Is that why you moved to the city?"

"That was only temporary. Anyhow, I left, didn't I?"

"I'm glad you left there, Denise. Otherwise, I would have missed having you help me look for a place here."

The sun could not have beamed brighter than her expression. Happiness bubbled out of her as she jumped into his arms and planted kisses all over the side of his face.

"A cabin," she said. "Secluded. It has to be in some remote area away from busy highways, congested cities, and any noise of everyday clamor. I don't want any distractions.

"The next thing is water. Flowing water. I prefer a river or creek over a pond or lake. It really doesn't matter as long as I can hear the water from the porches or through open windows. Nothing beats the sound of water bashing against or skirting around rocks. It's such a gratifying sound. Don't you think?"

Before he answered, she continued. "Also, the cabin must have a fireplace. One of those large stone fireplaces. If the cabin doesn't have one, then we'll have to build one. A cabin is not complete without the cracks and pops of logs on fire and the warmth of glowing embers on a cool, lazy evening."

"I was wondering if you were ever planning to take a breath."

"Oh, hush. Can't you see how excited I am? I love the idea of living in a cabin nestled in some far-a-way place where the worst thing that can happen is having to skedaddle critters off the porch. At night, the sounds of crickets and rustle of leaves as the wind blows through the trees on top of water splashing over rocks is enough to lull anyone to sleep. The smell of fresh air, cool mornings cuddled in bed with windows open and covers pulled up around your neck and days with nothing to do except enjoy the lavish scenery make me want to be there right now."

"I thought you were talking about a cabin for me to stay at when I'm in town."

"I am, silly. I'm hoping you'll invite me to spend time there with you."

"Do you need an invitation?"

"Do I?"

"Is that what you want?"

"For starters."

FOR THE NEXT THREE days, Denise and Daniel searched through classifieds, real estate books, and toured the countryside. A place to his liking had yet to be located.

"I've been thinking," Denise said as she and Daniel pulled into the driveway of her parents' home from their trip to the store. "Why don't we take a drive this afternoon?"

"Have any area in mind?"

"I was thinking about Kinzel Springs. The area would be great and we haven't looked there yet."

"Sounds good to me. What about your parents? Think they might like to tag along?"

"I talked to Mom about it before I left this morning. She said they have appointments this afternoon. Dad has a meeting at the office and Mom is meeting friends at the mall for some special something or another. Looks like we're on our own. We don't have to be back until about six for dinner."

"I can go for that. When did you want to head out that way?"

"I thought I would take you to Sal's for lunch. Then we'll go. You'll like Sal's. He's been in business a long time."

"Good food?"

"Great food. He serves hot and cold sandwiches, fresh vegetables, and homemade desserts like you wouldn't believe."

"Sounds like my kind of place. I could really go for some of that right now. I'm ready whenever you are."

"I'll be ready in a moment."

"Good. I'll tell your parents our plans and we'll see them back here in plenty of time for dinner."

Daniel walked around to the patio where Clifton and Connie lounged in the fresh air and a late morning breeze. "Denise and I are headed to Sal's for lunch if you would care to join us," he said to Connie.

"No thanks, Daniel," Connie said, giving him a smile. "We have prior engagements we have to take care of shortly and will be out for most of the afternoon. You two go ahead. We'll see you back here for dinner. I have a pot roast in the crock pot. There's chocolate fluff for dessert."

"Sounds tasty."

Clifton didn't bother to look up from his book. "If you're going to Sal's, check out the Reuben. It's the best around."

Denise pushed the door open and stuck out her head. The black short-sleeved pullover and jeans she changed into complemented her figure. The sight unfolded for Daniel a new meaning to the word beauty.

HALF AN HOUR LATER, Denise and Daniel sat down to a lunch of Reuben and open-faced roast beef sandwiches, homemade chips, and iced tea. They shared a slice of French silk pie way too large for one person.

"This is great. I don't think I have ever tasted a Reuben this good." Daniel wiped his fingers on a napkin.

"Sal has a way with food," Denise replied. "I knew you would like it. Wait 'til you taste the pie."

"Who exactly is Sal?"

"He came here from New York City about a year ago. He opened this place and has been here ever since. He has another one in downtown Knoxville."

"Well, New York is missing out on some great stuff. Check please," he said and motioned for the server.

She promptly brought the check and placed it on the table. "Excuse me. I think I know you. I've been racking my brain trying to figure out where I've seen you before. Is your name Denise Tyler?"

"Yes. Yes, it is. Why do you ask?"

"I'm Cherie, Richard's sister. It hit me when one of the other customers and I were talking after you came in. I think she must have known you from school. Said her name is Angela Donavan."

"Angela Donavan." Denise pondered a moment. "I don't remember her. Is she still here? Maybe I'd know her face." Denise stretched to look around Daniel. No one seated at any of the other tables or booths resembled anyone she knew in school.

"She told me she had to leave to pick up her son. Said to tell you hi, though."

"You be sure to tell her hello for me if she comes in again. Tell her I'm sorry I missed getting to see her."

"I will. Thank you for stopping in today."

Daniel paid the check and left a gracious tip for the young, pleasant server. "Nice girl," he said.

"College student. I know her brother," Denise said. "Don't you go getting any ideas now, you hear?"

"Not me. I found what I want."

"Good answer. I'm feeling lucky. I have a feeling we might find what we are looking for today."

"I hope you're right. Today could be our day."

Chapter 24

Denise pulled out of the parking lot, having taken the wheel of Daniel's Mercedes since she knew the area they were headed to. A few shortcuts through the hills and they would be there in no time at all. The September afternoon was beautiful. Various species of late-blooming flowers garnished yard after yard as if beckoning "look at me." A lad mowed the lawn at the next house. The scent of the fresh-mowed grass saturated the atmosphere as they passed.

"I love the smell of the outdoors, don't you, Daniel?"

"I sure do. There's nothing like it."

"You're right. I'm going to cut through here." She negotiated a right turn off the main highway. "This will take us straight to where we might find a few places to check out."

The newly paved trail of a road angled off and wound up at the foothills of the Great Smoky Mountains. Several Realtor signs could be seen on the side of the thoroughfare, but none of the cabins they saw seemed to be anything they were interested in. After a couple of hours riding and looking, they came up on a gravel-covered road leading off to the left. A Realtor sign had fallen over in the corner.

"I wonder where this goes," she said. "Let's check it out. I've got that feeling again."

"Sounds good to me." He glanced over and spotted a sign partially hidden by vegetation.

"Hey! Wait! There's a realty sign lying next to the road."

Denise slammed on the brakes. "You about scared me to death, Daniel."

"Sorry."

"It's okay. I'll ease down through here and we'll look."

Daniel leaned out the window and read aloud the information printed on the sign. "Judith Lanier, Agent, Tennessee River Realty."

Denise smiled when he read Judith's name off the sign. "At least the road looks to be in good shape."

The road narrowed to little more than a one-lane passage about a mile off the paved road. Three miles later, they saw a realty sign similar to the one at the intersection.

"This must be it," he said.

Denise stopped the Mercedes across the culvert at the entrance on the dirt drive and sat there for a moment, gazing at the scenery. Daniel glanced at the realtor sign, grabbed a pen from the console and wrote the information on a pad.

"Listen," she said in a tone barely above a whisper. "Do you hear that?"

"Sounds like rushing water." They looked at each other and grinned.

"Come on. We've got to check this out."

Denise pulled forward and followed the dirt drive leading to the cabin. The drive stopped about forty yards short of a cabin situated off to the right, nestled against the mountainside. A stone path led from the driveway to a wide set of steps attached to a spacious porch.

"Looks like we'll have to park here."

Daniel got out and surveyed the surroundings. Plenty of nature. White oak trees galore dotted the woods—the whitetails preferred food—among mixed hardwoods, a few pines and fir trees. Mountain laurel skirted the edge on both sides of the opening. "Seems secluded enough," he said, looking over at Denise who was now standing next to him. He reached for her hand. She threaded her fingers between his.

"Two down and one to go," she said, referring to the sound of rushing water and secluded nature of her surroundings. "This may be the one."

Seclusion was a priority, and this was secluded all right. The water running nearby sounded wonderful. Swift waters of a river cut its path on the far side of the cabin, only a few feet from the oversize screened porch attached on the northwest side. The aroma of Bathe's pink filled the air from both sides of the front steps while honeysuckle grew wildly around the cabin's right side.

The front door was locked. Daniel peered through the front window situated left of the door.

"Come look. Check out the size of that fireplace."

Denise walked up to the window and looked inside. A big grin broke free on her face.

"This is it," they chorused, looking at each other and then peering inside for a second look.

"We've found it! We've found our cabin," he said, grabbing and hugging her.

"We can't waste any time, Daniel. Good properties like this don't last long around here."

Daniel reached for his cellular phone. "I'll call right this minute if I have a signal. Good. Signal's strong enough. I can't believe the reception is this good way out here."

He quickly dialed the number he'd copied from the sign. "Tennessee River Realty, Monica speaking. How may I direct your call?"

"Hello, Monica." Daniel spoke in his professional manner. "My name is Daniel Baker. I am calling about the cabin Judith Lanier has listed off Hendrickson Road. Is Ms. Lanier available?"

"She sure is. Would you mind holding for a moment?"

"Not at all."

Anticipation was getting the best of them. What if it was under contract? Even worse, what if it had been sold?

"Hello." A different voice spoke on the other end. "This is Judith Lanier. How may I assist you today, Mr. Baker?"

"I was calling about the cabin you have listed off Hendrickson Road. Is it still available?"

"Yes, it is. The cabin was listed with us this past week; Tuesday to be exact. You are my first caller on the property, which I thought was odd, since it is in such a great location. I'm quite surprised no one has called about it sooner."

"Your sign was on the ground at the intersection where we turned off the paved road," Daniel said.

"That explains why I haven't had any calls."

"I guess so. My friend and I were riding the area when we noticed the gravel road and turned. As we were making the turn, I saw the sign lying beside the road. We checked it out to see if it was what we were looking for. When we saw the cabin, we thought we would call you about it."

"Your friend wouldn't be Denise Tyler, would it?"

"She's standing right here."

"I guess I'll finally get to meet you, Dr. Baker. My dad has high regard for you."

"Well, Denise brags about you, Ms. Lanier. I'd like some information about the cabin."

"Well, the cabin has a single bedroom with a loft and is on twenty-five acres. All utilities are underground, and sewer is a septic system. There is a live well on the property, and Little Tallassee River runs through about one-third of the acreage."

"How old is it?"

"A contractor from Maryville built it about three years ago."

"What's the asking price?"

"We have it listed at four eighty-nine."

"When will we be able to see inside?"

"I'm finishing with a client and have to work on a couple of things here in the office. How about forty-five minutes? Would that be doable?"

"Forty-five minutes would be great. Thank you, Ms. Lanier. Denise and I will be here scoping out the property."

"You're welcome, Mr. Baker. Thanks for calling. I'll see you then."

Daniel hit the end call button and slid the phone in the clip at his side. "Your friend is on her way."

"THIS IS TOO GOOD TO be true," Denise said, excited about the prospect. "Could it really be this easy? This place is exactly what we are looking for. It's like a dream coming true right before our eyes."

Thinking about the possibility of this cabin becoming theirs made her feel good inside. They walked around the cabin and over to the river's edge. They stood arm-in-arm watching and listening to the rushing water as it bashed against the rocky bottom. They turned after a few minutes and followed the east bank southward. The river wound down and around the edge of a clover-covered hillside bordering the western bank before entering the bosky bottom and out of sight.

A young whitetail buck with stubby, velvet-covered antlers leaped from his bedding area near the water's edge, paused momentarily, then with flag waving scampered off in the forest. "Whew. That startled me," Denise said, raising her hand to her chest over her swift beating heart.

Daniel laughed and extended his arms.

She stepped over and welcomed his embrace. Here, in his arms she felt truly loved. In his arms, she felt safe and secure. Nothing else mattered at the moment. Not even Jeremy. The time and setting felt right to her. "I love you, Daniel. I'm totally in love with you." She moved her hands up and down his muscular arms. "I love the way you take care of me. The way you hold me."

"I love taking care of you." Her heart leaped in her chest when he continued. "I love you, Denise Tyler."

The sound of approaching footsteps interrupted their moment. Judith Lanier strolled up to the couple and extended her hand. "Hello." Her hair waved in the breeze. "I'm Judith. Based on things Denise told me, you have to be Dr. Baker."

"Please call me Daniel."

Judith extended her arms to Denise. Denise extended hers and they hugged. "What do you think of the property now that you've looked around?"

"What we've seen is very nice," Denise said. "We can't wait to see inside."

"Come on then. Let's not wait any longer. I'll open it up. I think you'll like what you see. Inside looks like it hasn't been occupied."

Denise, Daniel, and Judith trekked up the hill to the cabin. Judith unlocked the front door and stepped aside for the two eager prospective buyers to enter. The door hinges made a little squawking noise as Daniel pushed on the door to allow Denise first entry.

Judith followed them inside, circled around, and pointed out several features in the cabin.

"The cabin is partially furnished, as you can see. These items are to be left for the new owner to do with as they see fit."

The cabin's décor seemed to welcome them as if they already belonged there. A limited-edition Thomas Kinkade canvas hung above the fireplace. The kitchen was in the right rear corner, complete with a double oven and dishwasher. And cabinets, lots of cabinet space, extended from the corner outward with antique brass fittings on a gunstock finish. An oak table with matching finish stood off to one side. Four matching chairs cuddled underneath around its perimeter. A four-poster king bed sat off-center against the left wall of the single bedroom. Triple-drawer nightstands were positioned on either side. A chesser, a combination of chest and dresser, with an oval mirror backed up against the inside wall.

"Nice. Very nice," Daniel said. "What do you think?"

"I love it. What I really like is this." Denise pointed to the oversized stone fireplace centering the back wall.

"This fireplace was built by special request of the contractor's wife," Judith said. "The stone was shipped in especially for this project. There is no fabrication here. This one is the real deal."

"Come look at this, honey," Denise said, only half hearing Judith's last statement. She stepped through the back door and onto the screened porch. "Look at this porch."

"Would you excuse us for a minute, please?"

"Of course. Take your time. I'll step out front and will be out there if you have any questions."

"Thanks."

Daniel stepped through the door where Denise was waiting.

"Come sit with me," she said, swinging on the five-foot swing attached to a beam overhead.

Daniel slid in next to her. A river at least twenty feet wide flowed within seventy-five feet of the porch and angled off at forty-five degrees.

"Isn't this lovely? I could sit here for the rest of the day if we had time."

"Me too. What do you think about this place?"

"It's perfect. I think you'll be making a mistake if you let it get away. What do you think?"

"I don't know. Maybe we should look some more—"

"Are you kidding me? I—"

"At the river, baby. I think we should take more time to enjoy the sound of that water and the cool mountain breeze."

"Don't do that to me. I was about to show you what a hissy fit is like. I thought you were serious."

"I am serious. I think you're right. I can't pass on this. I don't believe I'll find anything more to my liking."

"Okay then. Do it."

Together they rose, quickly kissed, and walked back through the cabin to the waiting agent.

"I would like to make you an offer," Daniel said. "Didn't you say the listing was four-eighty ...?"

"Four eighty-nine. I'm sure the owner will entertain any decent offer on the property. Tell me what you're willing to offer and I'll take it to them."

Denise and Daniel conferred for a minute.

"Four seventy-five," Daniel said.

"That's a decent offer. I'll draw up the papers and hopefully have an answer for you on Monday or Tuesday of next week. If you'll walk over to my car, I need to get some information from you and have you to sign the pledge to get the ball rolling. I'll be able to take care of the rest. I'll be right back. Walk with me, Denise."

"What do you think?" Denise asked on the way to Judith's car.

"It's a great deal."

"Not that. Daniel."

"Handsome."

"He's much more than that. He's everything I ever wanted."

"Are you sure?"

"Positive."

Judith stuck her head through the open door on the passenger side, reached in, and dug out a file from her satchel on the seat. "I met somebody."

Denise slowed her gait. "Oh, Judith. That's great. Who is he?"

"His name is Anthony Rubano."

"How did you meet him?"

"He came in the office looking for a house. Super nice. And gorgeous."

Denise stopped at the bottom of the stairs and locked her eyes on Judith's. "Be careful, Jude."

Judith nodded assurance. "I am."

"I want to hear about him."

"You will. You know I can't keep a secret."

They laughed and hopped up the steps. After taking care of the details, Daniel was on his way to owning his cabin hide-a-way.

"Thanks again. I'll call you as soon as I know something," Judith said.

Denise hugged Judith. "Remember what I said."

At one o'clock the following Friday, Denise and Daniel sat down with the owner, Judith, and the closing attorney to complete the purchase. They sailed through closing the deal without a problem. Every detail finished by one forty-five.

A weather front had pushed down from the north around eleven o'clock. Temperatures dropped ten degrees below normal for the last week of September. Denise and Daniel stepped out of the attorney's office into a snappish chill.

"We need to celebrate," Denise said, dangling the keys to the cabin in front of her face, her free hand tucked under her left arm. She whipped her head and let the wind brush hair from her face. The hair flipped and waved behind her. "This nip in the air makes me wish the temperature was another ten degrees cooler. I'd really like to try out the fireplace in the cabin."

"Why wait for colder weather? It's forty-nine degrees now and probably won't reach sixty today. We could build a fire and open the doors and windows if it gets too warm in there."

"You mean it?"

Daniel opened the car door for her to get in. He propped on the door while she settled in the seat. "Why not? We have the rest of the day to do whatever we want. I'm sure we can find some seasoned wood somewhere."

He leaned in and kissed her.

Chapter 25

Four weeks later, Daniel walked out of Jared's with a gift for Denise in his pocket. He settled in his Mercedes and opened the box for another look. Fervor to do this nudged his impatient side. It was already planned. Seven o'clock could not get here soon enough for him. He checked the time—six and a half more hours.

His stomach growled. It churned and griped all the way to Sal's. Daniel parked, took a peek again inside the box, and headed inside. Daniel dodged a line of diners rushing out the front door. A small boy showed off a baseball to the woman at the cash register. "He signed it for me," the boy said.

Daniel spotted the celebrity at a table next to one of the front windows.

"Carson Wright. How long has it been? Three years?"

"Four." Carson pushed back the chair with his legs and rose to greet his former teammate. A classic Carson Wright smile graced a broad face. "It's great to see you, Baker. Sorry I missed seeing you in Baltimore. Family in town wanted to get together. One of those things, you know. Have to take care of business. You're looking good. What you been up to? How's the knee?"

Daniel laughed and pulled over a chair from the opposite side of the table. The tables at Sal's Deli crowded the smaller, second location in downtown Knoxville. The service was great and the mouthwatering food every bit as good there as in the other location.

"Same ole Carson. Hyper as ever. It's nice to see you, and the knee's fine."

"Fine, huh? I doubt that. I know you, Baker. If you were fine, you'd still be out there with us."

"True, to a certain extent." Daniel glanced at the menu, slid it aside, and gazed out the window. He dropped his left hand to the pocket in his jacket to make sure the box was still there.

"What are you not telling me?" Carson crooked his neck around the window post. "Hold that thought a minute. I've got to get me an eyeful of that balm across the street."

"Which one?"

"Don't give me that which one nonsense. I saw you cut your eyes at her before she ever got out of her car." Carson shifted his chair to face the window and snickered. "Which one. Same ole Baker."

The two faced the window and watched the lady leave her Acura nosed to the curb between a green Lexus and silver Infinity.

"The usual?" the server asked Daniel.

"Yes. With chips instead of fries."

"May I interest you in a drink or appetizer?" She turned to Carson and placed a set of silverware on the table in front of him.

"Yes, please," he said, half turning. "I'll have a Miller draft, and for an appetizer I'll take the phone number of that beauty across the street."

The server looked at Daniel and raised a brow, perhaps waiting for approval.

"It's okay, Cherie. He's harmless."

"Who's harmless?"

After she walked away, Daniel sat in silence, waiting for his moment. He was curious to see Carson's reaction. Cherie returned from the bar, plopped a napkin on the table, and put the mug of beer on it. Carson spun in the chair, grabbed the handle, and guzzled half of the mug's contents. "Nothing like a cold Miller. Hey. You working on my appetizer?"

"It's right where I left it, Harmless," she quipped. "Hurry it up. I don't have all day to stand here."

"Huh?"

Daniel pointed to the napkin. "This?"

Carson lifted the glass and pulled out the napkin. He flipped it over.

"You wanted the number. Now you have it," Cherie said.

"Yeah, right. I'm no fool. This is probably the number for Hotties XXX or something."

Daniel could hardly contain himself. He wanted to blurt out everything that had happened in the past three months with him and Denise.

"No. It's the real thing."

"I don't get it."

"Could if you were the lucky one."

"Okay. What did I say that was so funny?"

"Nothing."

Carson pushed up in the chair and said, "Wait a minute. I know her. That's Denise Tyler. That baby doll definitely has class."

"I believe you, Carson."

"Yeah, right."

"I do. She is a classy lady."

Carson rolled his head. "I don't freaking believe this. You know her, don't you?"

Daniel's cell phone rang. "Hey, sweetheart ... Yes ... Guess who's here ... Carson Wright ... Sure ... See you then ... Love you too." To Carson, Daniel said, "She said to tell you hello."

"Who?"

"Denise."

"No way, man. You're hooked up with her? How'd that happen?"

"I met her in Baltimore. The first time I ever saw her was the night before my last doctor's appointment. And get this. She had on a replica of your jersey."

"Vols or Dodgers?"

"Dodgers."

"That's freaking great. Wears my name across her back and you're the one who gets to take it off. Go figure."

"You were right when you said she has class. She has, and a lot more. She's beautiful, intelligent, charmingly sweet, and incredibly special all in one amazing package."

"I concur, Doctor," Carson spouted. "You're one lucky guy, Daniel Baker. One lucky guy. I'm jealous. I really envy you. If only I could be so lucky."

"You will one day, my friend. I'm sure of it."

"Nah. Not since Judith. I enjoy being single. I like to flirt too much to settle down with anyone. No one woman would have me, anyway. Not the way I am. Especially not one like Denise."

"People change."

"No, Baker. Not really. They're always the same inside."

ANOTHER PAIR OF EYES followed Denise from the time she left her car parked on the street until she passed by the window. Her way of walking reminded Jeremy Guerdon of the many days he fell behind a step or two to watch her stroll along the sidewalks of New York City.

The rearmost corner of the diner offered a perfect line of sight to the sidewalk across the street, the front door, and the row of tables next to the window. It also provided access to the rear door in case he needed to slip out unseen.

Noise muffled the conversation between Carson and Daniel enough Jeremy Guerdon couldn't make out everything. He picked up on a reference to Denise. He watched with keen interest.

Jeremy watched Daniel's and Carson's reaction in the foreground. Fury flew over him when Denise blew the kiss to the man seated at the table with Carson.

The server treated him with the same kindness she showed the other customers, even though his words sounded gruff when he ordered, as if he was doing her a favor by being there.

"Is there anything else I can get for you, sir?"

He looked at the brunette with coal eyes glazed with hatred. "You can leave me alone for now."

He turned his attention back to the two men. For the next fifty minutes, he studied their movements and mannerisms. They acted as though he didn't exist. Like a ghost, Jeremy sat there alone and sipped coffee, his third cup, not counting two warm-ups.

"More coffee, sir?"

He wished she would stop bothering him. She blocked his line of sight, and he needed to keep an eye on them. He leaned to his right, pretended to reach for something so he could see around the waitress.

"Check please."

Daniel and Carson pushed back their chairs and turned toward the door.

"And be quick about it. I have some place to be."

The server gave him a puzzled stare, as if pondering his urgency.

He snapped his finger. "Now would be nice."

She sent him a half smile and plopped the ticket down on the table. "Come back now, you hear?"

A wood fence blocked the view from the street and line of sight of any onlookers who might pass by. Jeremy shuffled his feet and peered between slats in the fence. Carson loped around the corner.

"Take your time, next time, will you?" Jeremy said.

"Do you want my help or not?"

"Shut up and tell me what you found out. What's this guy all about?"

"You might want to get somebody else to do this."

"What the rhino crap are you saying, Cars? You'd better not back out on me now. Remember our deal."

"Okay, okay."

"I'm listening."

Carson extended his arm and propped on the fence. Two seconds later he shifted his weight, stuffed his hands in his waistband behind his back, and dropped his head forward. "Don't rush me. This is hard enough without you leaning on me."

"Listen to me, jock-head. You do as you're told." Jeremy whipped open his jacket to expose a Beretta tucked at his side. "Now say on."

Carson wet his lips, squatted, and retied the shoestring on his left Adidas.

Jeremy nudged him with a knee.

"You really picked a good one. We played ball together until he got hurt and had to give it up."

"Get to the point."

"His name's Daniel Baker. He's a doctor."

"And?"

"He works out of the CDC in Atlanta."

"Good to hear. I got the right one."

"Huh? You already know about Baker?" Carson swallowed hard.

"I've been checking on a few things. What else you got for me?"

"Her phone number." Carson flashed the napkin.

Jeremy snatched it from Carson's hand, saw the number, and flung the napkin in Carson's face. "Well, whoopee. It's the same number I have in my phone."

"That never crossed my mind."

"Well, how 'bout that. You didn't let on that you knew Denise, did you?"

"Of course not."

"You sure?"

"Yes."

"Good. Was anything said that I can use?"

"Yeah. He said he bought a cabin."

"Where?"

"I don't know exactly, but I know someone who might tell me."

"You find out then."

"Dalton Lanier's a friend of mine. He's Judith's brother."

"Arrange it. Get me over there. I want to meet Dalton. And find that cabin."

Chapter 26

The cabin was a perfect setting for romantic evenings with the love of her life, or maybe a place to get away from the clamor and hustle of everyday life in the city. Denise told Daniel she wanted to keep everything simple. No lavish décor. All her heart desired was a place to rest without interruptions while enjoying the serenity of mountain life and plenty of time to cuddle with Daniel.

Denise sat quietly on the rug in front of the fireplace. The rug turned out to be one of her favorite places to relax. The fire burned brightly on this late October evening. Light from the fire illuminated her magazine article published in the November issue of Trend. She was so involved in her reading that she hardly noticed the unclasped gold chain as it fell across her left shoulder and dangled against her chest.

Bewilderedly, Denise tossed the magazine aside and reached for the chain. Before she pulled it from her shoulder, a sparkling diamond ring slid down the chain and nudged her long, slender fingers. She quietly stared at the ring for a few moments and then turned to see Daniel's face beaming back at her.

"An attorney friend of mine once told me to always be sure you want to hear the answer before you ask the question."

Denise could not help but smile at his words. She remembered the promise. During one of their many lengthy telephone conversations, the subject of their future came up, and she promised Daniel that he would not be let down by her response. Even then, she knew that one day he would ask for her hand in marriage.

She had anticipated this moment, always curious about how he would propose. She wondered if it would it be in some typical manner or something romantically different and unique. Would it take place on some nice, romantic evening, maybe at dinner out at some fancy restaurant, or at the cabin? Whenever and wherever he would choose, she knew he would make sure that the timing would be right for the both of them and that he would do everything within his power to make the event special for her, an event that would become their lifetime memory.

Denise focused on the dimple in Daniel's left cheek, which looked like a small basin of allure fed from a broad smile. She could see the excitement and anticipation of her answer written all over his face. She was not the least disappointed. Daniel's timing could not have been more perfect, and the manner he proposed caught her completely by surprise.

"Yes," she said, full of vim. "Yes, Daniel Baker, I am yours forever." She patted the rug. "Come. Sit here with me. I want to cherish this moment with you, my love. This day, this moment, I will never forget."

"Nor will I." He eased down on her left side, facing her.

She gazed at the ring as he slid it on her finger. Floods of ecstasy rushed through her body. All the while her thoughts totally focused on the man crouched next to her—her soul mate. "I have an idea. After the ceremony, I want to put two red roses in the river. One for you and one for me. They'll be a symbol of our lives on the way to a sea of eternal love."

"Great idea."

"You've truly given me something greater than I imagined could ever be. From now on, we can look back on today and say that this day was one of our fondest memories." She leaned her head on his shoulder. "The firelight makes it look like it's on fire." She waggled her hand to see the sparkles. "It's so beautiful. It's perfect. I love it."

"When I saw it situated among the several rows of various settings, I knew this was the one for you. It had you written all over it. I've been antsy to give it to you. The meeting this morning was cut short because one of the guys had to catch an early flight out and the afternoon session was cancelled after the deadline for submission was extended. Since the afternoon was free, I drove across town and stopped at Sal's downtown to grab a late lunch. I was sitting at one of the tables next to the front windows when Carson Wright strolled in."

"I wonder if Judith knows he's in town."

"He didn't mention her. We were sitting there reminiscing when you drove by and parked across the street in front of Paragon. I saw you run your fingers through your hair and check your makeup in the mirror before you crossed the street and walked by the window.

"When you got out of the car, one look at you and I thought Carson was going to lose it. I don't think he recognized you at first. He kept his eyes on you and said 'Now that, my friend, is a beautiful lady. I can tell by the way she carries herself that she has class.' I fought to keep a straight face. I bubbled inside. Finally, a smile exploded on my face and I laughed. You should have seen the look on his face when you blew the kiss to me."

"What did he say?"

"He acted strange. Not like the Carson I know. He had a washed-out look in his eyes. We talked for a while, and he kept looking toward the back of the restaurant. He said he had to leave. We said our goodbyes, wished each other well, and he rushed out the door like something had spooked him."

"Maybe it was me."

"That's impossible."

"What then?"

"It doesn't matter. You're what matters now."

"You're sweet." She held up her hand and stared at the sparkling diamond on her finger.

"I'm glad you like it."

"Now I'll really be your queen."

"You are. You're my queen. I have something here for you I want you to read. I wrote it for you this morning."

On the outside of the envelope, Daniel had written "Queen." Denise removed the slip of paper inside and began to read:

Hey, Baby,

There comes a time in our lives when we meet someone who is special to us. When this happens, something deep inside our very being seems to click. It is as though a light is turned on inside and only this special one has the switch to turn it on. Once the light switch is on, it can never be turned off. For me, in my life, you are the special one. You turned on my switch.

You are the special one who walked into my life. Ever since that day, I have had peace in my heart, knowing beyond any doubt that you are the one I will spend the rest of my life with, knowing you are the one who excites me in such a way I can only imagine what lies ahead for us. There is no way I will ever let go of this one true blessing I have received. You are this blessing, and I will do everything in my power to show you every day how much you mean to me and how fortunate I am to have you.

You are the one I have searched for all my life. It is like when you are looking for something and you don't really know what it is, but you know when you see it. Well, I found it when I found you, Denise, and you have made me the happiest man on this earth. You are the one I am in love with. You are the one I want. You are the one I need. You are the one, the only one.

I love you. You are my baby doll, my queen.

Your honey,

Daniel

Denise carefully placed the note back inside the envelope and looked up at Daniel. His face beamed. The dimple showered its magic on her heart.

She caressed his face, touched the dimple, and said, "You've brought joy and happiness to my heart and life. You complete me. You wow me every time you look at me. Every time you touch me or hold me, every time you kiss me, every time you say, 'Come here,' and especially when you tell me you love me, I get the same feeling. Thank you for a love that exceeds any that I could have ever hoped for or dreamed of. You show me love that really wows me in more ways than I could ever express or that you could ever imagine."

Chapter 27

Dalton Lanier steered his shiny red pickup into the driveway of his Binfield, Tennessee, home at twenty minutes past his normal arrival time. The truck bounced side-to-side going down the rough dirt drive leading to the old farmhouse.

Dalton was the second child of Luke and Mary Lanier, who were lifelong residents in the Binfield area. Those who knew the Lanier family regarded them as well-respected, church-going folks who never have an unkind word to say about anyone.

Dalton inherited the same attribute of kindness, or so it seemed. He attended the local high school where he excelled in football and received a scholarship to play wide receiver for the University of Tennessee Volunteers, following in the footsteps of his older brother, Craig. On the days he had no classes or football practice, Dalton worked around the family farm taking care of the livestock or riding his prized steed, an appaloosa he named Wind Under Wing.

Already forty minutes late for dinner, he followed the drive down past his normal spot next to the back steps. He left class at the university around three o'clock and made a couple of stops before heading home. Instead of parking and going straight inside, he drove on out to the barn where he noticed the light on. His friend, Carson Wright, toyed with a 1957 Chevrolet truck inside the barn.

Dalton could see Carson working on his restored pickup stored in their barn. They grew up in the same neighborhood, although Carson had a few years on him, and spent time together during the off season. He pulled his truck to the side and switched off the ignition. He got out. Stopped to tie the laces on one of his boots.

"Danged laces won't stay tied."

Carson lay over the front fender of the truck adjusting the idle with a screwdriver. He looked up from across the hood of his truck as Dalton pulled up and parked.

"Hey, guy. Where were you? We've been waiting on you for pretty near an hour."

"Hey, Cars. Good to see you back in town. I've been out and about, you know. Going to school. Not doing nothing much. When did you get here?"

"Oh, a couple of hours ago, I guess. I thought I'd tinker with this baby 'til you got back. How do you like it since I've had her painted?"

"I was wondering where you had taken it off to. She's beautiful. You gonna show her soon?"

"If I can get her ready, I am. There's a show coming up in two weeks over in Pigeon Forge. I'd really like to make that one if I can."

"I'm sure if anybody can do it, you can." Dalton reached into his truck and pulled his new compound bow from the seat. He strutted over to Carson and presented his bow.

"How do you like this?"

Carson raised his eyebrows and reached for the bow. "That's nice. When did you take up hunting?"

"I thought I'd give it a try, you know."

"That's not like you. Can you hit anything with it?"

"I've been practicing a little."

"Nice outfit." The voice came from behind him. Dalton turned. "May I see it?"

"Dalton," Carson spoke up, "this is a friend of mine. He's from Jersey."

Jeremy's lean, muscular appearance and choice in clothing gave Dalton the impression that Jeremy was a few years older than

Carson. He stood about the same height as Carson, and his dark, straight hair fell on top of his collar. The man looked as though he stepped right out of GQ magazine. His physique really made his clothes look like they were tailor made. His aura appeared mysterious and somewhat reserved—definitely out of place in the Tennessee hills.

Dalton reached to shake Jeremy's already waiting hand.

"Anthony Rubano," he lied. "It's nice to meet you."

"Jersey, huh? Good to meet you." He acted nice enough. Big smile and straight, pearl-white teeth.

"Here. Have a look for yourself. If you'd like to shoot a couple, I've got some practice arrows over on that work bench." Dalton handed the bow to Jeremy and pointed to a makeshift piece of a shelf attached along the left side of the barn.

"Hmm, Reflex Rampage. Nice bow. What are you shooting?"

"Gold Tip XT with hundred grain Wasp Jak-Hammer SST. Go ahead. Try it."

"I'd like to, but it'll have to wait. Your mother said to tell you dinner is getting cold and to send you in if you were down here. I guess she heard you when you drove by. She acted like she was tired of waiting on you."

"You know my parents?"

"Had to use the facilities."

"Guess we better go. Y'all coming?"

"Yes, sir. Wouldn't want to miss out on Mrs. Lanier's good cooking," Carson said.

"Why not?" Jeremy said. "I never have eaten Southern cooking. If Cars says it's good, then that's good enough for me." To Carson he said, "You gave good directions, made it easy to find what I was looking for in this middle-of-nowhere countryside."

"You're pleased?"

"Let's have some chow."

Jeremy examined the bow as Carson and Dalton made their way to the house three strides ahead of him.

Dalton gave Carson a what's-up look.

"Later," Carson whispered.

Dalton nodded and stepped ahead to open the door.

Jeremy passed the bow to Dalton. "Do you have lots of game around here?"

"Sure do, if you find the right spot. It's pretty good west of here and the closer you get to the national park."

"I may have to try it."

DALTON HELD OPEN THE door and followed them into the kitchen. He propped the bow on the stairs before taking his place at the dinner table across from Carson and Jeremy.

One thing was for certain, Jeremy thought, seeing the table full of food. Moms in the South know how to put on a spread. Fried chicken and pork chops, mashed potatoes smothered with gravy, fresh corn, butter beans, and tomatoes all homegrown in the family garden. And the fringe benefit of hot biscuits with slabs of real butter stuffed inside. He could live with a little indulgence. Besides, this was a first for him.

Luke Lanier was already seated at the head of the table when the boys entered and filled the three remaining chairs. As soon as the boys and Mary Lanier were in their places, Luke bowed his head and prayed God's blessings for the food.

The next sounds heard were those of utensils clanging against dishes full of delicious victuals and ice popping in glasses being filled with sweet tea.

"Where's Judith?" Dalton asked; her empty chair was pushed up under the table next to their mom.

"She and Denise went out somewhere."

"What time is she gonna be home?"

"She didn't say. Why?"

Dalton rolled his eyes toward Jeremy. "Just wondering."

After dinner, they returned to the barn. Dalton stuffed his hands in his pockets and squeezed his arms against his sides. He pulled on the door to close it, flipped on a space heater, and sat it on the shelf.

Jeremy situated the bale of hay Dalton offered him next to Carson's truck. "Why haven't you ever told me about Dalton's sister?" he asked Carson.

Carson played along. "Oh, I don't know. I figured you'd hook up with one of those gals up around your area."

"Have you forgotten already? I used to date a girl from the South, remember?"

"Oh, yeah. Whatever happened between you and her?"

"I guess big-city life wasn't her thing. One day I arrived home and she was gone."

"Did you know she was leaving?"

"No clue. I gave her everything a girl would ever want. There was no reason for her to leave that way."

"No note or nothing?"

"Not anything."

"Man. That's terrible."

"Sure is," Dalton piped in. "Nothing like that'd happen round here unless you really messed up bad, like getting caught screwing around with some other girl or something."

"I don't mess up." Jeremy resented the implication.

"I didn't mean you," Dalton was quick to reply. "I'm talking general terms. Heck, what do I know anyway? I don't even have a girlfriend."

After having a good laugh, they settled down and spent the next hour chatting about the Great Smoky Mountains and things the area offered.

With a look at his watch, Jeremy got up and gave a friendly wave to Dalton. "I guess I had better take my leave. I enjoyed meeting and hanging with you this evening. Tell your folks thanks again for their hospitality."

"I will and you're welcome anytime, Anthony. Are you going to be around here very long?"

"I'm not sure. At least a few days. I have some things I need to take care of."

"He's looking for work." Carson glanced at Dalton with raised eyebrows.

"What are you looking for?" Dalton asked. "I'll keep an eye out for you if something comes up."

"Thanks, but no thanks. For starters, I'm planning to look for a teaching position at the university. I prefer to make my own contacts. I hope you understand. It's nothing personal."

"No, that's fine. Good luck. Hey. Maybe next time you'll get to meet Judith."

Jeremy nodded at Carson and walked out of the barn. Carson followed him to the Charger. Jeremy motioned for him to get in. Jeremy pulled out a wad of money and counted out fifteen hundred dollars in hundred-dollar bills. "I want a Reflex Rampage compound bow outfitted exactly like Dalton's and two dozen of the Gold Tip XT with hundred-grain Wasp Jak-Hammer SST Broad-heads."

"You don't hunt."

Jeremy glared at Carson. He didn't like his motives questioned, and Carson knew better than quibble with him.

"I do now."

"Okay." Carson snatched the money from the seat and stuffed it in his pants' pocket. "How soon do you need it?"

"No later than Tuesday or Wednesday."

"I'll try."

"Uh-uh. You do it. You got it?"

Jeremy watched Carson saunter to the barn. He wheeled the car around and eyed Dalton in his rearview mirror until he reached the road and turned the corner. He chuckled. Mysterious. Everyone he'd met lately said something along those lines about him. He wondered if Judith thought that of him. He planned to find out tomorrow.

Sometimes people have too much trust in others, especially the ones they don't know. He always tried to drill that into Carson. If only they knew the truth. He readily admitted that sometimes it was difficult to determine what the truth was. Wherever the truth was to be found, he was determined to be there.

Instead of turning toward the city, Jeremy steered his rented Charger south. Clouds dotted the night sky. A light breeze blew from the northwest. The moon was in its last quarter phase. It provided very little light on the winding Tennessee highway. Someone would be hard to spot on a night like this. Sneaking around in the woods would be easy.

The rpms dropped on the tachometer as Jeremy slowed the Charger to negotiate a left turn off the highway. Carson's directions led him exactly where he wanted to go. The cabin's location said to be less than a mile from the intersection.

A Blount County Sheriff's vehicle sat in the darkness off to the side a few feet from the corner. After turning, Jeremy glanced over his right shoulder and kept on his way. The sheriff's vehicle never moved.

Jeremy mentally noted the deputy's presence. He drove on through the area without stopping at the hide-a-way shelter he had commandeered. He would try again after his date with Judith.

Then he would return Friday to scout the area. He may have to stay out all night, perhaps camp there the entire weekend.

His idea would rattle the citizens of Blount County.

Chapter 28

"Hi, Judith."

Judith looked up from the computer screen at her desk. Jeremy Guerdon stood in the doorway.

A co-worker, blonde, thin, in her late twenties, removed her gum, dropped it into the trash can, waltzed in from an adjoining office, and said to Judith, "My next appointment's not for two hours. I can help him if you're busy."

Jeremy ignored the blonde's remarks. He kept his eyes locked on Judith, whose features he found appealing, captivating, more so than he remembered. He yearned to touch her, lusting for the part of her hidden beneath olive blouse and beige slacks.

"No, I'll take care of it. I've been expecting him."

The blonde whispered, "He likes you," in Judith's left ear loud enough he heard every word.

"Mr. Rubano. Have a seat, please." She turned to the blonde. "Shut the door on your way out and hold my calls."

The blonde raised her brows and grinned.

"It's just contract stuff."

"Uh-huh," the blonde said on her way out.

Judith slid closer to the desk. She propped her elbows on the edge and interlaced her fingers under her chin. "What brings you here today, Mr. Rubano? Is there something wrong with the house?"

He felt relief when she used Rubano instead of her way of saying Anthony—a minor detail considering he liked everything else he knew about her. "I feel lost in its massiveness, and being alone there intensifies it." He reached out and touched her hand. "I was wondering if you might keep me company this evening."

"You didn't have to come all the way here to ask me. You could have called."

"I misplaced your number," he lied. "Besides, I prefer inviting you to dinner in person. The odds of acceptance increase."

"It's true. It is much harder to give an answer face-to-face than it is over the phone."

"Is that a yes?"

"Yes. Isn't that what we planned?"

"We can't deviate from the plan now, can we?"

Their evening began with a drive along Foothills Parkway. They ate dinner at Chop House in Sevierville. They ended their date in Jeremy's bed.

Jeremy swung his feet off the side of the bed and peered at the clock on the nightstand: eleven forty. He looked over his shoulder. Judith's back was to him. He listened. Her breathing indicated sleep. He eased to the closet where he pulled on a pair of jeans and shirt. He picked up a pair of socks and work boots he had bought for this occasion, tiptoed out of the bedroom, and drove to the hide-a-way.

The shack looked eerie under faint moonlight. He pulled around the side and parked. Unkempt hedge bushes concealed the car from passing motorists after he doused the lights. No one knew he was here. The targeted area spread beyond the shed. Hundreds of acres of forest land provided ample cover. Soon to be filled with hunters.

Jeremy spent five hours scouting the ridges, gorges, funnels, and the river. He pondered every move, focused his effort on acreage surrounding the cabin owned by Daniel Baker, and figured out the best escape routes. When he departed, no one knew he had been there.

Judith stirred when he crawled in bed. She rolled over and cuddled in his arms.

"Miss me?"

"Sorry, I fell asleep. What time is it?"

Jeremy pulled her closer. Contact with her body excited him. "Time for whatever it is you want."

Chapter 29

Wednesday morning, Carson heard the cabinet door close and the sound of water running from the faucet in the kitchen. He shook his head as if it would make his hearing better and peered through half-closed eyelids at the door of his bedroom. The smell of something burning got him to his feet and along the hall to the kitchen, shirtless and wearing blue boxers.

"There you are."

Jeremy Guerdon washed ashes from part of a cracker box into the disposal. He wore all black and looked as though he'd been awake most of the night. He filled a ceramic mug and sipped water before speaking again.

"Saltines. Is that all you have to eat around here?"

Carson checked the sink and ran more water down the drain. "Why did you burn that? You could've set off the smoke detector."

"Got you out of bed, didn't it?"

"You didn't have to light a fire."

"I do things my way, remember? Now, where's the cabin?"

"How did you get in?"

"Simple." He tossed two saltines in his mouth, washed them down with the remaining water in the cup, and set the cup on the counter. "Where?"

"Daniel's my friend."

"I'll be your enemy if you don't tell me."

"I don't know if I can."

"Good thing baseball season's over, Cars. You'll have plenty of time to heal before you have to report for spring training."

"You wouldn't."

"This girl, Judith. How long did you two date?"

"She has nothing to do with this."

Jeremy pulled a chair from the glass table, sat sideways, and crossed his legs. "I might ask her to dinner."

"You wouldn't."

Jeremy raised a brow.

"Okay. Okay. Promise me you won't hurt her."

"I told you I don't make promises, remember? Now get dressed."

"Where are we going?"

"You're going shopping."

"Me? For what?"

Jeremy slammed a fist into Carson's face. "You know what."

"I haven't had time."

"You're out of time."

"Whatever."

Carson rubbed his left cheek once he was in the bedroom. He loathed the way Jeremy treated him. He hated the way Jeremy treated everybody in the family. He knew Jeremy wouldn't go as far as killing him, but one thing was certain: Jeremy Guerdon didn't mind inflicting pain on anyone.

He pulled on a pair of jeans and a polo shirt and slipped into loafers. He crossed the room to a closet where he had stashed the money Jeremy had given him to purchase the bow. He slipped the envelope of cash in his hip pocket and pulled the shirttail over it on his way to the kitchen.

"How do you live like this?" Jeremy poised in front of an open cabinet. "You need to get out of here and stay with me at my place."

"Move to Jersey? No thanks."

"I'm not talking Jersey, Cars. I bought a nice house here in Tennessee."

"What prompted you to buy here?"

Jeremy pulled open the door. "If you're ready, let's go. I have things to do."

By the time Carson and Jeremy reached the sporting goods store, Jeremy had explained his plan to Carson. Carson nodded he understood what Jeremy wanted him to do. Equipped with the cash Jeremy supplied, he strolled into the store and went straight to the archery department.

Cold sweat dotted his forehead. He liked Dalton. He liked Dalton's family. They treated him as if he was part of their family since the first date he ever had with Judith. If he went through with Jeremy's idea, Dalton and the Lanier family would be harmed. He knew the price if he failed Jeremy. What choice did he have? Pressure Jeremy put on him languished any will he possessed to do the right thing.

"I'll be right with you, sir." A middle-aged man wearing rimless glasses motioned to Carson from the far end of a glass display counter that looked to be about thirty feet long.

Carson turned his attention to the items displayed for sale. A countless supply of archery accessories and gadgets for any archer's budget lined the shelves. A row of new compound bows lined the wall above the man's workspace. He glanced at the bows from one end to the other, then perused the broad-head section until he located the packages of hundred-grain Wasp Jak-Hammer SSTs.

"What are you shooting?"

Carson lifted his head. Rimless glasses man stood two feet away.

"Looking for a Reflex Rampage."

"Nice choice. We have two in stock."

"I need a dozen Gold Tip XT cut to thirty inches and three packs of those." Carson indicated his choice in the display.

The man looked puzzled. "Thirty? You probably shoot at least a thirty-two with those arms."

"They're a Christmas gift," Carson lied.

"No problem. Checking to be sure, that's all. Once you cut them, you can't make them longer, you know."

Chapter 30

Daniel's travels through the last week in October sent him to four states before he ended the trek at the CDC in Atlanta and returned to Knoxville.

He phoned Denise from the airport in Knoxville and told her he should be at the cabin within forty minutes. He arrived an hour before sunset to waiting arms and a table spread with food.

Denise knew her way around the kitchen when time came to prepare a meal. She would take a backseat to no one, anywhere. She had prepared a moist and tender baked chicken, silver queen corn, green beans, and a sweet potato casserole. She definitely deserved an A+ for organization skills.

After the meal, Denise stacked the dishes on the table in front of her.

"I'll get those." Daniel reached for the dishes with one hand, rose, and pushed his chair back with his legs. "Why don't you take a few minutes to relax in the swing? I'll be there as soon as I can put these away."

"What do you think about taking a little walk before the sun goes down?" She got up from the table and started through the door leading to the screened porch.

"I'd like that."

Daniel quickly rinsed the dishes and placed them in the dishwasher. He peeked around the edge of the open door to catch views of Denise on the back porch swing. She looked great in her yellow tee and denim shorts. It did not matter what she was wearing.

She was naturally beautiful. Seeing her automatically made him smile.

She loved being out there on that porch. Between the back-and-forth motion of the swing and the serenity of the surroundings, she would often be found sound asleep, cuddled up on the swing with her head propped up on one of the plush pillows on either end.

The way she had decorated the porch reflected her warm and inviting personality. Two large wicker lounge chairs sat opposite the swing, each adorned with an afghan draped across the back with matching pillow cushions on the seats. A small, round, glass-top table stood between the chairs adorned with a floral arrangement blossoming from a porcelain vase. Being comfortable out there was no problem. She made sure of it.

"I think I'll take the camera with us. Would you mind getting it for me? I placed it next to the bed after I came in this morning."

"I don't mind at all. I have to get my shoes, anyway. Do you need yours?"

"I have them out here."

"Okay. I'll be right there."

"I want to get a few photos of the black bear and her cubs this evening if I can get close enough. I've been seeing them before sundown the past few times we've been here," she said as Daniel walked out on the porch with camera and shoes in hand.

"That'd be good," he said, sitting next to her on the swing, crossing his leg, and sliding on his shoe. "Maybe we will see lots of wildlife this evening. There's plenty of it around here from what I've seen. I'd like to get a glimpse of those wolves again that we saw recently."

"They terrify me."

"We'll be okay if we keep our distance. Soon enough, they'll get used to us being around," he said, sliding on the other shoe. "Now, I'm ready. Let's do it."

The area around the cabin was blessed with an abundance of wildlife. Black bear, whitetail deer, grey and red fox, raccoon, and grey wolves were observed frequently, especially in the early morning and late in the evening around sunset. Occasionally, a couple elk made an appearance.

An avid hunter as an adolescent and teen, many of Daniel's friends and family deemed him woods-wise. He was crafty for making the most of available material and learned to shoot early on in life. He was quite proficient with rifle and handgun and the use of primitive weapons. Most of what he learned came from his dad, who had served as a ranger and sniper before being transferred to intelligence. The rest of his skills came from hands-on, being-in-the-woods experience.

Daniel watched Denise tie the laces on her hiking boots, stand up, and walk back through the cabin and out the front door. His eyes followed her every move as he fell in behind her. She looked cute in her outdoor attire, not out-of-place at all. She fit right in with her surroundings. Wow, Daniel thought. Even in hiking boots, she moves with the grace of a lady. He was a lucky guy and he knew it. He never took her love or anything about her for granted. He loved everything about her and cherished her as his greatest treasure.

She must have felt him watching her. She turned around as she stepped off the bottom step onto the ground and welcomed him with her smile and outstretched hand.

"Come on, honey."

Daniel smiled back. He loved the way she called him honey. He knew she meant it from her heart.

"I love it here, don't you?"

"I sure do, baby doll. I don't believe we could have found a better place. It's perfect for us."

"I know. I feel the same way."

They strolled to the river's edge where they stopped to look at the water. The level had risen from the morning rain and now roared over the multitude of rocks scattered about the riverbed.

"It's loud," Daniel said.

"What did you say?"

"The water. It's loud."

"Oh. It sure is. We can walk along and enjoy it for a few minutes, and then I want to go over to the meadow where I saw the bears."

Daniel nodded, keeping in step with her. He looked to the west where the sun appeared to be about to kiss the horizon and put it to bed for the night. What a magnificent sight. The mountains reminded him of home in the Rockies. These were different, but no less beautiful.

The roar subsided somewhat two hundred feet downstream where the water deepened. Denise stopped and pointed across the river.

"There. There they are. Do you see them?" A black bear and her cubs ambled from the edge of the trees toward the river as if to say, "Take a look at us. We are wild and free."

"I see two. No, three. There's a third one over behind that bent-over tree."

"They're pretty close. I'm going to take a picture of them. Wait! There's another one. This is great."

Denise snapped six or seven photos of the bears and three more of a whitetail doe lingering inside the tree line.

"Do you see the deer? She would make a nice cover girl for Wildlife Times, don't you think? Look at her standing there. Isn't she beautiful?"

"She is at that."

Denise snapped a couple more photos of the doe, whirled around, and snapped a photo of Daniel caught up in the moment. "Gotcha." She leaned back and slapped her leg with an open hand.

"I'll get you back. You wait and see."

After a good laugh, they watched the sun disappear behind the mountaintops before heading back to the cabin. Denise changed the camera lens to a wide-angle setting and snapped a half-a-dozen photos of the sunset.

Daniel tossed a twig in the water. The stick rose and fell under ripples and floated away.

Denise jerked around to face Daniel. "I can see it now."

"What?"

"Two roses floating down the river. Like I said the other day, it'll be a symbol of our journey into the future."

A sense of being watched swathed Daniel. He stilled and tried to concentrate and listen to Denise and hone awareness to their environment. The stir stayed with him.

"What's the matter? Do you not like my idea?"

"It's awesome."

"Then what's wrong?"

"I'm not sure. I have a feeling we're not alone. Don't move. Whatever it is may be in the woods on the other side of the river. Turn this way and face me. That'll allow me to study the other side, and it won't be so apparent to whoever is out there."

Denise shifted around and leaned toward Daniel and propped on her left hand between his knees. Daniel looked into her eyes and smiled as if nothing was amiss. What he wanted more than anything at that moment was to ford the river and charge through the trees, catch whoever might be out there. Instinct and Grandfather's training held him back. He must act normal. He must not alert any would-be predator if, in fact, something or someone was out there.

"Maybe nothing. Perhaps it's me. I don't know. I don't want to take any chances on someone sneaking up on us."

"Then maybe we should go back to the cabin, honey." Denise inched closer and clung to his left arm. "It will be dark soon."

"I want to take a quick look around before we head back."

Daniel gathered a handful of stones within reach and tossed them one by one into the water. He worked his way left to right. He scrutinized the woods beyond each splash. When he finished, he hooked his arm under hers, helped her to her feet, and moved to her right side.

"Stay close."

They strode along the bank on their way back to the cabin. Daniel kept his face turned toward Denise and the river, pretending to lose himself in conversation while he studied the landscape.

Dim light of the setting sun provided some illumination. Streaks of light fingered under tree branches and hovered above the forest's floor. Although the shadows were lengthening with the passing moments, Daniel's eyes scanned the woods intently and curiously for anything he thought might be any exception to the norm.

By the time they arrived back at the cabin, shadows succumbed to the overtaking darkness.

"Honey, do you really think there was someone out there?"

"I don't know, baby. Why don't you go on inside? I'm going to check around the cabin to make sure things are okay. I'll be right in."

"Be careful, please."

DANIEL EDGED AROUND the east side of the cabin and disappeared as Denise ran up the steps leading to the front porch. A slip of paper neatly folded had been tucked in the screen door. Denise removed it. Once inside, she switched on the lamp and perched on the front edge of the sofa. A business card of Caleb

McCluskey, Deputy, Blount County, Tennessee, accompanied a form letter.

Dear Friends,

This letter is to warn you of a situation in the area that you need to be made aware of.

Bow season opened the third week of September, and the first three weeks went by without report of injury. Before the morning was over on the third Saturday, one hunter lay dead at the foot of his tree stand. The hunter suffered a fatal through-and-through shot with an arrow. Two more hunters were wounded in the same manner this past weekend. One died in his stand. The other collapsed near his truck.

None of the arrows have been recovered.

If you have any information, or if you hear anything pertaining to these incidents, please call the Blount County Sheriff's Office.

Thank you,

R. J. Price, Sheriff

Denise folded the letter and set it aside and placed the card on the table next to it. She crossed her arms and sat quietly for the next few minutes until Daniel opened the door and stepped in.

"Did you see anything?"

"Someone's definitely been here." Daniel lowered himself to the sofa and kicked off his shoes. "I found footprints leading from the road up to the cabin and tire tracks behind our cars."

"This was in the screen door." She handed the letter to him. "He also left this card."

DANIEL READ THE LETTER and handed it back to Denise. He dropped the deputy's card on the end table. Maybe the presence of the deputy was what he felt while they were down by the river this evening. No, he thought. It might be possible, but he didn't think so.

It had to be something else. What he felt was more than something from a friendly visitor. The stigma of Halloween hung in the air. Evil loomed. He didn't dare say a word to Denise about thinking it might be Jeremy.

Nothing had happened to either of them to indicate Jeremy's presence in over six weeks. That concerned him. He knew a man like Jeremy would not give up until he satisfied his desire for reprisal.

Denise interrupted his thoughts. "I imagine what you felt out there was probably the deputy coming by here. I hope so anyway."

"Probably. I wouldn't worry about it." He patted her thigh. "I'm sure it's nothing we need to be concerned about."

"I hope you're right."

"Everything's going to be fine." Daniel got up from the sofa, walked over to the window, and peered out into the darkness. Was that you, Jeremy? "I'll take care of you."

"I know you will, honey. That's another reason I love you so much."

"I love taking care of you." He returned to her side on the sofa, put his arm around her, and kissed her softly on the cheek. "You're my everything, baby. I can't imagine one day without you."

"That's exactly the way I feel about you."

They cuddled close to each other for several minutes without speaking a word. Crickets conversed outside the cabin, along with occasional hoots from a couple of owls.

Denise scooted forward on the sofa and turned to face him. "Do you really think you'll be okay out here tonight?"

"Yes, baby. I'll be fine. I'm going to check around again after you leave to make sure everything's secured."

"I think you should leave with me. It would make me feel better if you did. Please. I'm afraid for you being here alone, especially if somebody is lurking out there. You read the note. What if the man they're looking for comes here?"

"I'll offer him a plate of spaghetti and bid him good night."

She leaned forward and slapped his arm. "Smarty. This is serious."

"Don't worry. I'll be okay."

Denise slumped back into her comfort zone next to him and threaded her arm under his.

Daniel sat still for a few more minutes, stared through the front window into the darkness, and then rose and walked over to the front door. He checked to make sure the door was locked and paused in front of the window.

Moonbeams from a full moon lit the forest. Trees swayed in the breeze. Their eerie, finger-like shadows grasped at the edge of the porch.

Whatever had caused the feeling Daniel experienced earlier was gone.

JEREMY GUERDON WATCHED their every move for over an hour. The way Denise and Daniel frolicked disgusted him. His hands tensed, ached to clutch Daniel's throat. He yearned to hear Daniel exhale one last time. He wanted Denise to be there to see it.

Jeremy paralleled the couple from where they lounged on the riverbank to the clearing on the cabin's west side. Even though the roar of the rushing water would have made it difficult for anyone to hear him, he exercised caution and stayed on the opposite side of the river. The back light of the sun benefited him until it dropped below the horizon. Clumps of mountain laurel gave him ample cover from the couple's wandering eyes.

He waited ten feet from the bank until Denise entered the cabin. He sneaked to the edge of the river and forded the water only after her companion rounded the corner and was out of sight. From there, Jeremy slinked away under the light of the moon, curious about the man Denise rubbed against and kissed more times than he cared to see.

This was an added hitch to destroy. One he hadn't expected. He would get rid of him and crush her heart at the same time. Jeremy snickered at the thought of hurting Denise from a different angle. All he had to decide now was how to do it.

Happy Halloween.

Chapter 31

Rays of the rising sun effectively eked their way through the cracks in the wooden blinds covering the bedroom window. They reflected off the chesser's mirror onto Daniel's face. He squinted and shielded his eyes, again wondering what plagued them the previous evening.

What a night it had been. The ghouls and goblins had unleashed restlessness around the cabin. They lived up to their hallowed night. Sleep for Daniel had been off and on until dawn. He felt worse than times when he worked through the night and stayed up the next day.

Thank goodness he had the next several days to leisure at the cabin. Maybe he could get some rest. Relaxation was not normally an issue at the cabin. The setting provided the perfect atmosphere necessary to unwind. Getting rest? Now, that was a different story.

He looked over at the other side of the bed and wished Denise was there. The sad look she gave him when he left her at the Tyler's home close to midnight tore at his heart. He pictured the feather pillow cradling her head, covers tucked tightly under the chin. The vision of beauty warmed him. Confirmation of true love satisfied the longing that once existed in his heart.

Daniel slid out of bed. The hardwood floor on this first day of November felt cold to his bare feet as he picked up his jeans and shirt and headed out of the bedroom. He grabbed the shoes next to the sofa where he had left them and worked his feet into them. He wanted to look around this morning for anything left by the intruder.

Daniel removed a coffee mug from the cabinet, dumped in a packet of hot chocolate mix, filled the cup with water, and placed it in the microwave. He pulled on a lightweight jacket while the microwave heated his breakfast. He paced from room to room while sipping the hot chocolate. If evidence was out there to be found, proof to implicate Jeremy in any form, Daniel was determined to find it. He rinsed the cup and set it in the sink.

The outside air whipped through the open door and nipped at him. He stuffed his hands in his pockets and thought about getting a heavier coat. The air felt good though, and he knew walking would warm him in no time at all. Branches swayed back and forth from a northwest breeze.

Chirping finches moved from branch to branch as if they were competing in gymnastics. A fox squirrel scurried across the drive and latched onto a tree, barking as Daniel made his way toward the river.

Daniel trekked along the river to the place where they had been the previous evening. Once there, he followed the river farther south until he found disturbed vegetation and scuffed soil. A footprint indicated where someone had crossed from west to east. He climbed the bank and entered the forest, careful not to disturb any evidence he might come across. The forest floor still held dampness from a rain two days before. If something had been out there since then, Daniel felt sure any signs left behind should be identifiable.

Two hundred yards into the woods, Daniel noticed a broken branch on a small sapling next to a towering white oak tree. Overturned leaves surrounded the base of the oak. He squatted for a closer look. These were not the work of squirrels or turkeys in search of acorns. Tread marks in the disturbed dirt resembled those expected to be made by a hunting boot.

From this vantage point, anyone would be well concealed from the river's edge. Who was this intruder? Why was this spot picked?

What did this person have in mind to do? Daniel determined to find out.

A trail of disturbed leaves led away from the oak in a southeasterly direction. Daniel followed the trail, losing it intermittently and picking it up again. At nearly three hundred yards, he came upon a sweet gum tree. Cuts in the bark marked its trunk. They began some two feet above ground level and continued upward to eighteen or twenty feet. Someone had climbed the tree in a portable hunting stand. Freshness in the cuts indicated recent presence, probably within the past week.

Daniel scanned the forest. He eyed every part within sight and let out a sigh. "I'll get you, whoever you are. I'll get you for sure. You can count on it."

He made a trip to the cabin in search of things he could use to set traps for the unwelcome visitor. Finding what he needed, Daniel strategically placed branches and the items he had taken from the cabin near the injured tree in case the intruder returned. If someone walked within thirty yards of the tree, Daniel would know it.

It was time to pay a visit to Deputy McCluskey.

The lobby at the Blount County Sheriff's Office was vacant when Daniel arrived. He strolled to the window and waited five minutes before a woman shoved open the door opposite the front counter and entered the reception area.

The robust secretary jerked a chair from under the built-in desk. She snatched a pen from a tray and said, "I'll be with you in a minute," without even a glance at him. The chair squawked and whined when she plopped in it and spun to face a computer monitor.

Daniel waited, hands in pockets while the woman peered at the screen, tapped a few keys, and scowled. He picked up a copy of *Car & Driver* from a table and flipped through it.

The woman mumbled, "Stupid moron didn't enter the information like he was told." She twisted to her right and yelled,

"Hello, I need that data, and I need it now. Can anybody hear me in there?"

Daniel peeked over the top of the magazine. If they can't hear that loud mouth, they'd have to be deaf. A bawl like hers could wake the dead, he wanted to say.

He pitched the magazine to the table and leaned an arm on the counter. The secretary's gaze gave him the impression she didn't want to be bothered.

"I said I'd be with you in a moment. Have a seat."

A uniformed deputy stood at the front door. He held the door open for a boy who looked about ten to enter. "Sir, is there something I can help you with?"

"I'm Daniel Baker. I have a place out on Hendrickson. Deputy McCluskey left his business card and a letter about trouble in the area."

The deputy extended his hand. "I'm McCluskey, but please call me Caleb. It's very nice to meet you, Mr. Baker. Let me take care of one thing for my son here and we'll talk. This is Nate. His grandma's coming by here to get him. Come on back."

Daniel followed the deputy and Nate to the deputy's work station. McCluskey swiped the chair from the desk next to his and motioned for Daniel to sit there.

File folders, two empty coffee cups, an unopened sleeve of Butterfingers, and a copy of the previous day's *Knoxville News-Sentinel* lay scattered on the deputy's desk.

"Let me get Nate situated, and I'll be right back," McCluskey said.

The deputy and the boy pushed through a door opposite where they entered the office. A couple minutes later, McCluskey returned alone, pulled up a chair, popped a piece of Nicorette gum in his mouth, and handed Daniel a composite drawing of a white male.

"This is our suspect," he said, tapping the drawing with an ink pen. "It's not the best, but it's all we have to go on. The man in this composite was seen in the Hendrickson area this past weekend. Some guys on four-wheelers spotted him hanging around out there on one of the back roads. He flagged down one of the boys and said he was looking for an address. We checked the address and it doesn't exist."

"What about a vehicle?"

"The boys couldn't say what it was other than it had four doors and was a dark color. I think they were more interested in riding than anything else. They tear it up out there. There's no one to complain even if they did and they know it. Say, you're not the same Daniel Baker who used to play for the Dodgers, are you?"

"I am."

"Oh, man. I wish Nate was still here. Would you mind signing something for him?"

"Not at all."

"Great."

McCluskey pulled out a business card and flipped it over. "Sign the back of this. He's going to be so excited when he finds out."

Daniel grinned as he autographed the card. "Something like his dad?"

"You bet."

"I read the letter you left at the cabin. Any trouble around my place?

"None reported that I'm aware of. The first couple cases were three or four miles farther north of you. Why? Have you noticed anything unusual on your property? I'll be glad to come have a look."

"It's probably those kids," Daniel said, though he thought the opposite.

"Well, call if you need us. This guy is dangerous. Don't try to handle anything yourself."

Chapter 32

The next morning, Daniel's bare feet hit the cabin's cold hardwood floor at five fifteen. He pulled his shirt from the back of the chair post, threw it on, slipped into camouflage pants and out the bedroom door with a pair of Rocky boots in hand. He pulled on acrylic socks and the boots and stuffed the pants' legs inside before tying the laces.

Something had to be done about the hunter-hunter. The cops had no clues to identify the perpetrator. If they did, they weren't saying anything. Forget McCluskey's warning to stay out of this. The Constitution gave him the right to protect Denise, and himself, from any threat.

Daniel grabbed his lightweight jacket, slipped out through the back door, and crept to the river. The river had dropped to its lowest level in two months. He stepped carefully down the bank into the water and walked downstream. The rush of the water over exposed rock covered the sloshing of his movement.

After he'd gone about two hundred yards, he climbed out and sneaked through a cluster of mountain laurels. The southernmost edge opened up on the rim of a ridge. The natural fall of the ridge, dotted with huge pieces of granite, stretched for a quarter of a mile east of the river.

Supposedly, the latest incident occurred less than a hundred yards from where the ridge dipped and formed what hunters refer to as a funnel, a long, narrow depression between two ridges or similar land masses.

Daniel stalked across the ridge. His grandfather's old hunting knife was strapped on his right hip. He listened after each step on the dew-covered leaves.

After several minutes, the crisp air bit his fingers and cheeks. He stuck his hands in the jacket pocket expecting to find his gloves. They weren't there. He'd left them in another jacket. It didn't matter.

The way he looked at the situation, potential prey now lurked for the predator. He intended on taking a POW instead of notching a kill. Nevertheless, if killing became necessary, he would not hesitate. Athleticism and prowess put him in the mix against this unknown enemy. Determination fueled the desire to win. Training all but assured it.

Any disadvantage he might suffer forced him to stay alert. Knowledge definitely meant advantage, and Daniel figured the killer probably knew the area better than anyone. In Daniel's way of thinking, all things even out under cover of darkness.

At the pace he crept, Daniel reached the funnel in thirty-two minutes. He took the south side and followed it until he got to the hunter's tree some forty yards above the bottom. The poplar towered over the surrounding saplings. This was a perfect spot for hunting whitetail deer. Cuts in the bark indicated where the hunter had attached a climbing stand and ascended and descended the tree. The ground at the base of the tree had been raked clean.

A crackle of leaves broke the silence. Daniel stood motionless. A slight breeze touched his face. It brought with it an unmistakable odor: human.

Bears don't smoke.

A silhouette moved across Daniel's line of sight. It stayed cowered behind trees. When it moved, it skulked in straight lines from tree to tree. Prowling? Stalking? Whatever the person's plan, Daniel intended to find out and put a stop to it.

He mimicked the intruder's moves. He stayed downwind and kept the same distance of fifty to sixty yards between them as best he could. At one point, the intruder angled downward, crossed the funnel where the two ridges met, and cut across the opposite ridge. The distance between them shortened to less than fifty feet when the person snuck past Daniel's position halfway up the hill.

They were headed toward the cabin. Denise was supposed to arrive early since she had an appointment to get to by nine thirty. Taking the risk of being detected, Daniel closed the distance. Survival prompted him. He judged that if he could take two steps for each one of the visitor's, he'd reach the clearing at the cabin ahead of the prowler. Possibly.

Footfalls made minute sound on the damp forest floor. Only the occasional brush of a limb pushed aside marked the subject's location.

This person's good at this, he thought.

The thick leaf-covered ground worked against progress. Dew squelched the otherwise noisy crackle under foot. After another hundred yards, they closed in on the clearing. Ten yards apart. This was not good. Too much ground to cover prohibited any surprise attack. What if the intruder was armed? What then? And what would happen to Denise if he became disabled? Or killed?

The intruder dropped to one knee near the edge of the clearing. A flicker of light quickly was hidden beneath a hand. A faint glow escaped between gloved fingers. Daniel crouched and watched from the cover of a cedar tree. The light faded. The intruder rose, slipped something into a pocket, faced the cabin for a few seconds, and looked skyward. The black sky had lightened to gray. The intruder whirled and headed into the woods.

Straight at Daniel.

Crouched and on the move.

Closer.

Closer.

Tension rose in Daniel's chest. The ball of his right foot found the base of a tree behind him. Another ten feet and the intruder would be on top of him. The intruder stopped five feet away. Daniel fought to control his breaths. His heart raced. A cramp seized his foot. He winced and eased off the pressure from the tree. Dawn was coming. Another two feet and he'd be exposed.

The intruder shrank back a step back and sidestepped a cedar tree.

Relief. An advantage he had been waiting for. One more step. As soon as the person stepped away from the cedar, Daniel whirled and lunged in one motion. They crashed to the ground, arms flailing, each fighting to overcome the other.

Fingers latched onto Daniel's shoulders. A head-butt snapped his head back. A foot, which felt like a battering ram, slammed his chest. Another foot creased his right jaw before he hit the ground. He rolled to his feet. A glint of light on metal caught his eye. Not a good thing. He grabbed at the intruder. Clinched a handful of cloth. He jerked leftward, held on, and spun around as if he was in a body-flinging contest.

Something hard clamped his left wrist. Cold metal. A female's voice blared, "FBI."

Daniel couldn't believe his ears. He twisted the female's arm that held the other end of the handcuffs. He forced her forward and planted a knee in the small of her back. "You want to run that by me again?"

The woman squirmed. "You heard me! Let me up from here!"

"Why you're trespassing on my property."

"You've assaulted a federal agent, you idiot. There are three more agents—"

"You reek."

"It's part of my cover. Haven't you ever heard of fitting in? It's the jacket. Get off of me."

Light played on the treetops. It lit enough for Daniel to see the woman's face. He bent forward and sniffed her hair. It smelled of floral essence. Not a hint of smoke or body odor.

He eased his hold and removed his knee from her back. "Show me some ID. I want to know why you're here."

She whipped a handgun from under her jacket as she stood and pressed the muzzle against Daniel's side. "I'm after a killer. Looks like I found him. Now down on your knees."

"Don't you mean I found you?"

"You find this amusing, mister? Put your arms behind you."

Daniel did as he was told and tensed. Before she cuffed the other wrist, he stiffened his legs and pushed rearward as hard as he could. A twang. A zip. A broad-head slashed through the sleeve of his jacket. He stumbled to his left and sprawled on the ground, pulling the agent with him. He rolled and cupped his hand over her mouth. He peered into the woods from behind the cedar tree.

"Someone's out there."

The woman shoved away Daniel's hand. She elbowed his midsection, squirmed free, and whipped around behind him. She pressed the muzzle of the pistol against the base of his head. "Where?"

Pain jolted Daniel's arm and sent streaks down through his fingers when she clamped a hand on top of the injury. She jerked her hand away.

"You're hit."

Blood soaked the lower half of the sleeve and trickled across the back of his hand and off the fingertips. "I'm fine."

The agent gave him a puzzled look. "How did you know? Did you see somebody?"

"No. I heard something brush a tree and the twang of the bowstring."

"He may still be out there. I didn't hear him run away."

"How could you hear anything scuffling with me?

"What's your name?"

"Daniel Baker."

"Agent Angela Donavan," she said. "My apologies, Mr. Baker. Deputy McCluskey told me you lived out here somewhere. You're obviously not the man we're looking for."

"If it's that apparent ... never mind."

"No, say what's on your mind."

"Do you always attack innocent people on their own property without first checking for ID?"

"Who attacked whom, Mr. Baker? You came at me first, remember?"

"McCluskey didn't say anything." Daniel spotted movement near the bottom of the ridge. "There!"

JEREMY SUCKED IN HIS cheeks and grinned sheepishly when the target went down. Daniel Baker was only one of many to get in his way. Not for long. Nobody matched him for stealth. Nobody.

He faded into the dense woods and made his way over the ridge to an abandoned road. The road led to a shack built into the side of the mountain. A fallen tree hid all but one corner of the structure. The shack lacked the comforts of an extended stay but was perfect to house supplies and other necessities. The day he discovered it, he oiled the hinges, and moved rusted farm equipment out of the way to one corner to give him plenty of room to maneuver around without making noise.

He slipped around tree limbs and pulled open the door. Once inside, he checked for messages on his phone. Richie wanted to meet with him. Carson again pleaded for him not to hurt Judith in the second message.

Jeremy cleared the voicemails and hit the speed dial. He heard a soft "Hello" and said, "Count your days, Denise. I have them numbered."

Chapter 33

Daniel and Agent Donavan angled down the ridge as fast as they could on foot toward where they thought the shooter had gone. The shooter was nowhere in sight by the time they reached the bottom. They listened for any sound to indicate direction of travel—rustle of leaves, snap of a twig, anything.

Nothing.

Daniel cradled his arm against his side and propped on a tree.

"How's the arm?"

"Stings." He scanned the ridge. "How could he disappear like that? We were right on top of him."

"He knows something we don't."

It took twenty-five minutes for them to circle the ridge, drop off the other side, and work their way over to the river. Nothing indicated an escape route.

"What now?" Daniel asked. "Radio for assistance?"

"I'm alone. The only thing I can do is retrieve the evidence he left behind."

"The arrow."

"Yes. I'm curious to see if it matches the others we have."

"How did you know to look for him here?"

Agent Donavan stuck her left hand in the jacket pocket and came out with an envelope. She opened the clasp and pulled the flap open to show him the broad-head inside. Blood stained the blades.

Daniel peered in the envelope. He thought the broad-head looked like a Wasp SST.

"A doctor removed this last night from one of our victims. The man said he'd been hunting near here and drew me a map to the area where he had his stand on a tree."

"Did you find it?"

"Not yet."

"I think I might know where it is. I'll take you there after we look for your evidence."

"You're looking peaked. Maybe you should sit down and let me do this."

He insisted they continue. Agent Donavan followed Daniel through the trees back to where they first encountered each other.

"I need that arrow," she said.

They scoured through the leaves and underbrush for ten minutes before part of a yellow fletching beneath a bramble bush caught Daniel's eye. "Over here."

"Don't touch it."

He stood there, having no intention of pulling the arrow from its resting place. He wondered if the agent thought of him as a reckless dolt. He resented any implication of the sort and wandered off to the side while she slipped on a surgical glove. She pulled the arrow from the soil.

She studied the shaft and broad-head, rotating it back and forth with a twist of her wrist.

"I'll be back in a minute," Daniel said.

"Where are you going?"

He didn't bother to answer and strolled sixty yards to the river's edge. He stooped and washed his bloody hands in the cool water. He shoved the sleeve of the jacket up to the elbow. He had a gaping wound two inches long on the forearm. The wound angled toward his thumb, an inch and a half distal to the elbow. The tissue around the cut throbbed and burned. He stayed in a crouch and lapped water on the arm with his right hand until he heard leaves rustle from her approach.

"Let's get that arm taken care of."

Daniel stood and turned to face her. The agent had closed the distance to within fifty feet of the bank. "I'll see to it. First, I want to show you the hunter's tree."

"That wasn't a request." Agent Donavan pointed toward the cabin. "Go. You can show it to me after we dress that wound."

Daniel scrambled up the bank. He paused at the top to allow Agent Donavan time to get to the trail that paralleled the river.

"Getting worse?"

"Like the devil stuck me with his pitchfork."

"That's an understatement."

"How do you mean?"

"You've never met Jeremy Guerdon. And it's best that you never do. Let's say I'm surprised your friend Denise Tyler is still alive."

They trekked in silence to the cabin. Agent Donavan shed the odorous jacket on the porch and followed Daniel inside. She helped Daniel shrug out of his coat.

He tugged off the shirt and dropped it on the floor next to the back door on his way to the bathroom. Daniel returned to the kitchen with a first-aid kit from the bathroom closet in hand. He took a seat at the table. He flipped the latch and spread the kit's contents in front of him: gauze, surgical tape, syringe, needle, vial of medication, thread.

A smile played on the agent's lips. "I'd say you're well prepared."

Not in the mood for chitchat, he said, "Hold this." A vial of local anesthetic lay in his palm. Donavan took it, followed his instruction, and filled the syringe to ten milliliters.

Daniel injected the needle in his arm. His thumb reddened as he plunged the stopper into the syringe and dispensed the clear liquid on each side of the wound. He set the syringe aside and propped the arm on the table. Agent Donavan cleansed the cut and threaded a needle. The alcohol set the arm on fire worse than the slice from the broad-head.

He caught her eye each time she looked up from the task. Dirt and grime darkened otherwise fair skin on her cheeks and forehead. Evidence of their scuffle. Her irises blended into the pupils as if one color. They emitted mixed signals of a hardened officer of the law and the lady within.

"Hold still." Donavan shoved the needle under the skin on each side and pulled the edges together. Three sutures closed the cut. She applied an antibiotic ointment and taped gauze over it. "That should hold for the time being."

"Nice job," Daniel said when she finished. "Obviously, you have had some medical training." He gathered the unused supplies and stuffed them into the kit.

"I'd like to get cleaned up if you don't mind me using your bathroom."

"Through the bedroom door and to the right."

The sound of a car door closing alerted Daniel to Denise's early arrival.

The front door of the cabin opened a few seconds afterward. Denise darkened the doorway holding a white box in one hand and two Styrofoam containers balanced on the other. The aroma of breakfast wafted from the containers when she closed the door and made her way to the table and planted a wet kiss on his lips.

"I brought breakfast and picked up some chocolate-covered strawberries for this evening."

Her smile faded. She gasped when a stranger stepped out of the bedroom. Agent Donavan was buttoning the top two buttons of her shirt. Not a good sign.

"What's going on here?"

"This is Special Agent Angela Donavan from the FBI."

"I don't care about her credentials. What's she doing here?"

"I caught her roaming around the property. She came in and dressed my laceration after someone took a shot at me." He lifted his bandaged arm.

Denise chucked the Styrofoam boxes onto the table and marched to the refrigerator. "Oh, I see. Then she got dressed herself, I suppose. Adept and attractive." The refrigerator's contents rattled when she jerked open the door. The container of strawberries banged down on the rack. Denise whirled and stormed toward the front door leaving the refrigerator door open.

Daniel hurried to cut off her exit. "Wait. It's not like that."

"Move." She brushed aside his outstretched arm. She paused at the door with her hand on the doorknob. "Oh? What was it you told me about trust?"

"Will you please let me explain?"

The door slam gave him her answer.

"I'll speak to her." Agent Donavan half-sprinted to the door. She turned her head to look over her shoulder at Daniel. "You stay in here. I know how to handle things like this."

DENISE STOMPED TO THE end of the porch and bent over the rail. Nausea poked her stomach, making it feel like it rose into her throat. Breaths she sucked in came in short bursts. She closed her eyes and tried to reason. She tried reliving the past weeks, hunting for anything she might have done to cause him to cheat on her. She couldn't decide which was worse: anger caused by seeing Daniel with another woman or the belief that he betrayed her. What happened?

The front door opened. The screen door hinges groaned when it swung open and again before it tapped closed against the frame. Denise expected any moment to feel Daniel's arms slide under hers and him press his face in her hair. If he did, there would not be much she could do about it where she stood. The only escape led through him unless she opted to vault over the rail. She wasn't that desperate.

The slats creaked on the porch.

"Ms. Tyler."

"Leave me alone." Denise stared into the forest. The throng of trees stood still and quiet as an audience in wait to see the opening act of a Broadway show.

"I'm sorry. I can't do that."

Denise spun around to face the stranger. "Sure, you can. It's easy. I leave and you stay here with him, or whatever. Get out of my way."

Agent Donavan shifted a half step to her left. She knocked against the wall when Denise bumped the agent's shoulder on her way by.

"I know about Jeremy."

The statement froze Denise next to the support column at the head of the steps. An arm around the wooden post kept her from plunging down. She leaned on the post. A trickle of tears streamed down her cheek. She swiped at it with her fingers.

"That's why I'm here, Ms. Tyler. What Dr. Baker said in there is the truth. He caught me snooping in the woods before dawn this morning. I had a hunch Jeremy Guerdon might be around here somewhere. I was out there hoping to find some sign he'd been here. I thought I might get lucky enough to catch him.

"Jeremy, or someone, shot at us out there. If it wasn't for Dr. Baker's reflexes, one or both of us would most likely be seriously injured or maybe dead right now."

Denise looked up. "I knew he'd come after me, but what I can't figure out is how he found me way out here. Daniel just bought this place. No one other than my parents and my friend Judith even knows about this cabin. Now, we're both in danger. What am I to do? What can I do?"

"Let the FBI handle it, Ms. Tyler. We know all about Jeremy Guerdon. We've had an active file on him for more than a year."

Denise reached in a pocket and pulled out her cell phone. "He called me this morning."

"What time?"

She flipped open the phone, dabbed her eyes with the back of her hand, and checked the recent call list. "He called at six eighteen." She closed the phone and stuck it back in her pocket.

"Did your phone show the number he called from?"

"It displayed 'No Number,' like he withheld it or something."

"What did he say?"

"He told me to count my days. He said he is." Denise gazed into the forest and yelled, "Go away. Leave me alone." She slid down the post, covered her face with her hands, and sobbed. "Please. Just leave me alone. I'm so scared." Her voice trailed, stifled by lack of air from diseased lungs.

A hand slid across her shoulders.

"I'm here, Denise." Daniel pulled her to him.

She buried her face against his chest. "When will he leave us alone? When is it ever going to stop?"

"Soon," Agent Donavan assured her. She stepped around them down two steps, turned, and patted Denise's hand. "We'll get him, Ms. Tyler. I promise you. We'll get Jeremy Guerdon."

Denise lifted her head. She stared across the river at the nothingness of the open field. Was Agent Donavan's promise supposed to provide hope? If it was, it failed to change the way she felt. She decided the agent meant well and attempted to comfort her with words of support. Yet doubt slipped in and split her credence in the agent's promise. What would happen until then? What about Jeremy's vow? Would his onslaught overpower the FBI?

"He's sly," she finally said.

"Everybody makes mistakes. When he does, we'll get him."

Denise turned her face and gazed into the agent's eyes. "He'll kill you."

Angela smiled. "He doesn't know I exist."

"Don't count on it."

Chapter 34

Suspicion brought on by the incident at the cabin wormed in and out of Denise's thoughts all morning. By eleven o'clock, she decided she had seethed enough for one day. She stopped by her father's office building. She penned a message for her dad and left it with the receptionist at the front desk. What she needed was some girl-talk.

Denise adjusted her blouse and ran her palms down the hips of her slacks on her way into the FBI's field office. "I'm here to see Agent Angela Donavan," Denise told the woman on the other side of the glass partition.

"Your name?."

"Denise Tyler."

"What's the nature of your visit, Ms. Tyler?"

"It's about a case she's working on." Denise said it having no thought about what she was going to say next.

"May I have the case name?"

"Guerdon."

"Do you have a first name?"

"Jeremy."

"Please have a seat."

Denise slid into a chair where she could see out the front windows and the door leading back to the offices. Two men dressed in dark suits erupted through the office door. The door again opened. Agent Angela Donavan. The men bolted out the front door.

"Care to join me for lunch?" Angela asked from halfway across the room.

Denise accepted without hesitation. She wanted to know everything she could learn about Angela Donavan, the woman. She was curious about how the agent knew about the cabin. Did any secrets involving Daniel exist that she should know about? Either way, Denise figured lunch was a good start.

The comment Daniel made about trust on the day of the hit-and-run crossed her mind. So far, he had earned her trust. Nothing except finding Angela with him at the cabin besieged that trust. The time of day bothered her more than anything. Any other occasion wouldn't have been as threatening as an hour after dawn, although the reason they gave fit what she observed.

All those things aside, the main questions on her mind concerned Angela's investigation of Jeremy Guerdon. She wanted to know what instigated the query into Jeremy's dealings. How long had this FBI thing been going on, and what were they doing about it?

"Where to?" Denise asked.

"Some guys told me about a place near the mall that I haven't tried yet. I thought we'd go there. If we hurry, we might beat the lunch crowd."

"If you're talking about Crystal River, we'll have to wait awhile to be seated at this hour. Crystal River gets swarmed when it opens at eleven and stays busy until two or later. The food is worth the wait though, that's for sure."

The crowd was as Denise suspected on their arrival. Customers lined the walls back to the entrance. A dozen or more stood outside the double doors.

"You weren't kidding about them being busy," Angela said after Denise gave the hostess her name and asked for a table for two.

"It's usually worse."

Denise hoped they could get a table off to one side. Twenty minutes later, an available table put them near the kitchen between two tables jammed with college-aged kids, half of them in orange shirts with "Tennessee" in bold letters on the front.

"Maybe we should have eaten somewhere else," Angela said.

"What did you say?"

"I said I was hoping we could talk."

"Me too."

The way Angela smiled lifted her spirit. Fake or not, Angela's face beamed with enthusiasm. Angela settled in the chair and draped a cloth napkin over her lap. The clamor kept conversation to a minimum while they shared a fruit bowl and Crystal River's specialty salad. At the end of the meal, Angela folded her napkin and dropped it on the table next to her empty salad bowl. She signed the meal ticket and included a generous tip.

"How much time do you have?" Angela asked.

"All afternoon if necessary."

"Is there some place we can talk? I need to ask you some things about Jeremy."

The chance to choose where they would go pleased Denise. She wanted to be where she felt comfortable. "I know the perfect place. Take me back to my car and you can follow me."

Forty minutes later, Denise pulled up to the cabin. She stood at the driver's door of the agent's car before Angela shut off the engine.

"You guys have a pretty—"

"Hold on right there. I've got to say something, and I want you to listen and listen well. I've had time to think about this morning. I don't appreciate you being in our cabin alone with Daniel, whatever the reason."

"Okay."

Denise paced in front of Angela's car. "No, it's not just okay. Understand how it looked to me. I come in and find you there, him half naked, and then you walk out of the bedroom buttoning your shirt. How do you think that made me feel? You had no business being in there alone with him."

She glanced at Angela, who rested her wrist on the door through the open window. Angela wasn't wearing a gun where she could see it. Did she have it hidden somewhere on her person? Her guess was she probably did.

She felt angered and flustered at the same time. Stress—compounded by stewing about the incident all morning—brought on a bout of queasiness. Her brain reeled with "What ifs." Was there some way to blot those things out of her mind and focus on the promising things in her life? How could she not worry now that her future lay in doubt? Denise drooped against the car. She hung her head and let out a sigh.

"I deserved that."

The response was not what Denise expected. She anticipated more of a comeback from an FBI agent.

"Don't patronize me, Agent Donavan. I'm not in the mood."

Angela reached into the car and swept her gun and holster off the seat. She attached the holster's clip to the waistband of her slacks.

"What's this? Are you planning to shoot me now?"

"No. You're the one who's going to do the shooting." Angela pushed the door shut and pointed toward the river. "You won't exactly be shooting me." Angela popped open the trunk lid and removed a paper target. "You may pretend it's me. Or Jeremy. Whichever you prefer. Come on. Blast your troubles away."

Denise liked Angela's sense of humor. The gesture made her feel better, mind and body. "Are you serious?"

"Absolutely. Ever shot a semi-automatic?"

"Won't you get in trouble for this?"

"Not if you don't file a complaint." Angela raised the target and pointed to center mass. "I'll even write Jeremy's name across the top. How about it?"

Denise loved the idea. "Why not?"

Angela tossed a pair of ear protectors to Denise and grabbed another pair for herself. They strolled to the river where she set up the target using the opposite bank as a backstop. She handed the pistol to Denise and showed her the best way to grip the weapon in two hands and how to position her feet. She stepped aside and said, "Whenever you're ready."

The pistol thundered and jerked in her hand. The bullet nicked the silhouette on the left shoulder. Denise looked at the gun and then at Angela.

"What'd I do wrong? I aimed at the chest."

"You jerked the trigger in anticipation of the shot. Try again and this time increase pressure on the trigger slowly while you focus on the sight picture."

"My hand's shaking."

"Take a deep breath and let it ease out. Remember to line up the sights. Take your time and gently pull the trigger."

Denise nodded. She inhaled and released. Steadied her stance. Aimed at the target. The shot ripped the paper two inches to the right of the midline. A metallic sulphury odor filled the air.

"Nice shot. Now I'm mortally wounded."

"It wasn't you."

"Thanks. I appreciate that."

Denise fired two more shots into the kill zone, lowered aim, and drove one through the crotch.

"How did it feel?"

"Good enough that I wish Jeremy really was dead. Now it's your turn. Show me your stuff."

Angela grinned. "Show you or show off?"

"Show off." Denise wanted to see what the agent was capable of.

The eight shots Angela fired formed an outline of a heart on the target.

"Wow." Denise clapped her hands. "Now punch his heart out."

"Like this?" Angela inverted the pistol and pulled the trigger using her pinky. The bullet centered the heart.

"Incredible. How'd you learn to shoot like that?"

Angela popped out the clip, loaded another, and holstered the weapon. "Hours and hours at the range. We practice for every scenario. It's not how fast you are, Denise. A cool head and proficiency win in the end. Keep that in mind when you face the dangers in this world."

"You're referring to Jeremy, aren't you?" Denise felt her throat thicken. "I need some water. Come on. Let's go inside."

By the time Angela stopped off at her car and entered the cabin, Denise had two glasses full of iced tea on the table. Denise handed one of the glasses to Angela. She kicked off her shoes and settled on one end of the sofa.

"How did you get involved with Jeremy?" Angela sat on the opposite end of the sofa.

"I frequented a deli in Staten Island owned by his uncle. One day I was there, Jeremy came in. We had been introduced the week before at a dinner party. He spoke to me, and after a brief conversation with his uncle, he sat at a table next to where I was sitting. His Sicilian accent and those dark eyes wrapped in mystery charmed me. I found him irresistible. We went out, and before long we were engaged, and I agreed to move into his house. That's when things changed."

"How?"

"Interest in me dwindled. We'd go to one of his socials, he'd pamper me in front of everybody there until he was sure we were seen, and then he'd disappear for thirty minutes to an hour, sometimes longer."

"Did you know what he was doing?"

"Not a clue. He got furious when I finally asked him about it. He told me it was business and that I should mind my own."

"Do you think his lost interest was because of another woman?"

"Perhaps. I don't know. Have you two ever met each other?"

Angela maintained eye contact with Denise. "I saw him once at a party. A covert operation. I'm not allowed to elaborate on it."

"I didn't mean—"

"It's all right. Do you know anything about Jeremy's business dealings?"

"Nothing. I thought he was an investment broker. That's what he led me to believe. The things I saw in the file proved otherwise."

"Let's talk about the file. What was in it?"

"Names. Dates. Places. I realized then where Jeremy's loyalties were. One entry named me. He'd already planned to kill me."

Angela sipped the tea and cradled the glass in her left palm. She shifted to the edge of the cushion. "Any idea why?"

"None."

"Think," Angela said on her way to the kitchen where she dumped the ice in the sink, rinsed the glass, and set it in the sink.

"I have." Denise followed Angela and set her still full glass on the counter. "I've gone over everything from the day we met until the night I left him."

"Agents searched the house in New Jersey and another one he kept in upstate New York."

"I didn't even know he had another house."

"There are a lot of things you don't know about Jeremy Guerdon, Denise. You got away from him at the right time. Another week and your family would have been planning your funeral."

"If they'd found my body, right?"

"I wasn't going to say that, but yes ... if."

"That night somebody came to the house in New Jersey. I already had my bags packed and was lugging them down the stairs when a car pulled in the driveway. I just knew it was him. I've never been so afraid of anything in my life. If he'd caught me, then I'd been a goner that night for sure, even if he hadn't planned on killing me until later.

"I heard the clap of shoes on the walkway and knew it wasn't Jeremy. I couldn't remember if the front door was locked or not. When the door cracked open and the barrel of a gun protruded through, I ran out the back door and around the house to my car.

"Can you believe it? He sent some floozy after me. She's probably—"

"The door was locked."

"Huh? How would you know?"

Angela tousled her hair. She cocked her hip to one side. "Because I used a lock pick to open it."

Chapter 35

A hint of Clinique Happy swirled around the room when Daniel entered the office at ten o'clock the following Tuesday morning to check messages and return calls. He paused inside the door and inhaled, taking in the aroma of the perfume. Denise often used the same office in her dad's building. Her perfume of choice wafted around him. He wondered how it could be her. She was supposed to be out of town until late in the evening.

He sat down in his chair behind a small cherry desk and spun around. He switched on the computer. An envelope addressed to him lay on the desk in front of the monitor. He picked it up and opened it. The handwritten note also smelled of Happy. It said: "Seven o'clock at our special place."

Daniel leaned back in his chair. Anticipation for what would be waiting for him when he arrived at the cabin that evening gave him reason to smile. He brought out of her special feelings that she had tucked safely away, waiting for the right one with the key to unlock that part of her. He held the key to her heart. He knew it. She knew it too.

The phone rang. Daniel picked it up and heard Mr. Tyler's voice. "I'll be right there."

Daniel grabbed his jacket and hummed "I'm On the Winning Side"—a song his mother used to sing—all the way to the office.

Clifton Tyler stirred behind the desk, coffee cup in one hand, and opening and closing desk drawers with the other.

"Have a seat, Daniel. I'm glad you came in today. I have some good news for you."

"Judging by your exuberance, I'd say it must really be something."

Clifton set the cup on the desk pad and rose to his feet. "Then let me be the first to congratulate you on reaching the final stage." He extended his hand across the desk.

"They went for it?"

He held onto Daniel's hand longer than a normal handshake. He picked up his coffee, sipped twice, and chuckled. "You'd better get some pants with deep pockets, Daniel."

"That good, huh?"

"Better than good. Much better."

The phone buzzed. Mr. Tyler pressed the button to put the call on speaker. Before he had time to speak, the secretary's voice blurted, "Fire!"

"Where?"

"Your old office."

The news dampened the celebration of a deal involving Cyclodactin. Mr. Tyler's face paled. Daniel beat Mr. Tyler through the door. He raced down the corridor and reached the door to the borrowed office ahead of Mr. Tyler by two strides. What he saw froze him. A fog rose from the computer. The word *bye* in bold font flashed on the monitor. The body of a female lay curled in the middle of the room, arms and legs in a pugilistic attitude typical of fire victims. Only he knew this wasn't a fire that claimed her life. The lack of odor proved it.

Daniel covered his nose and mouth and slammed the office door.

The secretary stuck her head out in the hall. "The fire department is on their way."

"Call and tell them to get a Hazmat team here and notify the coroner," Daniel said.

"Coroner?" Clifton rushed the door. Daniel threw his arms outward to block his passage. "I need to get in there."

"Not now, Mr. Tyler. There's nothing you can do for her."

"She might still be alive."

"It's too late. We've got to get everybody out of the building."

Clifton hurried away. He shouted orders to every door he came to. He got on the intercom and ordered an immediate evacuation. Within thirty seconds, he caught Daniel about to head through the stairway door on the east end behind a horde of employees.

"You got any ideas?"

"Lots of ideas, but no substance to any of them.

"This is crazy."

"We need to get downstairs."

Sirens wailed to an abrupt stop near the building. Speakers in the trucks blared radio traffic. Firefighters scrambled for equipment.

Three members of Hazmat arrived in a separate vehicle. Two of them donned full protective gear. The third identified himself to Clifton Tyler as Captain Young. "Are you the one who called this in?"

"Yes. Clifton Tyler."

"Is everybody out?"

"As far as I know. I ordered a complete evacuation of the building."

"Tell me what happened."

"You'd best talk to this young man." He thumbed toward Daniel.

"Describe what happened up there and be quick about it."

"Smoke coming from under the desk, eggshell white. A female, mid-thirties, lying on her side in front of the desk. Cyanotic and pugilistic attitude."

"Thanks." The captain nodded appreciation. "That helps." In the radio, he said, "No one inside the building without protective gear and a breathing apparatus. Third floor, second office on the right from the east stairwell."

Questions ransacked Daniel's mind. What kind of substance could cause something like this? How did it get there? Who was the woman? Was she a patsy? If so, how did she get past security and up to the third floor without being seen? And how did she know Daniel used that office? Or did she know?

He scanned the crowd of employees among bustling firefighters and police for any sign of Clifton Tyler. The man was nowhere in sight. He noticed a police officer carrying a video camera. The officer aimed the camera at the front entrance and entered the building. Daniel wondered what might have been captured by the security cameras. Maybe one of them caught something useful.

He was imagining the video images when a police lieutenant got his attention. "Are you the one that discovered the body?" The lieutenant held a tablet and pen.

"Yes."

"What is your name?"

"Daniel Baker."

"Are you an employee here, Mr. Baker?"

"I'm working on a project with Clifton Tyler, CEO of the company."

The lieutenant scribbled something on the paper. "Have a seat right there." He pointed to a park bench between the sidewalk and a row of hedge bushes. "A detective will be here shortly to talk to you about your involvement."

The lieutenant turned his back to Daniel and headed toward a group of employees. He said something in his radio mike and called one of the females to the side and jotted more things on the pad.

A horn beep made Daniel look toward the street. Angela Donavan jogged across the street and up the sidewalk to the bench where Daniel sat. Her gait resembled the grace of an Olympic athlete, fine-tuned and ready for action. She looked quite different from the first time he saw her. She wore navy slacks and silk blouse the color of bone. Her hair was curled over the shoulders and emphasized her slender neckline.

Daniel rose to greet her.

She flashed a smile. "How's the arm?"

"Sore."

"You know what's happening here, don't you?"

"I suspect it's him."

"How this time?"

"My guess is poisonous gas. I saw an odorless fog coming from a CPU. I would have noticed the smell of a fire, especially if it was electrical. This one gave no warning."

"Fits his MO." She fidgeted with her holster, unsnapped the release, adjusted the pistol, and snapped the strap back in place. "Never strikes the same way twice. That makes him dangerous and extremely difficult to catch him. Jeremy acts, waits few days or even weeks, and goes at it again with more force than the previous time."

"The victim never knows when he'll come after them?"

"Exactly. He catches them off guard. What's so scary, he's a master at doing it."

"Inimitable."

"That's why we've had a hard time figuring out which crimes are his. We've never really been able to track him until now. Denise became our best lead when Jeremy turned his attention on her and now you. Jeremy Guerdon exudes jealousy, Daniel. He'll not deviate from his course this time. I'm sure of it."

"How do you know so much about him?"

"Personal ties I've made."

"With Jeremy?"

"Yes."

"Then he knows you."

"Yes. But not as FBI. I can't say more than that."

Thoughts about what Angela said buzzed Daniel's mind. He stared at the busy street wondering about the secrecy. Should he trust her? Their first encounter shouted yes. But what if it was all a setup? What if she had planned the opportunity at the cabin to get close to them? Her tie with Jeremy, whatever it was, bothered him. He balled his hands and pressed on his thighs. Maybe he should have confirmed her identity as an agent for the FBI.

Daniel rose to his feet, eyes straight ahead. "I need to call Deputy McCluskey."

"He's out of the office today. Tell me what you need, and I'll relay the message to him."

Without looking at her, he said, "Thanks, but I have to check on something."

"Okay. I'll be inside if you need me."

"AGENT DONAVAN, MAY I have a word with you?"

"Who are you?" Angela looked up at a man she had never seen as he neared where she stood outside the doorway leading into Daniel's temporary office. Investigators from the medical examiner's office wrapped the dead woman's body in a white sheet and placed her in a black body bag.

"You'll want to hear this in private."

"Things are pretty hectic around here, as you can see."

"This will only take five minutes. These guys will put you off longer than that. I'm ready to hear your input on this situation now, Agent."

Arrogance or confidence, which drove this stranger's ambition? Either way, the man portrayed an aura bordering on a god complex. To her, his demeanor appeared pushy. Nonetheless, he was right about the wait.

"Three minutes," Angela said.

"I'll squeeze four."

There it was again.

"This way, Agent."

He led her through one office and into an inner office with no windows. He closed both doors behind them. Before the man offered a comfortable chair to her, he began, "I've been watching you, Agent Donavan." Angela dared guess where this was headed. "You're equally personable and professional, an asset to the agency."

She waited in silence for him to continue, arms at her sides. Still no offer.

"You've shadowed Denise Tyler without her knowledge until the unfortunate run-in at the cabin the other morning."

"Who are you? How do you know about the cabin?"

"How doesn't matter."

His face gave her nothing to go with the voice. Had she seen him some time in the past and not realized it? She raised her internal defenses. "I covered it well."

"You got caught."

"Like I said, I handled it."

"So you say. Tell me, how did Denise react to your presence?"

"I fail to see what that has to do with what happened here or my status with the FBI. If you don't mind, I have a crime to investigate, whoever you are."

"Agent, this has nothing to do with the FBI. Believe me, Denise can handle herself. I have no doubt. Her ability has exceeded my expectation. All she needs is guidance. When she's ready, I want her."

"Look, I'm certain Denise Tyler will do just fine in whatever field she goes into. Still, the issue—"

"Have a chair, Agent Donavan."

"You've used up your four minutes. I'm leaving." Angela spun around and reached for the doorknob.

"Would you walk out on Simon One?"

A UNIFORMED OFFICER blocked Daniel's passage to the parking lot. "You can't leave until the detectives get a statement from you."

"I told Agent Donavan what happened."

The officer stepped closer. He shoved his hat up on his forehead and cut his eyes up at Daniel. "Good. Then you'll have no problem remembering what to tell the detective when he gets here, will you? Have a seat, bub."

"Never mind that, Officer," said a tall man with graying temples dressed in a khaki suit and light blue shirt with open collar. "I'll take it from here."

The man questioned Daniel for thirty minutes. He stepped aside when his phone rang, said, "Yes, sir," stuffed the phone into the inside pocket of his coat, and charged toward the main entrance. He ignored Angela Donavan's call to him as she exited the side door.

Angela slid onto the bench next to Daniel. "He's taking it better than I expected."

"How do you mean?"

"He's off the case."

"He's not working it?"

"It's ours now. His chief wants the FBI to handle this."

"He acted like he was on it."

"He's considered a temp. We let them gather what information they can, and then they'll turn everything over to us. It's more efficient that way."

"Do you agree?"

"Sometimes. Not always. He's a good cop. Levelheaded most of the time."

"And other times?"

"We all have our pride, Daniel."

"Are you keeping something from me?"

"What makes you ask?"

"Body language."

"You know everything I know."

The answer she gave fortified his theory about her. Whatever secret she was hiding, he wanted it revealed. He wanted to know if she really worked for the FBI or if it was all a façade. "Any ideas about the dead girl? Who was she?"

"Our agents located what they believe is her car or a car she might have used about a block from here. It's being towed for processing. The vehicle's registered to a business in Marietta, Georgia. Agents from the Atlanta office are running it down now. They're also going to check on a connection to the CDC."

"You think she worked at the CDC?"

"Something's not right. They found a CDC employee badge inside the car."

Chapter 36

Suite 600 at 710 Locust Street in Knoxville housed the field office of the FBI. Daniel wheeled onto Locust Street from W. Church Avenue and parked in the designated area in front of the building five minutes after talking on the phone to Deputy McCluskey.

He switched off the ignition and sat there for five minutes, unsure if he should go inside. Never had he faced a situation like this. Was he acting foolish by being here? What evidence did he have for doubting Angela Donavan's credibility as an agent of the FBI? Why had she lied about knowing Deputy McCluskey? The two of them never worked on anything together according to McCluskey. The deputy denied having ever met her.

He tried to picture Angela seated behind a desk, paperwork piled in front of her, supervisor demanding copy of her case reports, suspect handcuffed to a chair next to her desk, spouting obscenities and claiming innocence. He thought of how she was dressed at their first encounter compared to the way she looked when he saw her outside Mr. Tyler's building.

Cops. They have their ethics. They bleed blue and look out for each another.

Enough. Daniel knew he must find an answer to his foreboding. He shoved the car door open and pushed out, hesitated a moment, started to get back in to leave. He paused with his hand on the door latch release and gazed at the building.

"Ah heck." He shut the door and strode to the front entrance.

Angela pushed open an interior door and called to him before he crossed the lobby. "What took you so long?"

"How did you know I was even here?"

"Security camera. I saw you drive into the parking lot."

"Well, I wasn't sure if I should come in or not."

She grinned. "Intimidating, I know. Don't fret it. You're among friends here."

"I was among friends in front of fifty thousand fans, but sometimes it didn't make it any easier."

Angela laughed and held the door open. "I guess not. Come on in."

She led the way through a maze of desks and into a small room filled with cabinets and shelves. After offering Daniel a chair, Angela opened an evidence drawer and handed him a clear baggie containing the CDC ID badge.

"The people down at the CDC reported this stolen in August. The photo's been removed. Do you recognize the name?"

Daniel ignored the chair and glanced at the badge. "No."

She flashed a photo taken by the medical examiner of the dead woman from Clifton Tyler's office. "What about her?"

He studied the face in the picture. "No."

"Are you sure? Look again."

He stuck it under a desk lamp.

"No. I'd remember a scar like that." He pointed to the woman's chin.

"Let me see that." She peered at the face. "Hmm. I guess you would at that, Dr. Baker. I thought it was a shadow or something." Daniel tensed. He tightened his jaw to keep from spouting, Aren't FBI agents supposed to be observant? How could you miss something like this scar? "Any idea what might have caused it?"

He avoided eye contact. "It exhibits an unusual pattern."

"Like a man's ring, maybe?"

Daniel again examined the photo. "Maybe."

Angela pulled a case file from atop a stack on one of the shelves, dug through it, and pulled out a photograph of a Krugerrand coin ring and handed it to him. "One like this?"

A glance told him the pattern on the woman's skin had similarities to the ring.

"I wouldn't swear to it in court."

"But it's possible."

"It's possible. I'd prefer to make comparison with the actual injury and not from a photograph."

"Are you okay? You seem distracted."

Daniel dropped the photo on the file jacket and edged toward the door. "I'm fine."

"We'll get Jeremy Guerdon; don't worry."

"I'm not worried."

"Then what is it?"

A black-and-white photograph on the desk caught his eye. An inspiring sight. The snapshot showed a girl holding hands with a firefighter at the scene of a crash between a compact car and dump truck. The girl cradled a doll under her chin.

"Great photo," he said, lifting it off the corner for a closer look. "Was the little girl involved in the collision?"

"In the car's backseat. She was trapped in there for over half an hour. Her mother was the driver. Blood from the mother's head dripped to her knees and trickled down her legs the whole time she was in there."

Daniel returned it to its place. "How sad."

"I carry it with me. It reminds me why I do what I do. The incident destroyed the world I knew and birthed a new one in me the same day." Angela reached for it and clasped it in both hands. "Five years old. Memories from that age haunt and amaze me at the same time."

The scene in the photo tugged at his heart. He realized the significance of it when Angela cradled the framed art against her chest and rested her chin on it.

"I'm truly sorry."

Angela turned away and set the frame on the file cabinet next to the window. "That was a long time ago, Dr. Baker." She wiped her left cheek with her fingers.

Daniel noticed moisture glistening on her fingertips. Some pains never heal.

"Please, call me Daniel."

Chapter 37

Daniel arrived at the cabin Thursday evening at five minutes before seven. As he got out of his car and stepped toward the cabin, he found the first of many notes that would lead him to his soul mate. When he reached the door, Denise met him wearing a flowing white gown made of satin trimmed in black lace. Her long dark hair lay against her tan shoulders and chest.

She greeted him with a tight hug and a long passionate kiss.

"It's great to see you," she said. "I love you so much. Tonight, I will take care of you in every way."

At that moment, he knew what cared for meant. He saw it in her eyes and realized what he saw in Denise was love beyond measure expanding toward infinity. There was no need to wait for next Thursday to give thanks. For him, Thanksgiving began months ago in Baltimore.

What started with a flicker ignited a fervor they craved to share with each other and no one else. The scene set the tempo for a story only they could imagine. The future belonged to them. They knew its reality would surpass every expectation even they had dreamed of.

Daniel admired her magnificence in the firelight. The blessing of such an incredible person's love was without comparison. He was ready to commit to her and her alone and vowed in his heart to cherish her as long as he lived.

A portable stereo played Andrea Bocelli. Denise preferred Bocelli's soothing tone or the sounds of waterscapes to accent times of their togetherness. Nice, thought Daniel. The tenor voice energized the serenity of the moment, as if the flow of the melody carried them to another world. The ardor felt when he touched her bare neck and caressed the soft skin as he slipped the gown off her shoulder roused and warmed him.

"Have I told you lately how much I love you?" Denise said.

"Yes, yes, you have. And not only that, but you prove it to me every day. I have always imagined how our love would be, but never believed it would be as strong and sure as it is today. I see us getting closer every day and cannot imagine even one day without you. Nothing will ever be able to tear us apart because of love and you know what is said about love."

"Yes, I do, but tell me again."

"Love is the greatest thing in the world."

"I love you and I am yours forever."

"And I yours, baby." Daniel reached for her left hand and pressed her palm over his heart. "What we have is the greatest thing in the world."

Glass shattered, and something thumped the cabin wall above the sofa the moment their lips touched. Daniel pulled Denise to the floor and sheathed her with his body.

"What was that?"

"I don't know. Stay down."

Denise wriggled to a fetal position and turned her back to the broken window on the east side of the cabin. Daniel kept low, jerked the electrical plug from the outlet to stop the music, and shifted around to face the window.

"It has to be him. I know it. He's never going to leave us alone." She nuzzled the hand he braced with on the floor next to her face. Tears dripped to the back of the hand. He listened for movement. Silence.

"Move over there," he said, indicating the corner of the living room nearest the front door.

Denise crept to the corner and rolled to a sitting position next to the sofa. She pulled her knees to her chest and tightened her arms around them. She propped her chin in the cleft between her knees.

Daniel scrambled to the fireplace where he blew out two candles on the mantle. Reaching for the one centered on the table, he noticed an arrow in the wall three feet below the ceiling. He snuffed out the flame and wished he could somehow extinguish the burning logs in the fireplace. He dashed to the wall for a closer look at the arrow.

Something white and about two inches wide was taped to the shaft. He worked the broad head loose from the wood and slithered to the floor next to Denise. He peeled off the tape and unrolled the slip of paper.

He squinted to read the message by firelight. The typewritten note said, "A worthy adversary succeeds in some battles. I shall prevail."

"Where's McCluskey's card?"

"I think I put it in the first drawer on the left." Denise indicated the drawer with a tilt of her head.

Daniel slinked to the cabinet, pulled out the drawer she had motioned to, and peeked over the edge. "I don't see it."

He removed the drawer, dumped it on the floor, and scrambled through the contents with his fingers. "Here it is." He flipped open his phone.

"I don't have a signal. Let me see your phone."

"I left it in the car, and you're not about to go out there and leave me in here alone."

DENISE CRAWLED TO DANIEL and latched onto his arm when he pulled his leg under him and pushed to get up. "Daniel, no."

"I have to get help."

"He might still be out there. Please stay in here with me."

She heard him sigh.

"At least let me get my knife."

"Where is it?"

"Top of the closet."

She pulled him closer to her, afraid to let him leave the room long enough to get the knife and return. "Use one in the drawer."

He patted her hand. She accepted the gesture as assurance he would not leave the room and loosened her grip on his arm.

Daniel's dim figure crawled along the counter and reached the drawer where they kept the cutlery. He pulled out the largest knife in the drawer, tested its tensile, replaced it, and chose another. He returned to her side. Air poured through the broken window. The thin gown Denise wore provided no protection from the elements. She pulled the quilt off the arm of the couch for them to use for warmth until something could be put over the window opening. For the next forty-five minutes to an hour, Denise and Daniel huddled in the corner under the quilt.

The knife lay on the floor next to Daniel's leg.

Kisses on the head and Daniel's arm around her did little to dissuade the anxiety crawling through her. Etched in her mind was an image of the note discovered that day in the hospital exam room. It haunted her every night when she closed her eyes. She pictured an enlarged copy tacked to the ceiling every morning.

She focused on the broken window as if Jeremy might ooze through and slime her with putrescence as vile as purge from decaying flesh. She cringed every time the wind moved the curtains hanging over the broken window. In her mind, Jeremy's spirit disturbed the material. It reminded her of his persistence. He was going through with his plan a little at a time until he achieved the permanency of damage intended for her, for them.

Forget everything in the past and get on with her life. That's all she asked for. The ever-present threat unnerved her. She wasn't sure how much more of it she could take. And now she worried about what Jeremy might do to Daniel.

"I'm sorry our plans were ruined this evening."

"Don't be. This wasn't your fault. I knew what I was getting into months ago. I'm in love with you, Denise, and no one is going to take that away from us."

"He won't stop."

"Somehow, we'll stop him. I promise."

"Maybe Angela will catch him and chain him in a dungeon somewhere."

Daniel tilted his head. "Oh, it's Angela now, huh? Not Agent Donavan?"

"We had lunch."

"She didn't say anything about it to me today when she came to the office."

"I asked her not to. I wanted to talk to her about the other morning and asked her if she'd meet me. She agreed. We went to Crystal River and nibbled on fruit, ate a salad, and chatted a while."

"A while?"

"More like three hours, I guess."

"That was some chat."

"Actually, four hours. We talked about all kinds of things. Work. Family. Shopping." Denise paused. "I like her. Angela's nothing like I expected. I figured she'd be brash working with the FBI and having to put up with what any female would in her position, but she's not like that at all ... She likes you."

"She said that?"

"She didn't have to. A woman senses those things in other women. It's in our genes. She recognizes her bounds. I can tell."

"You plan to take on the FBI if she puts the move on me?"

"Ever witnessed a woman's scorn?"

"I trust I'll never have to if it's worse than what Jeremy's done and probably plans to do."

"That's nothing compared to what I'd do."

"I guess I'll have to be a good boy then."

"You are, Daniel. That's one reason I intend to keep you. Unlike Jeremy. You think he's still out there?"

"He probably left the minute the arrow crashed through the glass. Terrorize and leave the rest for us to deal with."

"Another hit-and-run. One day he's going to linger and finish us."

"He has one weakness, Denise."

"What's that?"

"He's human."

Chapter 38

Numbness in Daniel's left hand woke him from a nightmare. He flexed his fingers, checked Denise, and eased his arm from behind her back. The fingers tingled, reminding him of the feeling the dream brought when he lost the use of the arm during battle with Jeremy.

Darkness and the effect of the broken window compounded the realness of their foe. It put the cabin in a black hole. The fire had gone out, leaving orange and yellow embers aglow in the fireplace. Denise breathed slow, shallow breaths. She stirred when he shifted to get up.

"What time do you think it is?"

He turned and rested on his knees facing her. The blackness made it impossible to make out anything more than her silhouette, and even it blended with the end of the sofa.

"I'm not sure. We must've dozed off."

"You did. I've been awake the whole time."

Disappointment pulled at his viscera. How could he let himself fall prey to sleep when Denise needed him alert and aware of their surroundings?

"How long?" he asked, hoping it wasn't the way it felt—hours.

"Fifteen minutes, maybe. You twitched and jerked a couple times and moaned right before you woke up."

"I had a bad dream."

"Tell me."

"I was tumbling down a mountain. I crashed into trees on the way down and broke my leg. Then a guy loomed over me with a gun in each hand and blew off my left arm."

"The guy was Jeremy, wasn't it?"

"I don't know. I couldn't see a face. I apologize for falling asleep. I can't believe I did."

"You're tired, Daniel. You had a busy day."

"What if something happened while I was sleeping?"

She snickered. "I'd have used you as a shield. That would've gotten you awake."

"You'd better stay here tonight. Take the bedroom. The windows are high enough off the ground. I doubt he'd try to get through one on them. I'll push the sofa in front of the bedroom door and stay there 'til morning."

"Put whatever you need to in front of the door, but you're not leaving my side."

Denise climbed into bed only after Daniel checked every door and window and put something over the broken glass to keep out the frigid air. Daniel tucked the comforter under her chin and around her shoulders, situated himself on top of the cover next to her, and shoved the knife under his pillow. He faced her, pulled a plaid blanket to his shoulders, and stared at the double window in the bedroom.

He watched. Tensed and ready, he kept his ears tuned to the surroundings. Every time the clock chimed—on the hour and half-hour—Daniel rose and checked the cabin.

The sun threw the cover off of the horizon at 8:03. Every window and door in the cabin remained secured through the night. After getting a drink of juice, Daniel swept pieces of glass off the floor and dumped them in the garbage.

He returned to the bedroom, straightened the comforter on his side of the bed, and stood there watching Denise sleep. Breaths heaved her chest. Eyes twitched under her lids. Arms lay motionless on top of the comforter.

A kiss on the lips made her open her eyes. "What's wrong with me?"

"Not a thing." Daniel again kissed her.

"I can't move my arms."

"REM atonia. Rapid eye movement. It sometimes causes paralysis in the extremities to keep you from acting out dreams while asleep."

"I remember."

"Dream?"

"Yeah. Hold me." Denise opened her arms. He filled them and slid his arms under her. "I was trying to fight off Jeremy, but I couldn't move. Felt disconnected from my body. I'm afraid, Daniel."

"It's okay. You'll be able to battle him when the time comes."

"What if I can't?"

"Surprise him. Give him something he'll never expect from you. I've got to fix the window. I saw one in the cellar that I think will fit."

By nine thirty, Daniel had repaired the window and secured the arrow and note as evidence. He followed Denise to her parents' house and drove to the Blount County Sheriff's Office. He parked and got the package containing the arrow and the note off the backseat. As soon as the winds hit him, he pulled on his wool coat and turned up the collar. He tucked the package under his arm and stuffed his hands in his coat pockets.

Luke Lanier loped out the front door of the sheriff's office, head down, shoulders drooped. Wind flapped his unzipped jacket. He didn't act like he noticed. Daniel reached the juncture of the sidewalk and parking lot a few steps ahead of Luke. This was the first time he'd seen Luke dressed in casual attire.

"What's wrong, Luke?"

Luke shielded his eyes with the folder clutched in his left hand. "Dalton's been arrested."

"For what?"

"The hunter shootings."

"They don't really think he's the one responsible, do they?"

"The sheriff told me they have evidence implicating him in half a dozen cases. They searched our house at three this morning. Confiscated his bow and every arrow they could find."

Daniel thought about the arrow he'd pulled out of the wall at the cabin, the same one he intended to turn over to McCluskey. Though he would not mention last night's incident to Luke, he wondered if the arrow would match any taken from Dalton. He refused to believe it would. He knew the identity of the person behind this. It wasn't Dalton. He was sure of it.

"Something has to be wrong. Has Dalton said anything?"

"They wouldn't let me see or talk to him."

"I'm here to see McCluskey about another matter. I'll mention it to him and see what he says."

Luke shifted his eyes to the item under Daniel's arm, returned them to Daniel's, and shook his head. "You'd be wasting your time, Daniel. McCluskey's the one who arrested my son. He's strutting around in there like he's just been elected governor. Everybody's congratulating him with high fives and slaps on the back. Makes me want to puke."

"I know someone who might help."

"Who?"

"Somebody with more authority than McCluskey."

Daniel waved goodbye and secured the package in the trunk of his car. Luke was probably right. He saw no reason to waste time with McCluskey if the time could be used elsewhere.

Angela Donavan answered the phone on the third ring. She sounded pleased to hear Daniel's voice and agreed to meet him in the parking lot outside the FBI building. On the way there, he told her about the incident at the cabin and Dalton's arrest.

Bundled in a black overcoat, Angela hurried to the back of Daniel's car where he stood with the trunk open.

"Are you certain it's the same?"

"I got a good enough look at the one you showed me that morning to bring this one to you for comparison." He handed the evidence to her.

She turned her back to the wind and peeled a portion of the wrapping to have a look. "It's equipped with the same type of broad-head. Neither of you saw the shooter?"

"No, but you and I both know who it is."

"And now he's framing the Lanier kid."

"Without a doubt."

"How's Denise doing?"

"She's coping, but I can see this thing's beginning to take a toll on her mentally and physically. She said you two went out to lunch."

"We did."

"And spent the afternoon together," he added.

"Just chitchat."

"Well, whatever you said, thanks. She exudes a confidence I had not noticed in her."

"I like her. Denise is an intelligent woman. I'm sure she has loads of things that will surprise you. She's astute like her father. You keep on loving her, you hear me? She needs a good man in her life. Next week's Thanksgiving. Be thankful."

"I am. Believe me."

Chapter 39

The final two items on the list put a smile on Jeremy's face. He loosened the foil from around the chocolate kiss, careful not to rip it, flattened and smoothed it on all sides.

He dipped a tiny paintbrush in a tasteless solution he had mixed for the occasion and slathered the chocolate, starting at the tip, until he had coated the entire exposed surface. After it dried off, he applied a second coat. Then a third. He wanted enough substance to deliver death, but only after five to seven days of agony. A ten-day test on New York rats taken from the subway confirmed his objective: make Denise Tyler suffer with no hope of a known cure.

Jeremy chose white over the chartreuse to symbolize purity and cut a section of gift wrap to cover the three-inch square box that was to hold the surprise. The neon factor of the other paper might raise suspicion. He felt sure Daniel would choose white.

He measured and cut a length of half-inch ribbon at thirteen inches. The royal blue ribbon accented the white paper. He set the segment aside and cut a longer section to form a bow. Each loop fit perfectly with the others, one of the few decent things he ever learned from his mother.

A phone call to Glenda's Florist switched over to a voice recorder. The establishment opened at nine on weekdays according to the recorded massage. The shop was an hour away. That gave him enough time to finish what he needed to do at the house and be at the florist by the time they opened their doors.

A warm smile greeted Jeremy, along with a "May I help you, sir?" from the blonde behind the counter when he entered Glenda's Florist at a couple minutes past nine.

"Why, yes. You may."

Jeremy cradled the gift box in his left hand. His three steps to the counter would give anyone the impression he was in no hurry.

A woman, who Jeremy assumed was Glenda, dressed in a loose-fitting white jumper and with graying hair pulled back on one side, joined the blonde as Jeremy stepped up to the counter. She hobbled as if something was wrong with her foot, though the limp had no effect on her magnetism. He directed his attention toward her, although he was tempted to check out the blonde associate in view. He knew he must act the part. Otherwise, the florist might suspect something of him.

"I understand Denise Tyler frequents your fine establishment here and should be coming in sometime today or tomorrow to pick up flowers for Thanksgiving."

The older woman glanced at the box on the counter and returned her eyes to him. "You must be the fellow I've been hearing about. They said you're handsome. They were right. No doubt about that."

"Then she will be coming in?"

"I expect it'll be sometime today, probably this afternoon. She's such a sweet girl, don't you think?"

"Sweet as the finest chocolate. That's why I stopped in. I want to leave this package with you to give to her. If it's no bother."

"Oh, no bother at all. I'll be more than happy to see that she gets it." To the assistant, the woman said, "Put this with the Tyler's order," and handed her the box.

"One more thing, please. She can't know where it's from. Let it be our secret."

Glenda raised a crooked finger to her lips and rotated it clockwise. "Lips locked, handsome. Denise is lucky to have a fellow like you."

"Even when her luck runs out, I'll still be around," he said with a wink.

"How adorable. Anything else I can do for you? Flowers maybe? A girl can never get too many flowers. We have quite a selection to choose from if you're interested."

"I have everything I need for now. Thank you."

THE MONDAY BEFORE THANKSGIVING proved to be a busy day around the Tyler home. Thanksgiving was a revered holiday and was not to be taken lightly. The holiday was always more than gathering around the dining room table to feast on turkey and all the trimmings. Clifton Tyler made sure of that without exception.

For Clifton, giving thanks was a priority every day. This was especially true for Thanksgiving Day. A family devotion kicked off the day. Clifton would call everyone into the living room. There, he would sit on the hearth of the fireplace, read a few verses from the Bible, and tell some life-experience story. When he finished, it would be time for every family member and visitor present to tell what they were thankful for.

That was again the plan this year.

Connie and Denise left the house at eight thirty Monday morning to do some shopping and stop by the florist. Their spree ended after trekking through three different stores.

"I'm a little hungry," Connie said at the checkout counter at their last stop before going to Glenda's Florist. "How about I take you to lunch?"

"Sure. Anything in particular?"

"Armon's."

"Sounds good."

"It's better than ever. They have a new chef. From Chicago, I believe. Anyway, he makes this special dish with tilapia that you've got to try."

"I haven't had tilapia in a while."

"Well, you've never had any like his. It's the best I've had anywhere."

"Then let's go."

The hostess at Armon's guided Connie and Denise to a table overlooking an enclosed veranda. Denise noticed the multicolored flowers in hanging baskets and in pots used as centerpieces on every table.

"May we sit out there?" Denise asked the hostess.

"Certainly."

She looked at her mom, who gave her a go-ahead nod.

"It sure has changed," Denise said once they settled in their seats. "It's pretty out here."

Their server took their order without writing it down. Both chose the tilapia. Connie asked for iced tea. Denise chose water, extra lemon. He returned a minute later and recommended a bottle of house wine to go along with their entrée. Connie agreed and accepted a glass of wine instead of tea.

Denise stayed with water.

"Have a glass, Denise. They say it's good for your heart."

"Daniel's love fixed my heart, Mom."

"You love him dearly, don't you?"

"More than anyone. Anything."

When they finished lunch, Connie and Denise crossed the street. Connie went into the Hallmark while Denise checked on their flowers.

At one thirty-five, Connie slid into the passenger seat of her silver Lexus and shut the door. "Where did you get this?" She dropped her purse between her feet and picked up the gift-wrapped box on the console.

"Glenda said some nice-looking guy told her to give it to me. He dropped it off there this morning. Said he knew we'd be stopping by to pick up our order."

"Daniel must've gotten here early."

"I guess so. I wonder why he didn't call."

"See what it is."

Denise untied the ribbon and tore off the paper. She held the ring box in her palm and flipped open the top. She chuckled at the sight of a Hershey's kiss.

"Aw, that's sweet," Connie said.

A note was stuffed in the crevice. Denise unfolded the paper.

"Kiss for you. Bliss so true."

Denise peeled the foil and popped the chocolate in her mouth. It melted and coated her taste buds with its sweetness.

"I love Thanksgiving. I have so much to be thankful for this year."

"We all do, dear."

"I know. It's just so much has happened in my life this year, you know?"

Denise lifted the fingers of her left hand from around the steering wheel and focused her eyes on the diamond Daniel had given her. The stone glistened in the sunlight.

"He really loves me, Mom. He takes real good care of me."

"I believe Daniel will make you a good husband."

"He will. I know he will. If I didn't think so, I wouldn't be with him."

"And you will make him a good wife. I'm proud of you, dear."

"You've been a great role model for me to follow."

"That's one of the nicest things anyone has ever said to me before."

Denise looked over at her mother and smiled. She drove the last three miles in silence. Thoughts too numerous or maybe even too personal to share leapt for her attention. They were nice to think about. One thing Denise was certain of: Daniel. She had found her soulmate.

The Tyler's black Lab, Splendor, jumped around and circled the Lexus as soon as it stopped outside the garage. When Denise opened the door, Splendor stuck his nose inside to greet her.

"Hey, girl. Glad to see me again? We weren't gone that long." She rubbed Splendor's neck.

Splendor licked her hand, spun around, and followed Connie toward the house.

"Denise, will you get those things in the back for me, please?"

Denise acknowledged with a wave and reached to open the rear door. A sharp pain shot through her body. She pulled her arms in close and bent forward. She used the car for support and tried to yell for help. The words refused to come out. She lifted her head and looked toward the house. Everything looked as though she was seeing a 3-D movie without the aid of those special glasses. Heat flashed through her body. Her legs wobbled. Knees buckled. Her body sprawled on the lawn.

Denise stared at the sky through bare tree limbs. Their boney fingers clawed at the air above her. In a moment, the face of her mother emerged on the screen. *What has terrified her? Why is she screaming?* Another face lit up the frame. *Hey, I know you. Your name's Daniel. I didn't know you had a cameo in this movie. You act well. That worried expression looks real. Wait! Don't drop the curtain. The movie can't be over yet. I haven't seen the ending.*

"DENISE!" DANIEL HEARD Connie's scream. The sound of horror rattled her voice. "Cliff. Daniel. Call nine-one-one."

Clifton Tyler rushed into the living room in response to his wife's screams with Daniel close behind. Daniel noticed Connie running across the yard. Something on the ground next to the driveway seized his attention. Denise.

"Go." Clifton said to Daniel. "I'll call."

The sight of her was all the prompting Daniel needed. With a leap from the front porch, he sailed over the azaleas and landed with a thud on the concrete walkway. A slight twinge behind his knee cautioned him to be careful, but the pain wasn't enough to stop his resolve to get to Denise.

Connie knelt on the near side. Tears flowed as she rubbed Denise's arm.

When Daniel dropped to his knees on the other side, the first thing he checked was her eyes. They were open but had a faraway look in them. He moved his hand back and forth across her eyes, blocking sunlight, checking her pupils. The pupils reacted sluggishly. He felt for a pulse and discovered weak carotid and radial pulses.

"Denise." He tried for a verbal response. None.

"Denise. It's Mom. Can you hear me? Please answer. Please, baby."

Denise failed to respond to any verbal or painful stimuli, including sternal rub.

"An ambulance is on its way," said Clifton, clambering up to them and hunching over Connie's shoulder. He handed Connie a blanket and slid a pillow under Denise's head. "How's my girl, Daniel?"

"She's not responding." He repositioned the pillow under her neck. "Her breathing's shallow. She has a faint pulse. How long will it be?"

"They said ten minutes tops."

Better pray for five. Daniel eyed a group of thunderheads creeping upon them. Tension swelled inside his chest. *It's that bad.*

He said to Clifton. "Give me the phone."

Chapter 40

"Which one of you is Dr. Baker?" The pudgy EMT with thinning sandy-colored hair shifted his eyes from face to face.

"I am." Daniel shifted to one side to allow them room to work. He gazed up at the man, wondering how the man knew his name.

The EMT raised a brow. "You must really have some pull with the system, Doctor. Life Flight has been cleared to fly. They're on their way."

Doppler showed a line of severe thunderstorms headed into the area. Lightning, hail, and high winds loomed. The storm was due to hit within the next quarter hour.

"You must have me confused with someone else."

"You didn't call them?"

"No."

"Somebody did."

"I did," Clifton said. "Take her to Blount. I want Crissman working on her."

The EMT slapped pads on Denise's upper and lower chest and hooked the leads to a monitor.

A second EMT stared at Denise as she applied a blood pressure cuff to the left arm. Her eyes widened as she frantically pumped the bulb. "Denise Tyler?" She looked for confirmation in Connie's face.

"Yes. I'm her mother."

"What happened to her?"

"We don't know."

"BP ninety over fifty," she said to her partner.

"Tachy," Pudgy said and shoved a needle for an IV in the right forearm.

"ETA two minutes," said a voice on the talkie.

"Let's load and go," she told the other EMT. "We need to have her there when they land." To Daniel she said, "They're meeting us at the intersection."

"I'm going with you." Connie clasped Denise's hand.

Daniel held the IV bag while the EMTs lifted Denise to the gurney.

"Not enough room," the EMT said. "We need the doctor with us."

"Has she had anything to eat?" The slender flight nurse turned her brown eyes up to meet Daniel's once they were airborne.

"No. I don't know. She went shopping with her mother earlier."

"Find out."

Daniel called Connie's cell phone and asked when Denise ate last. "Less than two hours ago," Daniel relayed to the flight nurse. "Broiled tilapia with mixed veggies ... And what? ... Water with lemon ... Anything else? ... That's all."

The nurse nodded, intubated Denise, rechecked her vitals, and conducted a secondary assessment. The helicopter landed at Blount County Medical Center after a seven-minute flight.

A man identified as Dr. Crissman waited in the grass off the edge of the helipad. Two emergency room nurses accompanied him. The flight nurse rattled off her findings to Dr. Crissman on their way from the helipad to the ED.

Daniel clung to the side of the gurney and listened to the nurse. He knew he had to let them take care of Denise with no interruption from him unless they asked for his input. A couple times in triage, he caught himself on the verge of blurting out things he believed they should do next for Denise. Intensity forced him to the brink. He was a doctor, for goodness' sake. Doctors help people.

Three nurses entered the gray-walled room within the first two minutes, assessing, grabbing supplies, leaving, and coming in again. The last nurse to enter shot hard glances at Daniel. "Sir, you need to leave."

He ignored her.

"Did you not hear me?"

"I'm a doctor."

Hands on hips, she said, "Not here. Now please go."

Daniel sidled to the right a foot and crossed his arms.

"He can stay," Dr. Crissman said to the nurse. "He fights for our side. Do we have a bed yet?"

The nurse jerked the chart from a short-haired brunette in purple scrubs. To her she said, "Go check on a bed. I'll handle this."

Crissman's face reddened. Without looking up from his task, he said. "I told you to do it, Nurse Bickers. I need her in here with me."

Daniel stymied a grin. The name fit her perfectly. Let her bicker all she wished. It made no difference to him.

Nurse Bickers thrust the chart to the woman in purple scrubs. She spun and careened off the door when it bumped against Clifton Tyler.

"Can't anybody watch where they're going?" echoed off plastered walls outside triage.

Dr. Crissman saw Clifton standing outside the door and held up a finger.

"Breaths shallow at eighteen. BP ninety over forty," the nurse read aloud to Crissman.

Daniel's spirit dropped another level. He watched Denise. No response to stimuli. Nurses drew blood and tapped the catheter for urine. IVs dripped. He followed Crissman through the door to the hallway to hear what he was going to tell Clifton.

Clifton went straight to the point. "What's the word, John?"

"We won't know for a while. I've ordered a whole battery of tests. We'll have to wait and see."

To Clifton, Daniel said, "Mrs. Tyler?"

"In the family room. She's in a bad way, Daniel."

The lab needed time to process samples and Daniel knew it. Desire to stay with Denise urged him to return to the exam room. Knowledge as to cause prompted him in another direction. Answers were out there somewhere. He had to find them to save her.

"I'll be in the waiting room."

Chapter 41

The door leading into the family room closed without a sound. Connie Tyler sat on the forward edge of the cushion, head lowered, shoulders drooped, mouthing words. Daniel waited for her to acknowledge his presence. He watched, agonized over the same dilemma expressed in different ways. This was an unfair exchange from earlier in the day. Connie rubbed her cheeks, brushed a tissue under her nose, and smoothed her hair before lifting her head.

"Any news?"

"Still early. You can help her."

"How?" She rotated on the sofa, crossed her ankles, and patted the cushion for him to sit with her.

He lowered himself to the sofa, angled to face her. "I need to know where she went this morning, everything she came in contact with, what she had to eat. Even if it's something you might think insignificant."

Connie leaned back and stared blankly toward the door. "I don't know. We were together all morning." She said it as if pleading for something to jog her memory.

"Try."

"We got what we needed for Thursday and the weekend. Normal stuff, you know. We ate lunch. I told you about that. We then went to Glenda's Florist and home."

"What time?"

"Which one?"

"The florist."

"Twenty, twenty-five minutes before we got home. Glenda's was our last stop. You think something there ..."

"I don't know. Maybe."

"Nothing's ever happened before. She's not allergic to anything."

"Something is different this time. I'm sure of it. I can feel it."

"No. We ordered the same thing we always do for Thanksgiving. Oh, wait." She stressed the point with a raised finger. "Denise went to the florist while I went into the card shop next door."

"Did she come out with anything other than what you ordered?"

"Only the box you left there for her."

"Box?"

"It was a small gift box. I wasn't supposed to say anything until she talked to you first."

"Did she open it?"

Connie nodded. "A Hershey's kiss was inside."

"Where is it?"

"She ate it."

"Stay here."

Daniel bolted from the room and sprinted to triage where Dr. Crissman hovered over Denise. He was checking her pupils.

"Check for bacteria and poisons!"

Crissman whipped his head around. "What symptoms?"

"Look at her."

"I don't have any evidence. Don't know that any exists either."

"How do you know if you haven't looked?"

Crissman glowered. "We're wasting valuable time here, young man."

"Whose? Yours?" He pointed to Denise. "Or hers?"

Crissman turned to Clifton, who stood in the corner. A grim expression said all that needed to be said: *Try anything.* The frown on Clifton's face remained unchanged.

The next afternoon, Doctor Crissman met with Clifton, Connie, and Daniel in Denise's room. His expression matched the drabness of the room. The look failed to convey the hope they expected. Wanted.

"Although we've conducted exhaustive tests to learn what is going on with Denise, the best thing we can do right now is wait." He opened the chart and propped it on his left arm.

"We've been waiting, John," Clifton said.

Daniel leaned forward and clutched the footrail of the bed. "Any poisons?"

Dr. Crissman frowned and sucked in his lips as if attempting to squelch what might be conceived as a confession. "Burundanga." The word spewed from Crissman's mouth. "I'm sure you've heard of it before."

"Unfortunately. I studied three cases of it last year at the CDC. Two of the three laced with morphine induced twilight sleep. They were victims of a robbery. The other was a victim of sexual assault."

"I hate to admit when I'm wrong, Dr. Baker, but you seemed to have picked up on this long before I would have. I apologize for my smugness."

"That's not all, is it?"

"No." He looked from Daniel to Clifton, to Connie, and back to Daniel before he continued. "Her symptoms mimic a mycotic infection. Stephen Ballard, a specialist in microbiology, thinks it may be a rare form of invasive aspergillosis. Clinical manifestations point to a form of mucormycosis. Truthfully, we don't know what it is or how long she's been a host."

"I don't see how that's possible," Clifton said.

"Believe me, this thing has us all stumped. The fact that she has Sarcoidosis doesn't help matters any either." Turning to Daniel, he said, "Did you know about the Sarcoidosis?"

"She told me."

"We're having to deal with that, too. The disease is really putting a strain on her pulmonary system. The antibiotics and round of steroids we've tried have had no effect, and her situation is worsening by the hour. A risk of life-threatening hemorrhage is definitely critical at present." He turned to Clifton and Connie. "We're doing all we can to combat this. We have one more regimen to administer; however," He turned to Daniel. "we're not sure even that will work."

"Something has to work," Daniel said.

"I agree something should. It would if ... The problem lies with her body trying to decide which disease to fight against while a host of intruders battle it out to see which one will kill her."

Chapter 42

Daniel spent Thanksgiving morning sitting in a chair next to the hospital bed. Unresponsiveness maintained its clamp on Denise since Monday afternoon.

"Daniel." He turned to see who called his name.

Connie Tyler stepped in the room. He rose from his chair. Connie hugged him and planted a soft kiss on his cheek. "How is she doing this morning?" She stepped bedside.

"No change. I'm waiting for the doctor to come by. The nurse said they were still waiting on the results from the last battery of tests they ran late yesterday. So far, they still don't know anything. I've racked my brain and have come up with zilch. I have a call in to the CDC, but with the holiday, who knows when we might know something. Hopefully, we'll be able to find out something soon." He paused. "We're all trying."

Connie grasped Denise's hand. "Her hand's cold."

"I've been trying to keep her covered to conserve her body heat. Her circulation is being diverted from her extremities to her vital organs. It's the body's natural defense system at work."

Connie opened her purse, removed a piece of paper, and handed it to Daniel.

"What is this?"

"Something Denise wrote for you. She intended to give it to you today. I've got to run out for a bit. I wanted to drop this by. I'll be back in a little while. Call me if there's any change."

Daniel waited for her to leave the room and the door to close. He shifted the chair closer to the bed. He opened the paper. On it, Denise had written a poem.

Thoughts of You
There are so many thoughts dancing around in my mind,
Thoughts of one special man who is one of a kind.
Thoughts of the future and of present day
So much to be shared and so much to say.
I think of a prayer I have prayed so long
To find such a love so true and strong.
My heart overflows of this dream come true,
Giving thanks for this blessing I will certainly do.
The man I have prayed for has come passing my way
And I will love him forever as much as today.
Our future looks bright with a commitment steadfast
A true love to be shared that will forever last.

Daniel kept his eyes fixed on the paper. The bottom was spotted with tears. The words sank deep inside him. They burned across the surface of his heart. *Thoughts of future and of present day. So much to be shared and so much to say.*

Daniel envisioned Denise putting the poem on paper. He pictured her face, the way her lips curled upward in a mesmerizing way when she wrote, eyes sparkling with love emitted from her heart assembled into words intended solely for him.

Disease and infection threatened everything beyond the present moment. An assault on her existence tomahawked the rapt enjoyment of what once thrived between them. Life remained in her, but at what cost? What about the future now? How could he be thankful for this?

"We still have things we haven't shared or said." Daniel choked out the words and gazed at Denise in hopes she might perceive his garbled speech. "I need you, Denise. Come back to me. If you can hear me, I'm going to read your poem to you."

Daniel placed his hand on hers. Tears streamed down his cheeks. He read it aloud from beginning to end, leaned over, and kissed her lips.

"Thank you, baby. Your words are precious. I wish I could hear you read them to me."

A nurse tapped on the door and entered the room without waiting for a response. "Excuse me. It's time to change her IV. Dr. Crissman called and said to tell you he's stopping by the lab before he comes in. He'll be here as soon as he can."

Daniel dabbed his eyes with the sleeve of his shirt and backed away from the bed. "Good. Thanks. I'm going to step out to my car for a minute while you're in here. I'll be right back."

"Go right ahead. This will take me a few minutes."

Daniel rode the elevator to the main floor. The stainless walls heckled him in an eerie sort of way. The doors opened to freedom from their mocking reflection, dropped him off into an aesthetic nothingness between there and the hospital's front entrance.

Daniel removed a legal pad from his attaché case from his car. He strolled back inside, along the lonely hallway, and back up the same invariable elevator to the room where Denise still clutched to life with heartbeats of hope.

A fresh bag of Solu-Medrol dripped into the IV. There was no news from his contact at the CDC.

Once he and Denise were alone, Daniel fixed his eyes on the blank page of the pad and let his heart guide the pen. Line after line, the pen scrolled until two pages and part of another displayed his heart's reflection.

Denise,

I've had the fortunate opportunity to have met many prominent and important people. Without a doubt, having met you has left an indelible impression on me as a person and on my heart.

You belong in the inner circle, far above and beyond many other important figures in my life. To me, you have become the special someone. To me, you are incredible.

I love the way you smile and the twinkle in your sparkling eyes.

I love your touch, to feel the softness of your skin. The determination of spirit I sense in the grip of your hand. You hold on tight, not wanting to let go of mine. It is security I feel when we hold each other close.

The way you move causes me to follow wherever you go.

You made me to take a closer look at myself, who I am, and the person I want to be. To become this person, I have been led down a path I never knew existed. I found this path because of you. You took the time to believe in me; to trust me with your life and other issues, we faced together in the most recent past.

Now, the path ahead is leading us into unknown territory. We do not know where this path will lead or what obstacles might be in our way as we travel. Nevertheless, what we know is by faith we will make it through every day with Father's guidance. It will be these steps of faith that will get us through. We trust each other, but most of all we trust Him.

I thank God for the harmony of our special relationship and the love shown as we travel on our way to a future brightened with anticipation, hope, and trust. Because you are now a large part of my life, and I yours, an indescribable sense of inspiration and fortitude has set up its abode within us.

As we travel on our way, it will be side-by-side and hand-in-hand. Every hill will be climbed together and each valley will be entered at the same time. When the rains come, it will rain on us both. When the sun shines, we will share its warmth. When the winds blow, we have each other to hold on to. As long as we have each other, we will never be alone. We are never farther apart than our thoughts one for the other.

The world was made to be inhabited, and this world is a better place with you in it.

Though try as I might, words afford limited conveyance to true feelings deep inside my heart, leaving a plethora of emotional, physical, and spiritual feelings yet to be opened up to you. In time, you will discover more and more of them. I want you to know that you are cherished as an irreplaceable treasure. You are one of a kind. You are needed, and even more so, you are loved and wanted. Even the stars of heaven shine your way.

Thank you for loving me the way you do; for needing me in ways I might only imagine; and being my best friend.

I love you,

Daniel

Daniel pulled the pages from the pad, neatly folded them, stepped over to the clothes locker, and placed them with her belongings.

Before again taking a seat, he leaned over the bed's edge. He kissed Denise on the cheek and whispered in her ear, "When you wake, I want you to read this first thing. It's something I had to tell you. Something I want you to know."

He lifted her hand and placed her palm over his heart and put his right hand over her heart. He could feel her faint heartbeat through the gown.

"Your presence in my life has made an immeasurable difference in me. To really express to you in words how much you mean to me and what a difference you have truly made in my life would be difficult to impossible. So, when you get out of here, I'll compose my remaining years to giving you the paramount love and attention you deserve. Rest easy, my queen. I'm here for the duration. No matter what happens."

Daniel picked up the chair and moved it to the corner. He walked around to the other side of the bed where he glanced at the monitors and then at her. Denise had been comatose since the moment she collapsed without even a hint of coming around despite the staff's efforts to provoke a response.

"Reach out to me, baby. Give me some sign of what's going on so we can help you. You can do it. You have what it takes to get through this, and we will. I'm right here with you and—"

A nurse rapped on the door and entered the room. "It's time to take her vitals and draw blood."

"Any word from the doctor?"

"He called a few minutes ago and said he would be delayed in coming by because of an emergency with another patient. He said he would be here as soon as he could break away. He knows the urgency of Denise's condition and has ordered additional tests. That's why we need this blood. He wants it all done before he gets here."

Daniel turned his attention back to Denise. Without saying a word, he glanced at the monitors again. No change. She was still weak, but at least she was hanging in there.

"I'm here, baby. I'll be right here."

He slumped to the chair, lowered his head, and stared at nothingness.

Chapter 43

The afternoon hours passed without a word spoken by anyone, even when the nurses came in for hourly checks. They went about their duties checking vitals, administering medications, and updating the chart without a word.

Daniel repositioned the chair where he could monitor Denise and see out the window. The view out there on this day of thanks lacked appeal. Hardwood trees raised creature-like limbs in attack mode around the building and parking lot. Their ominous stance signified permanency. They would hold their ground unless threatened by a tornado, lightning, or some redneck logger wielding a chainsaw. The hardwoods thrived similar to two things his mother taught him—have deep roots of unwavering standards and bear fruit worthy of the finest markets.

He still worked on both.

At four thirty that afternoon, a woman he'd never seen in scrubs rushed in the room. Daniel edged forward on the chair.

"We got it," she said.

Angela pulled her left hand from a front pocket. In it lay a syringe containing the first official dose of Cyclodactin. Months of research, trials, and failures condensed into ten milliliters of potency—enough to save the life of the one person worth more than anything in the world to him.

A thrill zapped him. He leaped to his feet and started to ask her how she had gotten possession of it. Right then, it didn't matter.

"Would you like to do the honors?"

"You bet I do."

Daniel clutched the syringe and fed the needle into the IV line.

Angela watched from the other side of the bed as Daniel injected the Cyclodactin in short increments. When he finished, she said, "How long do you suppose it will take for it to work?"

"It depends on her system. I expect to see some results within three to four hours. Beyond four hours, we'll know it's not going to work."

Daniel dropped the used syringe in the sharps container and returned bedside.

"She looks at peace."

"It's a façade of serenity because of being comatose. If bacteria and pain were visible to us, we'd see micro-throngs of carnivorous terrorists setting off charges, destroying her body from the inside out. Their mission is wiping out specific targets to keep the body from functioning as designed. For the past three days, her body has been engaged in a losing effort and begs for reinforcements."

"How much pain does she feel?"

"No one really knows. With the state she's in now, she's unable to express anything other than what is displayed on the monitors. Her spirit may be drawn into another realm where she is encountering pleasantness, or possibly her worst nightmare."

Across the bed, Angela dug her hands under her arms and appeared to shrink into herself.

"Cold?"

"No."

He noticed Angela's eyes water and recalled the photo she kept on her desk. She blinked away the tears, prevented them from spilling onto her cheeks.

"Angela?"

"My mom was not much older than Denise when that jerk crashed into us and took her from me. Is she going to die?"

"I ... I don't know."

"If she dies, Jeremy wins."

Chapter 44

A few minutes after 6:00 p.m., Dr. Crissman arrived with Denise's chart in hand. The doctor stood next to the bed, pushed a couple of buttons on the monitor, and scribbled yet more notes on Denise's chart.

"So far every test we've run has come back either negative or inconclusive," Crissman said. The doctor tightened his lips. Daniel could see he was trying hard not to look discouraged. "The nurse said you got the package from CDC. I really hope this Cyclodactin will work for her."

"Nothing yet," Daniel said.

"Give it time. We'll see what happens."

Time was not a luxury Denise had available in her present condition. Every minute that passed stretched Daniel's patience. He felt Crissman's hand on his shoulder. Instead of looking at the doctor, he kept his eyes on Denise.

"Call me if anything changes."

Crissman hung his head and walked away. The frown on the doctor's face said everything. Every avenue they had tried led to dead-ends. Daniel shared Crissman's disappointment.

Fully understanding Crissman's position, Daniel sat quietly for the next fifteen minutes while tightening his grip on the one thing he still had: hope.

At six thirty, Daniel looked at his watch. It had been two hours since he had given her the Cyclodactin. He leaned over and gave

Denise a kiss. "Hold on, baby. Please don't let go. I'm going to call Mom. How late will you be able to stay?" he asked Angela.

"Midnight."

Somehow, he got the impression Angela wasn't referring to the hands on a clock.

The empty hallway was quiet except for the squeak of his shoes on the polished tile floor. The lobby doors slid open. Winter's grip encased him. Daniel's coat definitely lacked overdraft protection. Humidity razor-sharpened the iciness brought in by the jet stream. The cold found every crevice in and around Daniel's coat and sliced its way through. What a day not to have zipped in the liner.

Gust of fifteen to twenty-five miles per hour flounced the county. The temperature dropped to twenty-six degrees. Clouds hid the sun. No wonder his muscles ached. They tightened beneath non-insulated layers of skin to keep his bones warm. He hunched forward and turned to the wall to break the arctic swirl chasing him around the corner of the building.

Ordinarily, he would have ducked into some out-of-the-way spot to place a call. Forget the no-cell-phones-allowed rule in hospitals, especially in this weather. The problem Daniel faced stemmed from lack of reception inside the building. It forced him outside.

Fracture lines forced their way across the edge of hope. The only thing left to do now was pray. That's what he would ask of his mother. Then he guessed he should phone her friend Ann and ask her also to pray for a miracle.

He finished the conversation with his mother and placed a call Ann Brotherton to let her know about Denise. Every minute or so, he switched the phone from one hand to the other and stuffed his free hand deep inside a pocket.

"Daniel," Ann said in her own affirming way, "I knew you would call. Your mother told me about Denise, and we're planning to have a special time of prayer for her at five o'clock. Let's see, I guess that'd be seven your time. Our original plans were to meet at eight tonight for our regular Thanksgiving prayer, but I felt like we shouldn't wait until then. I've called some others and we've moved it up to five. I was just on my way out the door to meet them.

"There's no need to worry now, Daniel. God made our bodies, and you can be sure He knows how to fix them when something goes wrong. I imagine He enjoys watching doctors scratch their heads. Trust Him, Daniel. He's called the Great Physician for a reason."

Ann's optimism raised his spirits. She seemed to always know what to say at any opportunity. He thanked her and hurried through the glass doors. He stomped his feet on the mat inside the doors to remove the snow clinging to them and adjusted the collar of his coat. The trip back to Denise led him by the hospital's chapel. The chapel door opened as Daniel was about to pass by and stood ajar, as though inviting him inside.

Trust Him, Daniel.

Daniel stuck his head in long enough to see if anyone was in there. Warm air from inside caressed his cheek. It calmed the shivers. He stepped inside and admired the décor. The room was small but plush. One row of five pews, each probably six feet long, lined the right side. A cherry table stood against the wall on the left. An arrangement of lilies filled a crystal vase, flanked by inspirational-type literature.

A stained-glass window centered the wall opposite the door. The podium beneath it held an open Bible. Light from the outside fused through an image of a dove in the stained glass and poured onto it. Curious, Daniel edged closer and scanned the pages. A highlighted passage in Luke chapter seven held his attention. *To him who asks it will be given.*

He sat down on the second pew, bowed his head, and mused on the verse.

After about an hour of teetering between fear and faith, the door to the chapel opened. Someone called his name. "Sorry to bother you like this," the nurse said. "I need you to come with me."

Chapter 45

Frost-bitten grass crunched under Daniel's feet as he plodded across a well-manicured cemetery three days later. The smell of freshly turned dirt greeted him. Head down, he stared at the ground and stood motionless at the foot of the new grave. Wind from the nearby snow-covered Rocky Mountains whistled across the hillside.

Images of Denise's frail, sickly frame lying in that hospital bed were now stored with other memories in Daniel's mind. What if he and Denise had met with a different outcome? To date, he had not discussed with her the reason Clifton Tyler was picked to handle the Cyclodactin account and had yet to let her in on Simon One's interest in her.

A pat on his left his arm tapped his heart. A freshet of words gushed out.

"I'll never forget the look on your face and how I felt so helpless the day you fell ill. You had a cold, blank stare in your eyes and were unresponsive to any stimuli. I stand here now and all I can think about is you, our time together, things we've shared, and plans we made.

"After diligent efforts, the hospital staff continued searching for answers. Expressions on their faces gave us the impression that answers might never be found. I can still see Dr. Crissman's face and will never forget his words when he told me they had done all they could do for you. He turned away with his head low, walked out of your hospital room, and closed himself in his office.

"Your beautiful face turned ashen. We tried everything possible to restore your health, but nothing seemed to work. I felt like I was trapped in a maze." Daniel paused, sniffed. "I stood next to your bed and held your hand as I watched shallow breaths enter and leave your body. Your hand felt so cold. Death's fingers inched closer and closer. They brushed by me to get to you.

"I sat down on the edge of the bed and talked to you about the time we shared, hoping you could hear me and maybe somehow respond. I had hoped the sound of my voice would give you strength to fight a little harder. I know it was selfish of me, knowing your pain, but I didn't want to let you go. This was one thing I planned to fight for at all costs. I knew then what I had to do. I took a chance and gave you the Cyclodactin. I phoned one of Mom's friends. Mother had told me to call Ann if I ever needed anything. Even though it was Thanksgiving, that day I felt like I dangled by a rope and an angel of death loosening what the other end was tied to.

"I ended up in the chapel and began to think about what Ann told me. After I thought about her absolute concern, I looked down at my watch. It was five o'clock in Colorado. Ann's optimism about your situation reached across the expanse, and if anyone could find an answer, it would be her. With that in mind, I whispered to myself, 'Hold on, Denise, help is on the way.'"

A gloved hand touched Daniel's cheek and brushed away a trickle of tears.

He took the hand and placed it inside his coat against his chest. He knew she could feel every throb of his heart. A sense of satisfying solace engulfed his soul. Hot tears of joy dropped on Denise's forearm.

"She's alive today thanks to you, Ann," he whispered in a broken voice, looking up at the new headstone of his mother's friend. "Your prayers surpassed the far reaches of the heavens and were heard by the Great Physician. I imagine He is smiling at you for your faithfulness. I wish I could have thanked you in person for all you've done. Who would have known you would have been taken from us before I got the chance?

"I wanted you to know that while you were praying, I clung to that grain of faith you shared with me. When Denise's nurse came to the door and called my name, I knew that had to be it. I knew Denise was gone. I turned around and saw a huge smile on the nurse's face. I followed her down the hall and recognized that sweet voice before I ever reached the door. Pure joy poured over me when I saw Denise sitting on the side of the bed, wearing her trademark smile. Thank you, Ann. Your memory will live forever in our hearts."

Denise and Daniel turned and faced the evening majesty. The snow-capped Rockies loomed high against a blue Colorado sky.

"How could anyone possibly look at scenery like this and say there is no God?"

"If they would only take the time to look, really look, they would never deny His existence," Denise said. She looped her arm around his waist.

"I'm happy to have another chance to share life's blessing and being here with you to enjoy this wonderful place, a world He created for us."

"I really thought I was going to lose you."

"You'll never lose me, Daniel." She whirled to face him. "I'm here to stay. By the way, don't we have some unfinished business to tend to?"

Chapter 46

Denise scrambled around her parents' home all morning trying to make sure she had everything ready for the wedding. New-fallen snow dusted the Tennessee hills. A weather front brought with it temperatures that dipped fifteen degrees below the norm.

Three weeks had passed since her miraculous recovery. This morning when she awakened, she felt stronger in body than she had before the poisoning. She heard the phone ring and rushed to pick it up, expecting it to be Glenda calling about delivery of the floral arrangement for the rehearsal dinner.

"Ms. Tyler, Ms. Denise Tyler?" the caller asked.

"Yes, this is Denise Tyler."

"My name is Anthony Hoskins. I'm calling you from Denver, Colorado. I'm a friend of the Baker family and I've tried to reach Daniel's mother, but no one answered the phone."

"How did you get my number? What's this about? Has something happened to Daniel?"

"I'm sorry, Ms. Tyler. If you could please try to get in touch with Mrs. Baker and have her call me, I'd appreciate it."

"You didn't answer my question. Who are you? What's happened? Is Daniel okay?"

"I can't discuss this with you, Ms. Tyler. If you would please have Daniel's mother call me. You may want to turn on CNN or Fox News." The man disconnected the call after reciting a phone number to her.

Denise quickly called Daniel's phone. She glanced at the clock on the mantle. It was two forty-five. That meant Daniel was already on the flight to St. Louis. Eager to find out what was happening, Denise flipped on the TV.

The news walloped like a sledgehammer. Unexpected. This was the last thing Denise believed would ever happen at this point in her young life. Denise felt her heart pause. She knew what was coming next. She tried to swallow, but the neck muscles shut down that avenue. They squeezed her airway. The most air she could take in wouldn't half fill the upper lobes of her lungs.

"... The flight developed some type of mechanical problem shortly after takeoff and was attempting to return when it went down. The incident is currently under investigation by the National Transportation Safety Board and the Federal Aviation Administration. There are no known survivors."

Denise bit her lower lip and listened for a few moments before she finally dropped to the sofa in her parents' den. Her cellular phone bounced off the cushion and landed on the coffee table. The caller didn't have to say anything more. The plane crash near Last Chance, Colorado, shortly after its departure was the lead story on the news. Daniel was scheduled for that 12:10 flight from Denver to St. Louis.

The anchor's words played over and over in her mind. No known survivors. This could not be happening. Not today. Not on the eve of our wedding. She refused to believe it. She snatched the phone off the table and turned off the TV. A tone followed by a recording on the other end of her call sent her straight to Daniel's voicemail.

She tried the number Mr. Hoskins gave her. "Red Crags Bed and Breakfast, this is Tiffany. How may I help you?"

"I'm sorry," Denise said. "I must have dialed the wrong number."

She checked the number she had written against the number she had called. They were the same. She thought maybe she misheard

Hoskins when he gave it to her. She knew she should have repeated it to make certain she had it right. Why didn't she? Now she had no way of contacting him.

The next call put her in contact with Daniel's mother. "Have you talked to Daniel?"

"I've been out since early this morning. I just walked back in when the phone rang. Hold on a minute, will you, dear? Let me call the front desk to see if he's left a message. Hold on. I'll be right back." Denise heard what sounded like a one-sided conversation and the sound of the receiver placed on the hook. "They said no one's left any messages for us," Mrs. Baker said when she was again on the line. "Have you tried his cell phone?"

"All I get is voicemail."

"I'm sure he's all right. He's probably busy trying to get back here for tonight."

"I guess so." Denise tried to sound upbeat.

"Keep trying his phone. He'll answer for you when he won't answer for anybody else."

Not knowing what was going on with Daniel tore her up inside. Denise languished on the sofa, arms squeezing a pillow as she pressed it to her face. The house stood in silence. No TV. No sound of floors creaking under footfalls. No whimper out of the blonde Lab her mother had taken to the vet. Alone, yet surrounded by a poignancy like a barrier of clamor around her.

She tried again to reach Daniel. No luck. Denise carried the phone into the bathroom with her. She closed the door and turned on the shower. She turned up the ringer so she could hear it if Daniel called, stripped out of her clothes, and stepped under the spray.

Water soaked her hair and mixed with tears as Denise adjusted the tap to a cooler temperature. She braced her hands on the shower wall and watched the water swirl around the drain and plunge into darkness. Anxiety and fear snaked her until dizziness and nausea sucked her toward despair.

"IMPRESSIVE."

Jeremy Guerdon draped a black overcoat across his forearm and handed Hoskins ten one-hundred-dollar bills. The office near the airport in Colorado Springs was barely large enough for the two of them, a couple of chairs, and a two-drawer desk.

"You think she believed me?" Hoskins swigged the rest of the scotch in his glass. His hands shook as he poured another.

"What does it matter now? You've been paid to do a job. You performed well. You even convinced me. Why concern yourself with her? This unfortunate incident worked to my advantage and your good fortune."

Hoskins stuck the money in his shirt pocket and gulped more scotch. "It makes me feel all yucky inside. Using the deaths of those innocent passengers. It's not right."

Jeremy pulled on a pair of leather gloves. "Neither is this." He removed a switchblade from the coat pocket and slit Hoskins's throat. The gaping wound gurgled.

Hoskins mouthed words. His face was stricken with horror as life leaked from his body.

Jeremy removed the money from the dying man's pocket. He pulled the top bill and pasted it over the gash in Hoskins's throat. "You love Franklin a little too much."

He pulled off the gloves inside-out and stuffed them in the glass. The finale comes.

Chapter 47

A car crash on US 24 at Interstate 25 in Colorado Springs blocked all lanes. Police restricted access to the interstate with their cruisers. Fire engines and an ambulance filled lanes on either side of an overturned SUV.

Daniel slowed to a stop behind a line of vehicles and checked for a way around the chaos. Half a dozen cars cruised up behind him. There was nowhere to go. Five miles from the Colorado Springs airport. Ten minutes at most to get there. The clock on the dash displayed 12:55 p.m.

Drivers around him got out of their vehicles. Some stretched their necks. Others trekked to have a closer look at the crashed Explorer.

He called Denise's cell phone. "Hey, gorgeous," he said to her voicemail. The phone beeped. He figured the beep signaled a low battery and didn't look. "I'm on my way to the airport here in Colorado Springs. I couldn't make it to Denver, so I had to charter a plane. I'll see you when I get there. Love you."

A second ambulance arrived. The clock displayed 12:58.

He sat in the rented Malibu and checked the clock every couple minutes. He turned on the radio. Nothing appealed to him. He switched it off. He squirmed on the seat. Checked the time on his watch and compared it to the time on the dash. The clock displayed a minute slower than his watch.

When the police finally opened up a traffic lane, the clock on the dash showed 1:20. His charter was scheduled to depart in ten minutes. Denise. Their rehearsal was set for seven. Now what?

He arrived at Municipal Airport and dropped off the car in front of the FBO. Employees dashed in and out of the building. News of the downed aircraft played on the flat-screen in the waiting area.

"Where?" Daniel asked, motioning to the TV.

"Outside of Denver," the blonde behind the counter said.

"What flight number?"

"We're still waiting on confirmation. Now, about your flight. One of the pilots set to fly you got news his sister was on that plane. We're waiting on another pilot to get here."

He felt like saying, *What else can go wrong today?* "How long?"

"Fifteen minutes. Oh, one other thing. There's a gentleman who needs of a lift to Knoxville. We don't have another plane available. He said he would cover the cost if he could fly along with you."

"Where is this person?"

"He was sitting over in the corner."

Daniel turned and scanned the lobby.

The blonde said, "I don't see ... There he is."

"Mr. Baker, I presume?"

"Yes."

"I'm Ethan Pierce. I trust my presence on the flight will not inconvenience you."

"I cannot imagine anything dissuading me today."

"Sounds like you're an indomitable man."

"Today I am."

"Confidence is a good trait. I value a man of self-assurance in my company, especially when things crumble around him." Jeremy Guerdon swiped a chocolate chip cookie from the plate on the counter. He waved it at Daniel. "That goes for ally or foe."

"No matter what, Mr. Pierce, I'm ready for either."

Daniel excused himself and again tried Denise. The network buzzed a busy tone. He tried to get through to the Tyler residence. Temporarily unavailable. Phone lines jammed with calls.

They boarded the jet, taxied onto the runway, and were airborne in a matter of minutes.

Mr. Pierce kept quiet during most of the flight. He studied papers from a black leather attaché, or stared out the window. Daniel got the impression this Ethan Pierce was not one for empty conversation. The man seemed focused on other things.

Daniel kept a watchful eye. Something about the stranger looked familiar. He knew he had seen the man somewhere. He leaned his head on top of the seat back and half closed his eyes. Before realizing it, he drifted off into dreamland.

Everyone dressed their best. Hair in place. Shoes shined. Ties centered under collars. Tuxedos buttoned. Boutonnieres in place on lapels. Pews filled with family, friends, and those extending congratulations by their mere presence. The rear doors opened and in stepped the bride, a veil covering her face. Denise clutched a pomander with both hands. She took deliberate steps toward him. Finally, close enough to see her eyes. A commotion in the back of the church wrenched his eyes from hers. Denise stumbled. His eyes returned to her. Red grew out of the white on the front of her gown. She screamed, "Daniel."

Daniel's body jerked, waking him. The pilot was calling his name. "Twenty minutes, gentlemen."

When Mr. Pierce responded, Daniel remembered. The guy from the hotel in Baltimore. The same rude fellow that bumped into him in the stairway now shared a flight with him. The man with the gun. Daniel wondered if he had one on the plane with him.

Three hours and forty-six minutes after their flight left Colorado, the plane touched down in Knoxville, Tennessee.

Mr. Pierce bid Daniel farewell. He hopped in his rented Lincoln. The man smiled and waved as he and headed to the exit gate.

Daniel took two steps toward the FBO. The face. It was him. The identity of the man behind the disguise with whom he had just shared the flight was not Ethan Pierce.

It was Jeremy Guerdon.

Daniel dropped his bag on the apron and sprinted after the Lincoln. The Lincoln drove through the open access gate. The electronic gate began to slide closed. Daniel leapt through the gap two seconds before it seated in its closed and locked position. The Lincoln raced forward, turned ninety degrees, and merged into traffic on the access road.

Daniel called Agent Donavan. "Jeremy just left TAC Air in a black Lincoln headed east." He rattled off the license plate number.

"I'm on it."

Luke Lanier met Daniel inside the FBO. "Luke. What are you doing here?"

"To take my second favorite passenger wherever he wishes to go. Why did you come in through the front entrance? Where is your carry-on?"

Daniel pointed to the apron. "How did you know I was coming in here?"

"My favorite passenger told me I'd better be here to meet you."

"I imagine that is—"

"Me!" Denise ran into Daniel's arms and pressed her trembling body tight against him. She smothered him with kisses. "They said you were dead, but I refused to believe it."

"Who told you I was dead?"

"The man said his name was Hoskins. He called me trying to locate your mother. He wouldn't tell me why, just that I should watch the news. That's when I heard about the crash."

"Why don't you two talk about it on the way?" Luke said. "It's already five fifty. I'll get your bag. You don't want to be late."

In the limo, Denise clung to Daniel and relayed everything that happened.

"I called the airlines. It took me a while, but I finally found somebody who would give me some information. The lady told me you never checked in. She confirmed you weren't on the flight that went down and said maybe you'd changed flights or chartered a jet or something. She couldn't tell me any more than that but I didn't care. I never felt so relieved in all my life." Denise laid her head on Daniel's shoulder. "I was so scared."

He kissed her forehead and gazed out the window.

Wondering.

Chapter 48

Close friends and family greeted Denise and Daniel with handshakes, hugs, and kisses before lining the table set up for the couple's rehearsal dinner at Burke's Steak & Seafood. Aromas from the kitchen filled the restaurant. Denise had gone without food all day. One whiff of the new chef's cuisine made her stomach growl for anything edible.

Soon she forgot about everything that had happened earlier and focused on why they were there. In less than twenty-four hours, she would become Mrs. Daniel Baker. Excited, Denise sat in the chair Daniel pulled out for her and slid close to the table. Daniel occupied the chair to her left.

Once everyone was seated, the staff rushed to fill water glasses and take drink orders. By the time the beverages arrived, they were ready to order entrées.

Laughter followed story after story. Attendees reminisced things from their past. Denise felt like the guests were leaving nothing they remembered unreported. Neither she nor Daniel escaped onslaughts of jest, many girded with embellishment. Moments they hoped were long ago forgotten surfaced to the delight of everyone else at the table and often by diners at tables within earshot.

"Thank goodness the food's here," Denise whispered to Daniel as the entrées were placed in front of them. "This should squelch them for a little while."

"It could get worse. They'll figure out a way to do both at the same time."

They did. Once into the meal, words found their way out amidst mouthfuls of food quickly washed down by drink, one trying to outdo another, each wanting to be heard, acting the part of a jester. The worst came from Denise's uncle, a brutish man in out-of-style clothes and stringy hair matted with what looked like hummus. He became the recipient of a note passed to the table by their server.

The uncle opened the paper as if it was meant for him and rested his hands on his protruding belly. "Humph." He looked at Denise over fuchsia rimmed glasses. "Who in the fifth dimension is Jeremy Guerdon?"

"Never mind, Manny." Connie Tyler snapped at her brother. "Let me have that."

"What makes you think I'd give this to you, sis? Besides, there's some raunchy stuff here. I doubt you'd be interested." He ogled Denise. "It's amatory. That means—"

"I know what it means. Now give it to me."

JEREMY ENJOYED DINING at the same restaurant as the rehearsal dinner. An entrée of filet of sole seasoned and broiled to perfection, a glass of sauterne, and tiramisu whet his appetite and more than satisfied his taste buds.

He watched Daniel from across the restaurant. Having shared the flight from Colorado Springs to Knoxville provided Jeremy with the opportunity to observe the man he planned to kill. He expected Daniel to present a challenge when provoked. It bolstered his ego to know he was about to prevail over a man of Daniel's caliber.

At eight forty-five, he downed the last sip of wine, paid the bill, and waited for the rehearsal party to get their check. No one in the group gave any indication of seeing him seated at a table in the far corner away from the separate dining room and distant to all traffic to and from restrooms. If all went well, he would pass on congratulations and dispense a final endowment to Daniel within an hour of midnight and dole out a parting gift to Denise shortly thereafter.

Guests and family rose from the table, continued their mingling, and chatted another five to ten minutes. They tendered the usual clichés and said good night with waves, handshakes, or hugs.

Jeremy checked the time. He began to wonder if they were ever going cease all the chatter. He had business to tend to.

At five minutes before nine, Denise jumped up from the table. A grim look molded her facial expression as she snatched something from one of the guests and stormed in Jeremy's direction. She threaded her way between tables and along a chest-high partition adorned with greenery. The panel separated Denise and the table from which Jeremy watched her pass by, turn ninety degrees, and dart to the ladies' room.

Denise paused at the restroom door. She glanced to her left and vanished from sight when the door closed.

DENISE LATCHED THE stall door and leaned her back against it. She drew her arms to her chest. Closed her eyes. Her left hand tightened around the paper. Tension surpassed anxiety threshold.

Why do people have to be so tactless? A reasonable person would put from his mind as a bad idea the things Manny let guide his actions. She wondered if Uncle Manny's heart rated as good as what her mother said more times than she cared to remember. If good lived in his heart, it definitely beat an awkward rhythm.

Aching fingers reminded her why she squeezed them. Enduring her uncle's gobbledygook proved minor compared to reality. The foundation on which future life with Daniel rose from lifted her spirit.

"This is what I think of you, Jeremy Guerdon."

Without caring what was written on it, Denise released her grip on the paper and tilted her hand. The wad rolled off her palm into the toilet bowl. She pushed the flush button and watched the porcelain mouth gobble the note.

Chapter 49

Jeremy slipped out with eight diners leaving the table next to him as if they were together. The valet brought the Lincoln to a stop in front of the restaurant. Jeremy tipped the attendant and turned around when he felt a tap on the arm.

"Hi! I thought that was you I saw in there," said Judith Lanier.

Stunned at her presence, he fumbled out a, "Well, hello." Jeremy took a fleeting look at the door beyond her and added, "You look fantastic," to cover his slipup.

The compliment broadened her smile.

"I wish I'd known you'd be here. I'd a got you to come over to our table and meet my family and friends. My best friend is getting married tomorrow. Why don't you come back inside and I'll introduce you?"

"I'd like nothing more than to spend another evening with you, but I'm headed to the airport." He hurried to get in the car, watching the restaurant's front entrance in case Denise or Daniel appeared. "Please understand."

"Only if you call me." She followed him to the driver's door. "Soon."

Jeremy jerked the door closed. The front of the car lifted with acceleration and shot along the drive to the street. Zeal electrified desire inside him. He had vexed Denise and Daniel for weeks. Now, the blip he had long awaited signified the end.

Thirty minutes later, the Lincoln rolled to a stop behind the shack Jeremy had appropriated as a temporary center of operations.

He shut off the headlamps and sat in the darkness long enough to let his eyesight adjust. And to be certain that no one had followed him, or loomed near the hideaway.

He reached up to the dome light. The lens popped off with ease. He removed the bulb, tossed the lens cover and bulb in the glove box, and closed the lid. The driver's door opened without a sound. He eased it closed, leaving the doors unlocked.

Jeremy turned his back to the car and listened to crickets and other things of the night. They alternated calls as if in a contest to outdo each other. Things some considered creepy, Jeremy enjoyed. The noise covered any misstep he might make on the way to the cabin.

A humph came from the trunk latch when he pressed the release button on the key fob. He retrieved a satchel, gathered the few supplies stowed in the shed, and returned the bag to the trunk.

A full moon lit the woods enough for him to traipse through without need of a flashlight. Prior visits taught him the lay of the land between the hideout and the cabin. He followed the ridge to the funnel, crossed the bottom, and angled up the other side to within earshot of the river. That put him about a hundred yards from the clearing. He knew then to turn right and parallel the river to the cabin.

The vibrating mode on Jeremy's cell phone indicated an incoming call. "Cars, I told you not to call me."

"This is important. Where are you?" Carson Wright whispered, barely audible over the sound of rippling water.

"I'm busy."

"The police are knocking on my door. They're all over the place. What am I supposed to do?"

"Keep your mouth shut."

"But—"

Jeremy thumbed the end call button and slipped the telephone into his pocket.

The phone vibrated a second time. Jeremy rammed his hand in the pocket and came out with the phone and answered it without looking at the caller ID.

"What?"

"You're not going to like this. It's about Angela," Richie said.

"Don't tell me you haven't found her."

"Oh, I found her all right."

"Okay. What's so bad? She got a husband or something?"

"Lots of something, Jere. She's FBI."

"Contact her. Invite her to my party next week."

"Are you nuts?"

"Bonkers, my man. Have her there. I'll take care of the RIP."

"You mean RSVP?"

"No. That's your job."

"RIP. Ah. I get it. Rest in pieces."

Lights inside the cabin suggested someone's presence. The cabin harbored darkness at other times when he scoped the woods around the structure and along the river for ease of access. Jeremy slinked near the clearing and followed the edge around to the right. He paused, exhilarated by the sight of the Acura parked in the driveway. He wanted to pump his arms and let out a hurrah, but allowed only a wide grin to express the gut-washed feeling inside him.

Denise. Inside the cabin. Alone.

No one around to stop him.

Chapter 50

"Where is Denise?" Judith asked Connie Tyler. Judith waved the flat box she held in her left hand.

"She's already gone."

"Home?"

"The cabin."

"Oh, no. I was supposed to give this to her. Is Daniel still here?"

"I think I heard him say he was going out to the car."

Daniel overheard the last part of their conversation on his way from the restroom where he had changed into Levi's, a long-sleeve pullover, and navy and grey New Balance shoes. The dress clothes he had taken off hung over his left arm. Brown loafers dangled from two fingers on his left hand.

"You ladies looking for me?"

"Good, you're still here." Judith held out the box. "I forgot to give this to Denise. Will you take it to her?"

"Certainly." He took the box from her hand. "It's heavy. May I ask what's inside?"

"Sure."

"Well?"

"I can't tell you. And don't you look either. It's something Denise and I promised to do for whichever one of us got married first. It's rigged, so don't open it. She'll know it if you do."

He rotated the box in his hand. A clear seal was attached to each end.

"It must be important."

Judith cocked her head to one side and grinned. "You'll see."

TRIP AFTER TRIP, DENISE unloaded the Acura and carried their gifts into the cabin. The closet was barely large enough to hold the pile of boxes and other essentials given them by their family and friends. She wanted them out of sight when Daniel arrived. There could be no eyesores or anything out of place. Everything must be perfect.

She checked the time and guessed she had maybe fifteen minutes to prepare the cabin the way she wanted it and get out of there before Daniel's arrival.

She lit a butter crème-scented candle on the chest in the bedroom and another on the counter next to the kitchen sink.

The contract for Cyclodactin lay on the table, compliments of her dad's connivance. He had arranged with the pharmaceutical company to have it there in time for the wedding, along with a cashier's check payable to Daniel for an advance of 2.5 million dollars.

She double-checked the setting.

A chocolate-covered strawberry wrapped in cellophane centered Daniel's pillow.

Cover turned down, no wrinkles. The fresh smell and feel of clean sheets waited their entry.

A bottle of V-8 V-Fusion Peach Mango chilled in a bucket of ice on the nightstand, a reminder of their first days together.

Denise flipped off the lights and extinguished the candles. Excitement boogied through her body. By this time tomorrow, they would be on their way to Aruba.

The porch floor creaked. He's early, she thought. She fluffed her hair and posed against the counter, expecting Daniel to come through the door any second. She waited. The darkness abated somewhat from the small amount of moonlight filtering through the drapes.

Creak. Someone lurked at the door. In the darkness. No rap on the door. No "Hello" or "Anyone home?" came from out there. Fifteen feet away. A wooden door on hinges attached to the jamb with screws stood as the only barrier between her and certain demise, if her hunch proved correct.

A drone. The tone sounded male. Definitely not Daniel.

Her throat tightened. She threaded her arms around her torso and grabbed handfuls of the silk blouse. The clock on the mantle chimed once for the half hour—ten thirty. It startled her. She twitched. Her breathing increased to pants. The hinges on the screen door squawked. The doorknob jiggled. Please, let it be locked. She couldn't remember either way.

The distance between where she stood and the door troubled her. Her panting intensified. She felt exposed, even though she was consumed in darkness. There was nothing to hide behind if the person out there got in the cabin.

She feared making noise if she moved, but she had to try. She eased to the bedroom and shrank behind the doorjamb far enough that she could still see and yet slam the door and lock it if the man entered through one of the outside doors. The locked door might slow him long enough to slide the latch on the bedroom window, open it, and escape before he reached her.

Maybe.

The man stayed at the door. The hum continued softer than before. The sound terrified her. She hated not being able to see what he was doing out there.

A minute later, silence. Denise hovered at the bedroom door. She crooked her neck around the jamb. She listened. Why did he stop?

The next sounds explained it. Footfalls on the steps. A pause.

Daniel.

DANIEL'S ARRIVAL OPENED the valve of adrenalin that shot Jeremy Guerdon soaring to a height greater than the one time he introduced cocaine into his system. What better way to end a culmination of fear-instilled events than to have Denise and Daniel at their place of serenity for the final act? With his back to the cabin door, Jeremy rolled his shoulders and let his arms rest at his sides. He flexed and relaxed fingers on both hands. He readied his mind-set for the moment of attack.

The plan included humiliating Daniel before death separated spirit from body—tie a rope around Daniel's ankles, strip him of clothing, dangle him over the river with the rope looped around his unit and neck, make a spectacle out of the once celebrated athlete. Let everyone believe he was demented by narcissism.

Attack.

Conquer.

Humble and destroy Daniel while Denise watched.

Chapter 51

A presence as imposing as a pagan god blocked Daniel's access to the cabin. The menace—unlike the blonde lad known to terrorize Mr. Wilson—enjoyed trickery far superior to a boy's mischief.

Daniel halted halfway up the steps. All he could see was the shape of a man, a black hole with eyes motionless at the front door. The man stood frozen in time. The second night of the full moon afforded Daniel enough light to see what he imagined was the ooze of Satan's heartless bosom.

Unarmed, Daniel vaulted the handrail intending to lead the man away from the cabin. He hoped Jeremy would follow him. He wondered if he was too late to save Denise. A twinge in his leg when he landed reminded him what the doctor had told him: try not to wrench the leg. The doctor's advice no longer mattered. All he could picture was Denise sprawled on the cabin floor injured or dead.

Jeremy jumped him from behind. The down force bowed Daniel forward. Momentum rolled him away from Jeremy's grasp. Daniel dropped the box Judith had given him and braced for the fall by tucking his right shoulder. He rolled on contact with the ground and scrambled to his feet. That put him eye level with his assailant.

Moonlight turned Jeremy's color pewter. The white of his smile reminded Daniel of tainted chrome. Jeremy no longer resembled the handsome, debonair man he pretended to be. The man's aura likened him to a phantasm in human form.

Daniel knew Jeremy would counter any move he tried and used a least expected one. Swift action worked best. Daniel dropped his shoulder, pumped his legs, and caught Jeremy mid-chest. Momentum drove Jeremy backward toward the porch. He beat both arms, hands clasped together across Daniel's back. The effect came too late. The overhanging floorboards caught Jeremy's back in line with his kidneys.

Daniel tugged Jeremy's collar and slammed the man's head against the cross-rail. A dull thump of flesh on wood precipitated blood's acrid smell.

Jeremy cursed. A backhanded fist fanned Daniel's jaw. Daniel followed the head-slam and missed counter from Jeremy with a left hook to Jeremy's face and an uppercut to the abdomen. Jeremy shoved Daniel away and unleashed a barrage of jabs, punches, and kicks.

Aches erupted from Daniel's jaw, ribs, and abdomen. He scrambled to maintain his footing on the dew-covered grass. The volley from Jeremy's outburst and the slippery surface beneath his sneakers proved to be too much to overcome. Daniel lost his balance and landed on his back.

Jeremy stood motionless. He was no doubt reserving energy like a true professional, tensed and ready for anything.

Daniel got to his feet and stared into Jeremy's eyes. He altered his stance and hunched forward in preparation of what he knew was coming.

Vapor from Jeremy's mouth and nose made him look like a fire-breathing dragon ready to pounce and destroy its prey. Hate emanated from him in snorts, snarls, and snickers.

"You're nothing for me," he said, circling Daniel, focused and braving the cold as if it had no effect on him. "I'm going to mangle you and then I'm going to kill her. You'll watch her die."

For Daniel, protecting Denise mattered more than anything Jeremy might do to him. He must keep a clear mind and not panic to overcome the undertow of force. He sensed Jeremy's hatred. If Jeremy allowed hate to dictate his actions, it might distort his thought process. Hate alters and often kills those who harbor it. Now he knew he needed any advantage he could get.

Daniel and Jeremy tumbled, rolled, jabbed, pulled, punched, and kicked for the next three or four minutes. Neither showed any sign of weakening or giving up.

Jeremy countered everything Daniel threw at him with agility and strength superior to anything Daniel had ever seen. A flat-handed blow from Jeremy to the xiphoid process dropped Daniel to his knees. He imagined Jeremy had intended to strike the solar plexus, but missed high. He doubled over and pretended to suck in breaths that refused to comply with his need. Then, nausea gripped his viscera. His will insisted pushing to his feet. His aching muscles tensed but obeyed no order to stand.

A blow to the ribs from Jeremy's right foot rolled Daniel down the riverbank. Mud shifted under his weight. Daniel struggled to stay near the top, but the soil gave way and sent him to within inches of the rushing river. Dampness seeped through his shirt. Cold acted like leeches, sucking body heat and strength from his battered body.

He attempted a foothold against a rock. The rock dislodged and he slipped farther downward. Water rushed over his feet. The frigidness drained more strength. Daniel clawed to gain a handhold. His hand brushed across a crag. Something familiar was wedged between two rocks. Was this real?

Mother Nature's talent given to him at birth needed no further coaching. Muscles trained and kept fit for a time like this readied for what he required of them. The sensation at his fingertips stirred his vitality. He wrapped his fingers around it and rotated it in his hand until the seams felt in place against his fingertips. With his feet planted against the rocks at the water's edge and every bit of strength he could muster, Daniel focused on the target and hurled the baseball.

A thump signaled a solid hit. Leaves rustled. Tree limbs cracked. Daniel waited on the thud.

Jeremy crashed to the ground.

THE COMMOTION OUTSIDE the cabin drew Denise to one of the front windows. She pushed aside the drapes and peeked out in time to see Daniel charge and pin someone against the porch. The person's head bobbed rearward when he banged into the porch. She recognized him. She knew that the darkness where she stood made it impossible for him to see her. Still, she felt Jeremy's dark eyes lock on her. A black fire lurched from them.

Denise jerked the drapes closed to stave the inferno. She put her back to the wall. Weakness crept up her legs. She slumped to the floor and covered her ears to block the sounds of the battle: grunts, strains, shuffled feet, fabric ripped.

Outside, her soul mate fought with a man she knew had no intention of losing this fight.

No. This is not going to happen to me. She threw open the door and rushed down the steps.

Panicked by seeing Daniel drop to his knees and Jeremy kick him, Denise stiffened. What was she to do? The situation looked hopeless from where she stood. Things looked bleak for Daniel as he rolled down the bank out of sight.

Jeremy glanced her way. He hobbled two steps in her direction, paused, and changed direction. He was headed to the river.

Denise tried to scream a warning to Daniel. A whisper was all she could get out. She needed a miracle.

A thump drew her attention to Jeremy. She watched as he teetered mid-stride and crumpled against a tree. A baseball rolled to within ten feet of where she stood.

Denise peered toward the river, hoping to get a glimpse of Daniel. She had to help him.

That is when she saw it. Moonlight glinted off the foil ribbon around the box. She darted to the end of the porch. There on the ground lay what she considered a priceless wedding gift. "You remembered. Thank you, Judith."

Denise snapped off the ribbon and ripped off the paper with one pull and flipped the box top off to the side. She tore through the packaging. Grasped the item in her right hand. And sprinted toward the river.

Chapter 52

In Daniel's hazy mind, the collapsed enemy was surrounded by police and FBI led by Special Agent Angela Donavan. Flashlights waved. Light cut holes in the darkness, carried by those eager and willing to dispatch the evil man to his end. Fulfillment of being rescued in an operation carried out to perfection.

He blinked and realized he needed to get to the cabin. He had to get to Denise. First, he had to make sure Jeremy was down. Daniel crawled up the riverbank and mustered enough strength to drag his legs under him. He staggered toward Jeremy. Ten feet to go and he would finish him. He had the advantage. He planned to rid Denise of this scumbag any way his strength would allow.

The slide of metal on metal dashed the optimism of a rescue. He recognized that sound. A gleam of moonlight swept across the pistol in Jeremy's right hand. The silver silhouette of a predator closed in on him.

Daniel braced against a tree and tried to ready himself for the assault. Strength in his legs waned. He hugged the tree and mouthed a prayer for Denise's safety from this hellion.

"Thank you again for the flight this afternoon, Dr. Baker. I wouldn't be here in time to do this if you had said no. Now get down on your knees. I want to hear you beg for your life."

Jeremy raised his arm and leveled the pistol at Daniel's head.

A scream wrecked the silence.

Gunshots in rapid succession boomed. Four shots close enough that they sounded like they were right next to his left ear. Three flashes lit the night near the front corner of the cabin. They did not correspond to the blasts near him. He figured one of the two had to be Agent Donavan. The other was probably her backup.

Jeremy jerked and twisted every time the guns fired. He staggered and tumbled against a tree. Though hit, he raised his right arm and squeezed the trigger.

Additional shots rang out all around.

One bullet struck Daniel's left thigh. He cringed and clamped his hand on the burning and throbbing muscle. He kept his eyes on Jeremy. The man slumped around the tree trunk and crashed to the ground. He mumbled something Daniel couldn't quite make out, coughed, and exhaled a gurgling breath.

Daniel swiped his eyes with the back of his right hand and peered over his left shoulder. He expected to see Agent Donavan standing over him with her gun drawn and held at arm's length in front of her. The outline of the person looked nothing like Angela. He pushed up on his right elbow. A shift in the breeze delivered a whiff of Happy to his sense of smell.

"Denise?" He slumped to the ground.

"Daniel!"

Denise ran to him. She dropped to her knees and threw her arms around his neck. She clutched a pistol in her right hand.

He reached for the gun. "Let me have that."

She jerked, turned toward Jeremy, and pointed the gun in his direction. "Is he dead? Please tell me he's dead."

Mustering strength and wanting to be sure, Daniel overcame the throbbing pain in his thigh and crawled to Jeremy's side. He shoved the pistol beyond the man's reach. A sucking chest wound marred Jeremy's chest near dead center. He was still alive. Blood from half dozen other wounds saturated the man's clothing from shoulders to knees.

"I know who you are." Jeremy turned his head to face Daniel. His eyelids fluttered. "You work for ..." The gurgling wound silenced. Air escaped his lungs.

"What is he talking about?" Denise wanted to know.

"No need to worry about him, Ms. Tyler." Angela circled the downed man while keeping her gun trained on him. She squatted, put her fingers to Jeremy's neck, and holstered her weapon. "You won't be bothered by him after tonight."

Denise let the pistol fall from her hand. She buried her face on Daniel's shoulder.

"How did you know he was here?" Daniel asked Angela.

"Police arrested Carson Wright less than an hour ago. He told them about Jeremy's plan to ambush you tonight. He also told them about the woman who died in Mr. Tyler's building. Where are you hit?"

"My thigh. What about the woman? How did she fit into all of this and get a CDC name tag?"

"I've been wanting to know that too," Denise said.

"She was one of Jeremy's and Carson's cousins who had an acquaintance that used to work at the CDC. Hold on and let me get some help for you." Angela notified the authorities of the shooting and requested an ambulance. She picked up the pistol Denise had dropped and stuffed it in her jacket pocket. "Do you have any peroxide? Alcohol? You need that sanitized and wrapped 'til we can get you to the emergency room."

"In the bathroom," Denise said.

"Be right back."

While they waited, Daniel said, "Where did you get the gun?"

"Judith."

"That's what was in the box?"

"Yep."

"I guess I'll be minus one groomsman tomorrow. I never really trusted Carson. Now I know part of the reason."

"I don't care about that. I just want you to be all right."

"I'll be fine."

The leg throbbed. Daniel stuck his thumb through the defect in the fabric, clenched the cloth with his other hand, and ripped the pants' leg exposing the gunshot wound. Pain engorged the thigh in defiance of Daniel's finger probing in and around it.

"Shine the light down here," he directed Angela, who held a flashlight in one hand and items from the cabin with the other. A quilt draped one arm. A towel hung across the other.

Angela let the quilt fall to Denise, who draped it around Daniel's shoulders.

Daniel eased the leg up to look. Filth from crawling through muck on the riverbank soiled his hands and the front of his slacks and shirt.

Denise leaned forward and winced at sight of Daniel's leg.

"Pour some of that on my hands first."

Angela uncapped the peroxide and tilted the bottle. Daniel wrung his hands under the flow as she poured the clear liquid. He signaled enough when he no longer felt the grime and stickiness from the mixture of soil and his and Jeremy's blood. He tugged the towel off Angela's arm and dried his hands. Daniel palpated the thigh six inches above the knee and back to the hamstring.

"Through and through."

"Is that good?" Denise asked.

Daniel nodded. A pass-through gunshot wound meant less chance of additional damage to the leg for a projectile removal. The possibility of damage to the healed tissue below the gunshot concerned him.

He cupped his hand next to the entry and motioned to Donavan. Red-tinged foam bubbled and spilled out of the wound as she poured peroxide into it. The liquid worked its way through the path the bullet had taken and seeped out the exit.

Denise applied antibiotic ointment to the leg and wrapped a bandage around it. The sensation in the leg reminded Daniel of the injury that ended his baseball career. Except then, a hot poker hadn't torn through the leg.

As she finished, he noticed a wheeze in her breathing. Shivers jolted her from head to feet.

"Come here." He dried his hands, repositioned the quilt to cover her, and drew her to him.

Daniel looked up at Angela. "I have something I believe belongs to you."

"What?"

"You're not really FBI, are you?"

Denise jerked her head around. Daniel felt the inquisitiveness in her stare.

"What makes you say that?"

"This." He dug his left hand into his pocket and came out with the tracking device he had removed from Denise's car. He opened his hand and showed it to her.

"What is that?" Denise pulled his open palm closer to her.

"Shall I tell her?" he asked Angela.

Even though moonlight provided the only illumination on them, he saw the uneasiness on Angela's face.

"I ... Um ..."

"What's going on here?" Denise prodded.

"A little added protection, right, Angela?"

"He insisted," Angela said.

"Who insisted what?"

"Your dad," Angela and Daniel chorused.

"What does my dad have to do with this? What makes you believe he was involved?" She asked Daniel.

"I'm a federal agent, Denise, just not FBI," Angela said. "I work for a man known as Simon One. He's the person who called the sheriff's office when you and Daniel were detained by Blount County Sheriff and demanded your release. I was hired by your father to make sure you got safely away from New Jersey and Jeremy. Everything else you and I talked about before was all true. I came here to do a job and had to let Daniel know about the investigation, since he had become one of Jeremy's targets. I apologize if you think I misled you and please don't harbor any ill will against you dad."

"And the disk?"

"It was an easy way to keep up with you. I had a notion Daniel found it. I didn't want to involve him any more than necessary."

Angela strolled to the cabin and sat on the steps. Daniel respected the way Angela covered for him by taking responsibility.

"It's all over now, baby." He kissed Denise on her forehead.

A shift in the wind put them downwind of Jeremy's body. "I despise that smell."

"What smell?"

"His cologne."

"Mixes well with the other scents."

"What scents are those?"

"Blood and death."

She lifted her eyes and flashed a smile. "I concur, Doctor." The response brought a chuckle out of him. "Is this what I have to look forward to for the next four, five, or six decades of marriage?"

"What? Are you talking about honesty, trust, genuineness, and a smidgeon of wit?"

"Maybe. As long as you have no secrets I need to worry about, I'll be able to trust you."

"There is one thing," Daniel said.

Denise cocked her head and shied back. "Oh?"

"All I can say is, you'll have to trust me."

"Earn trust, remember?"

Caught up in the moment, neither one noticed Angela standing at their feet until light reflected off the side of the pistol Judith had given to Denise.

"Something was engraved on this."

Daniel looked at Denise, who shrugged. "What does it say?"

Angela presented the side of the barrel and hit it with light for them to see the engraving. "'Achieve your goal.'"

Chapter 53

The next evening, Denise strolled along the worn path toward the river on her way to fulfill a promise. A rose filled each hand. The trees stood still, branches bare, yet taking nothing away from the beauty of this perfect display of tranquility. Cold, swirling wind brushed locks of hair merrily back and forth across her shoulders.

Thoughts of Daniel danced inside her head. They sent a warm, peaceful feeling to her heart. She strolled alongside the river and reminisced how she and Daniel had discovered this place. She dropped the roses on the water and watched them float away. Tears welled in her eyes. "I love you, Daniel. I'll always love you."

Water dashed against the rocks. The evening majesty of the sun faded behind snow-covered peaks. Shadows crept along the bosky bottom below while a hawk soared high overhead. A smile formed on lips as she remembered his words: "Love is the greatest thing in the world." The light of the setting sun continued to fade as the first of many stars peeked through the amethyst sky.

"They are shining for you," she had heard him say many times before. The reminiscence made her feel whole inside. "Love," she said to herself, gazing at the starlit heavens. "Soulmate love."

Denise turned and made her way up the steps to the mammoth front porch and through the cabin's front door. The swelling fire inside the old stone fireplace welcomed her entrance. The small wood table was now garnished with an evergreen centerpiece. The glow of twin candles flickered in the breeze from the open door against place settings for two, purposefully arranged. At that moment, she knew how special this evening would be.

She kicked off her shoes before stepping on the plush, oversized rug in front of the stone hearth. Standing motionless, she watched the flames as they embraced each stick of wood. After a few moments, she eased down on the rug facing the fire.

What was, what would have been, and whatever could or should have happened did not matter now. She was where she needed to be, where she longed to be. She had waited her entire life for this moment. Now it belonged to her.

Her quietness was interrupted by the light touch of a hand on her shoulder. Without turning, she closed her eyes, relaxed in the comfort of knowing she belonged to the one person in the world for whom she really loved. Chills raced up and down her spine as the hand brushed her long, dark hair away from her neck. Lips softly pressed against the back of her neck. She cherished the warmth of his breath on her shoulder while he continued to lightly touch his lips to her skin.

Slowly, he lowered his sore body next to her, set the crutches aside, and wiggled to face her right side. He brushed her cheek. Denise opened her eyes and shifted to face him. His face beamed. He pushed her hair away from the side of her face and gazed into her eyes. "You have the most beautiful eyes," he whispered.

He wrapped his strong arms around her and pulled her close. He held her firmly, but gently, as if they were about to say a final farewell. But this was not goodbye.

"Am I dreaming? Are you really here with me?"

"Yes, baby, I'm really here. Thanks to you. You saved my life."

Denise tightened her arms. "I feared you were gone, honey."

Daniel eased back, reached for her left hand, and held it up. The diamond on her finger reflected the firelight. Earlier that day they were united in marriage.

"I love you, baby," he said, "with all my heart."

"I love you too, honey."

He shifted around to face the fireplace, cupped her head in his left hand, and eased her back on the soft rug.

Denise reached up, touched the dimple on his face, and smiled. She pulled him to her and held on as if her life depended on it. The seal on her heart confirmed their future. It was a done deal. A total commitment. The day's ceremony was only a formality to make it all legal.

The new moon phase made for an extremely dark night in the mountains of east Tennessee. It became a perfect backdrop for the night sky to eloquently display its innumerable stars. The only light inside was that of the flames from the fireplace and two half-burned candles on the kitchen table. The wind calmed outside and all was quiet and peaceful inside the cabin.

The diamond on her finger winked at them in the firelight. She felt Daniel's heart rhythm. Thanks to destiny, love worked its magic in their hearts. They gave her the freedom she prayed for: freedom to live, freedom to love.

Denise slipped her hand in her pocket and came out with a pair of handcuffs dangling from her fingers. "Agent Donavan sent these. She told me not to let you get away. Said since I got the real thing, she'd settle for a clone."

"You have all of me there is to share."

"Good answer."

Denise cuddled in Daniel's arms. She watched while he opened an envelope Angela hand-delivered to him at the reception. "Congratulations" was written on the card in blue ink.

Denise pointed at the signature. "Who is Simon One?" Daniel tossed the card and envelope in the fire. "I understand if you can't tell me."

"He's the man I work for."

"You, too? What about the CDC?"

"The CDC is only a temporary assignment."

"What happens when you finish your work there?"

"It depends on your dad."

"My dad? How does it involve him?"

"He is Simon One."

The End

Don't miss out!

Visit the website below and you can sign up to receive emails whenever Steve Rush publishes a new book. There's no charge and no obligation.

https://books2read.com/r/B-A-DDZR-IJCWB

BOOKS 2 READ

Connecting independent readers to independent writers.

About the Author

Steve Rush is an award-winning author whose experience includes tenure as homicide detective and chief forensic investigator for a national consulting firm. He was once hailed as "The best forensic investigator in the United States" by the late Joseph L. Burton, M.D, under whom he mastered his skills, investigated many deaths alongside Dr. Jan Garavaglia of Dr. G: Medical Examiner fame, and was part of the development team for Quincy Technologies, an automated case management system designed for coroners and medical examiners. Steve has investigated 900+ death scenes and taught classes related to death investigation. His specialties include injury causation, blood spatter analysis, occupant kinematics, and recovery of human skeletal remains.

Two of Steve's manuscripts placed first and third in the 2022 Public Safety Writers Association Writing Competition. His book Kill Your Characters; Crime Scene Tips for Writers, published by Genius Books on June 7, 2022, tied for first place in the 2022 PSWA Writing Competition's unpublished nonfiction category. Steve won joint first prize in the 2020 Chillzee KiMo T-E-N Contest and longlisted in the 2022 Page Turner Awards.

He lives in Metropolitan Atlanta, Georgia, with his wife Sharon. Read more at www.steverush.org.

Milton Keynes UK
Ingram Content Group UK Ltd.
UKHW010727130923
428592UK00004B/200